SHOWDOWN IN BEANTOWN

A CAVAZUTTI CRIME NOVEL

CARLO CAVAZUTTI

ISBN: 978-1-68046-778-9

Melange Books, LLC
White Bear Lake, MN 55110
www.melange-books.com

Published in the United States of America.

Cover Design by Lynsee Lauritsen

I dedicate this book to my fifth grade teacher, Blanche Toole. She instilled in me a love of reading and learning. Through her entire life, she remained a lifelong friend, mentor, scholar, and lady. Sadly, she passed away this past year on my birthday. May God keep you safe in the hollow of His hand.

To my Pops. You left us all too soon. Thanks for being a great role model, husband, and father. I know you are no longer in pain, but you live every day in my heart.

PROLOGUE

She sat in the back of her chauffeur-driven limo, her right knee ratcheting like a jackhammer. The corners of her mouth were turned down taking away from the face that other women envied. Bloodshot eyes were glazed over with tears; her right fist pressed against her face completed the look. She thought about lighting a smoke to ease the tension and instead removed several cubes of ice from the built-in freezer-fridge. Then she dropped them tinkling and spinning into the hand-cut crystal glass and topped them with the clear alcohol that was her choice of poison for the moment. God, she thought, a Xanax would be so good now. She was aware of the ever-present whining still audible from the outside of the well-insulated car, like a mosquito buzzing around one's head that one could never seem to swat. She couldn't ignore it nor tune it out with animated conversation as she took calls or gave commands to her driver. Maybe she noticed it because of the eerie, dark quiet.

It was another two hours to Boston, another two hours to endure the tension that built inside her like a rubber band about to burst. Her sister promised a glimmer of salvation, but she felt nailed to a tree. She would be damned or die before she turned over everything she had labored and worked toward all her life. She wished she was in her old neighborhood church where she felt peace and calm, like when she was a little girl and Gramma took her each Sunday in her white dress. But life had taken her on a voyage far away from those days in South Carolina and far away from those casual days as a young girl.

CHAPTER ONE

A New Start

I had enjoyed the previous ten years since I retired from the police department. I was sick of the bullshit and lies so I picked up and moved to Boston. A lot of people were surprised I went riding off into the sunset, but I looked at it as riding into a new sunrise. I kicked around in a few different jobs working for other people, but I was tired of the same old shit over and over, just like the PD. I didn't have a filter, so I didn't bite my tongue, and those were the times I had to pay a price. Those that tried to tame me, well, let's just say I've outlived them all. But I don't ever look back, as regret is for fools. I have lived as an outlaw and I have lived within the law, and even both at the same time. Sure, I worked in a lot of gray areas and walked a line that was razor-thin at times to make a case, and I didn't hesitate to bend or break a few rules.

So, I decided to get my own ticket and work for myself. Now

the only people I had to argue with were the voices in my head (ahh, that was a joke but coming from me one never knows for sure). As a civilian, either cops hated private sector people like me, or they got along well and at times worked together. As far as I was concerned, we were all of one blood, and someday they would be in the same boat as me, retired and looking for something to do. I made friends, some better than others, and then there were those I wouldn't have helped if they begged me. To me it was cut-and-dry, no in-between with people. If they laid down with dogs, they got fleas, and I wasn't about to start scratching an itch.

CHAPTER TWO

TEN YEARS LATER

CHEZ RENDEZVOUS WAS NOT THE TYPE OF PLACE THAT ONE would think had decent food. It was located in a less than desirable part of Dorchester, Massachusetts, along Dorchester Avenue, and had changed hands several times in the last twenty years.

There were Vietnamese and Chinese businesses sprinkled all along the street, with the cacophony of languages, and the neighborhood seemed to be struggling to make a rise from the ashes. But, Chez Rendezvous was a neighborhood icon as it has been owned for the last ten years by Tony "Sly" Green. Sly was a no-nonsense type of guy with a big-barreled chest and a head as bare as a billiard ball, but he knew how to make a good steak and BBQ at excellent prices found nowhere else in the city. It was a neighborhood secret. Sometimes I think Sly's supplies fell off the back of a truck, but I didn't ask and he sure as hell wasn't going to tell. Sly was well connected throughout the city and could get anything for a price. He knew who ran what and where they ran it, and he could reach out to any of them at any time. The big man had a knack for making things happen.

But, more importantly, Sly knew how I liked my steak and he served them not quite mooing but still bleeding when cut. There was nothing like a large slab of rare steak after a heavy workout, and I still managed to move the tonnage at 60 years of age. In the gym I lived by the motto, *Lift Heavy or Go the Frig Home*!

Across from the dining room and near the dance floor was the bar. It was all mahogany, built in the day when craftsmanship meant something. Behind the bar Sly had a sweet young sista girl named Britiney mixing drinks. Every brother, white and black, was strutting their swag, trying to lay their best game on her, until what they hoped was another sure thing walked through the door and in this area, there were plenty of those types. Britiney, a bedazzler in her own right, didn't give these boys the time of day and was able to rebuff their advances with her own cool style and sweet Southern charm. Sly hired her as a favor to me and she had yet to disappoint either of us.

Of course, no respectable club would be complete without bouncers, or should I say, "security staff," and Sly had six of the biggest, baddest mo-fos in town. They all looked like they were front linemen for the Dallas Cowboys. I hate to say it, but some of them made me look small. Sly had them all in tuxes to add some class to the place and they treated all the guests with respect unless they had to get down and dirty. Every one of them was loyal to Sly, as he had given them something much better than they had before. The "before" was hustling game on the street whether it was drugs, whores, guns, or money.

As for myself I was about as much out of place here as an Aryan Brotherhood member at a Jewish wedding. With a shaved head and sleeves down both arms and chest, built like Hulk

Hogan, I looked more like a 1%er than a career homicide detective. But since that time, I was working as a private investigator and/or bodyguard doing what I do best. No one really bothered me as my reputation as a no-nonsense cop preceded me. They all knew that I concealed at least my Glock 21 in a custom holster fitting neatly in the small of my back, and I wasn't afraid to use it if the occasion arose.

More than a few of the clientele that frequented the club had gotten locked up as a result of my investigations, whether for stealing from their employers or slinging dope at their places of work. But some still gave me tips on street stuff going down that proved useful in my investigations, or I confidentially passed it on to a trusted detective on the job. Of course they were compensated well if the leads turned out. Good information was worth something and I had learned that practice early on, even if it meant taking cash out of my own pocket.

It was about 9:30 a.m. and the crowd began to grow. The music grew louder as DJ Tee, hottest female DJ in town, cranked up the latest R&B, hip-hop, and old school tunes enticing the crowd to the dance floor. It was amusing to sit back and watch these young boys trying to score with some hoochie, whether dancing like they were something or buying them drinks. A few of the more unsavory characters would exit through the front door occasionally and walk down the block to conduct some devious "business" just around the corner. Sly tried to keep it cleaned up but just like cockroaches they all came back. Everyone had to get paid somehow. Brothers not talking or dancing with the fine ladies in the place were talking smack to one another while a few old-timers sat stationed in their usual spots complaining about anything and everything when they could get someone to listen—you know the type, they're in every bar in the world. For the most part they were harmless, babbling to themselves after having had a few drinks too many. Sly took care of these older men as half the time they didn't have a dime in their pockets. He also made sure they had a warm meal and warm clothes when needed.

Sly personally saw to it that only the best girls served my meals. He always took care of me. He would chastise the girls if they forgot and gave me a check. That usually just happened once. I gave up arguing with him over the lack of a check, as Sly was as stubborn as they came, next to me. Sly's hospitality was in thanks for bringing his son's killer to justice after I had retired and gotten my license. His son, Donny, had been gunned down in the alley out back when he stumbled upon the wrong guy—a pimp—giving one of his ho's a beatdown for holding out on him. Donny intervened and was shot six times at close range for trying to help the girl. Vice later identified the girl as a 16-year-old runaway from Philly. Human trafficking was abhorrent to me as it was to one other very dear "sweet" lady. The young prostitute was found three days later facedown in the Charles River, but that is another story for another day.

Anyway, I digress. I always made sure I tipped out the girls at least for the price of the meal. They all appreciated it and always made sure I had the best of everything even competing amongst themselves to see who would serve me. Not everyone in this place tipped well except for the bros that liked to make it "rain" to impress some hoochie or their entourage. But I was totally unprepared for what would happen next.

CHAPTER THREE

SHE'S A BRICK HOUSE
The Commodores

SLY HAD TAKEN A SEAT NEXT TO ME AT OUR USUAL TABLE, which positioned us with our backs to the wall. Old habits are hard to break. Any gunfighter knows that it is deadly to get caught in crossfire and at times I likened myself to an Old West gunfighter with his gun slung low on the hip and tied at the leg.

Sly and I shot the shit for a while sipping Kona coffee laced with Booker's—my favorite Bourbon and quickly becoming Sly's, discussing the finer attributes of each and every lady in the place. Yeah, we were a couple of dirty old men but then who could blame us for looking at what they flaunted. Some of them barely kept their private parts covered. As he talked, he pulled out what I thought were his usual superb Arturo Fuente cigars, proclaimed by some to be the best handmade cigar in the world. Instead, Sly laid out two Cohiba Siglo VI with a 52 gauge.

"You bastard, Sly, you been holding out on me?" I stated. "I know those babies didn't fall off the back of a truck!"

"More like a boat and a fast one at that," responded Sly with a loud laugh. His grin was like the Cheshire cat's and who knows, he may have gone down the rabbit's hole for these. Sly and I fired up the fine cigars and began to puff away. Yeah, we fired them up even with a *No Smoking* poster from Boston Health Commission on the wall.

We were not prepared for what was about to happen. From our seats we could clearly see through the windows and out onto the street. It was something I insisted on when Sly and I became friends as an added security measure, plus all the motion-sensing cameras equipped with infrared for nighttime.

"Sly, you see what just pulled up outside?" Sly looked out and saw the blue and gray Rolls Royce Goodwood ease up to the curb. The cigar smoke curled above our heads. Cars like that are not seen in this neighborhood, as the clientele owning them are usually deca-millionaires and not many of those are in this area. This baby had to run $350,000 if a penny. The chauffeur exited the vehicle, went to the rear passenger side, and opened the door. This guy reminded me of the "Odd Job" character from the James Bond movie, *Goldfinger*. If this dude was anything like the movie character, he was a walking, talking, killing machine. As a detective friend of mine, Jimmy K (since deceased), always said, "Nothing new is good." This certainly was new here and was definitely not good.

Due to Odd Job's mass, the lady that exited the car could barely be seen, but when the front door opened and she walked in everything seemed to stop, get quiet, and go into slow motion. Like in the movies. It wasn't due to Odd Job filling the doorway not allowing egress or exit, or the slight bulge under his coat concealing an MP7 that did not escape my attention. Readers, FYI, the MP7 is a short-barreled, fully automatic assault weapon usually used only by Special Forces teams. The music seemed to be a distant sound off somewhere far away, and everyone, including the women who gossiped, stopped talking and appeared mesmerized by the *lady*. Even Sly and I had stopped in mid-sentence as our eyes were fixed on the dark-skinned goddess who walked through the door. The devil may wear Prada, but this goddess did too, from head to toe. Just her clothing cost more than most people made in several months and the handbag, a Hilde Palladino, had to go for at least $35,000, not that I am into handbags, but you don't get far in my line of work not noticing the small stuff. Lack of it can get you killed fast. You're either the quick or the dead and I chose the former.

The black leather mini-dress showed every curve of her voluptuous toned body and she had legs that would not quit with muscles sculpted as a result of much hard work. Her hair cascaded in tumbling black rivers of curls down her toned shoulders looking like Angela Bassett did in the Ike and Tina movie.

God, was she hot!

If there ever was a perfect ten, this heavenly creature was it. This goddess stood six feet two in the five-inch Giuseppe Zanotti stiletto heels, and the way she moved was all business. As she walked by the crowd at the bar with a style and grace usually never seen here, she held up a hand letting everyone know she had no time for any of them. It was clear that everyone in there was out of her league. Her league existed somewhere far, far away where people made wads of money and spent it just as fast. Inside I began to smolder.

Britiney let go with a cry of delight and called out, "Sis, you're here," loud enough for anyone near the bar to hear. They greeted one another with a huge hug and a kiss. The goddess began to talk to Britiney, and I could see that it was serious as Britiney cleared the end of the bar and motioned for Sly to take over. As the two talked, I saw tears begin to well up in Brit's eyes. She was obviously upset, and she was not one to upset easily. Her sister, I soon found out, had come looking for help. I saw Sly shaking his head as he overheard some of the conversation and gave me the look that it was not good.

Brit asked Sly to make her sis a drink, a Long Island Tea, and she proceeded to my table leaving her sister at the bar with her drink and Sly as company.

Tonight, my life would be changed forever, I just wasn't sure how.

CHAPTER FOUR

The Problem

Britney took a seat across from me. The welling in her eyes turned to tears and began to run down her face, spilling in small splatters onto the table. She told me that her sister, Lady Tatiana, had come here looking for help. Britney had told her sister that maybe I could help her find a way out of a very dangerous situation.

"Carlo, my sister told me that there are very bad people trying to muscle in on her business and they want a piece of the action. She didn't tell me who because she feared for my safety and didn't want me involved any more than I had to be. Will you help her please?" Britney pleaded still crying.

"Baby girl, I'm not sure what I can do until she tells me exactly what the extent of her problem is, and she has to tell me *everything*. If it is bad as you look right now, it is going to take more than me to settle this. Have her come over and talk to me."

"Thank you, Carlo…and Carlo, she has a hard time accepting help from others so don't be too hard on her if she is a little difficult." Britiney then gave me a huge hug, spilling a last few tears on my shoulder and returned to the bar. And, "difficult" regarding her sister, dear reader, is the operative word.

What am I getting myself into now, just how bad can this be? Is this just a bunch of lowlife punks or is there more to worry about like a mob takeover? From my long and colorful career, I knew that any of the ethnic crime families loved taking over businesses and laundering their illicit gains. I thought to myself, all the while not being able to take my eyes off Lady Tatiana. Brit spoke to her in hushed tones and then I saw Lady Tatiana walk to my table leaving Sly and Brit to talk and make drinks. I could see that her confidence was shaken, and her exterior was starting to crack. I was about to find out just how bad it was and precisely who she was.

I stood and started to signal for a waitress, pulled out her chair, and asked if I could refresh her beverage. Lady Tatiana placed her hands on the back of the chair stopping its movement, glared at me, and stated, "I am not here to socialize nor be flirted with, so do dispense with the niceties and let's get down to the matter at hand. If you can't help me tell me now so I don't waste my time. I'm all about business!"

I dropped my hand, waved off the waitress, and with a WTF look on my face spoke in a low terse tone so only she could hear, "I don't know what they do where you come from, but I was raised to treat all women like a lady until they prove otherwise. If you object to me assisting you to your seat and getting you a drink then fine. But you came here with hat in hand looking for my help, so knock off the attitude because now you're in my backyard. You may put up a rocky facade, but I can see that you're just a scared little girl right now and if that pisses you off then so be it"—my finger pointed up at her face—"but you will

14

play by my rules if you want my help. Now sit down and start talking." I motioned to the chair.

I waited for a storm of anger in her reply, but she got the hint after I read the riot act to her, taking the last of the wind and stiffness out of her sails. She began to cry and placed her arms around me begging for help. I don't think anyone had ever talked to her that way and gotten away with it. Crying was something I don't think she had done in a very long time. Now I felt bad. Carlo, you jerk, you made her cry. God, why does this always happen with women?

I gave her a minute to compose herself, got her some tissues, and yes, a fresh drink which she surprisingly thanked me for. So, I thought, she can be polite.

"Miss Tatiana…may I call you that?" I asked as I pulled out her chair and she took a seat. I sat down across from her.

Lady Tatiana looked up, mascara streaks running down her beautiful face, and she said, "I'm sorry, but I'm scared, and I apologize. You may call me Lady Tatiana for now, and may I call you Carlo?"

I told her that was fine as that is what everyone called me plus a few other choice names. That almost got a smile out of her. She must have an amazing smile when she did smile.

"So, Lady Tatiana, what brings you here and why do you think I can help you?"

Lady Tatiana stated, "I am a media producer of up-and-coming artists in the hip-hop and R&B genres. I also produced video, movies, and TV shows and am based in New York City. Several months ago, I was approached, softly at first, with an offer to buy 51% of my company, Devine Productions."

I did note that the name was familiar as my education in different genres of music wasn't a waste of time.

"After I turned down the first offer the pressure began to turn up to sell and I was then visited by several unsavory characters of Albanian ethnicity." More on them later.

Now this is where the story goes from a small-time problem to major drama. I'm thinking to myself, *frigging Albanians,* if this isn't a pile of shit to step into. Now my mind went into overdrive thinking of the favors I needed to call in to raise a standing army that a Third World nation would be proud to call its own. I knew a little about the Albanian mob and as they say, a little knowledge can be a dangerous thing.

Lady Tatiana continued to pour out her story and said, "The pressure began to get nasty with threats of physical harm to me and my family, and several times I found damage to my property and cars along with one of my guard dogs being poisoned. Several of my employees had also been assaulted, and I first thought the events unrelated but soon had misgivings for my previous misconceptions."

These guys play for keeps, but I didn't want to lay that on her yet. She went on. "They knew pretty much all about me and had apparently done their homework and knew I had a sister here in Boston. They said they needed an outlet for "investment purposes."

"And I bet your business was the perfect vehicle. I'm guessing they were expecting an answer soon and *no* would not be an option they were willing to accept, am I right?"

From what I knew, the Albanians were involved in human trafficking, narcotics, and pornography. It all added up—what a setup to launder their illicit profits and a ready-made place to produce more "art."

"Yes, you're dead on and I am so frightened."

I asked her, "What about Odd Job?"

Lady Tatiana looked at me and asked, "What do you mean?"

I asked about the solar eclipse standing in the doorway and if she was sure about his loyalties.

She stated, "He's but just one man and he would die for me if need be."

Yeah, I thought to myself, I can see why.

"Lady Tatiana, fat chance you might know these Albanians, their names?"

Lady told me, "I know they are out of NYC but that was all I have."

I knew these guys didn't give names but only intimidated and hurt people or killed them if necessary, to get their way. The Albanian Organized Crime families were even pushing LNC (La Cosa Nostra, for those that did not see *The Godfather* or were living in a cave for the last ninety years) out of long-held territory, and there was no love lost between them and the Italians.

"Is anyone else in your corporation able to sell off part of the business without your approval?"

Lady stated, "No, I have total control. No one else can make any decision like that except me."

I asked if anyone may have been bribed and she stated, "Anyone can be bought for a price, right, Mr. Carlo? So, what is your price, and what will it cost me to get rid of this problem?"

So the feistiness returns and she looked dead serious.

"Let's not worry about that now, Lady Tatiana. We need to make a plan and we can talk money when this is all over."

Little did she know, I would not have taken a red cent.

Now I knew the shit-storm I was stepping into was hip-deep. I had a bad feeling that this was going to turn into World War III and turn sideways before it was all over, and a lot of people would die. The cops wouldn't be any help at all except to clean up the mess.

My smoldering had turned up a notch and I could feel myself falling for this woman. That was not a good sign. Never fall for a client!

Now, to form that plan…

CHAPTER FIVE

The Plan

"First off, you and your sister are not leaving here and going back home or anywhere else except a safe house. That car of yours stands out way too much and if they are here, which I'm sure they are, they will find you in no time. A little money can go a long way," I said. "But now to get you to a safe place, and I know just the person to help us with that."

I called out to Sly and on his way over Lady Tatiana began to ask if I could trust him and I stopped her mid-sentence stating, "Yeah, I trust him with my life and so will you if you know what's good for you. I've known him for ten years and he has always had my back. Besides, you think I would let your sister work for him if I couldn't trust him?" I said, almost with a leering look.

Lady Tatiana replied, "Sure, Carlo, whatever you say, you're in charge. And thanks for keeping my sister safe." She sounded almost relieved to be unburdened from worrying about what to do next.

"Sly, we need a safe house and we need it yesterday. Lady Tatiana and Brit need a place to lay up and we might as well include Odd Job. We're gonna need a place to hide that Rolls also if we want to keep them both safe. You got a safe house somewhere?" I asked almost half-joking.

Sly got this big shit-eating grin on his face and said, "Follow me, I know just the place and it's all set for guests."

"No, Sly, I mean like for real and now!"

"Carlo, man, you doubtin' me?" he said still with that shit-eating grin on his face. "First let's get this place empty." Sly went over to DJ Tee, grabbed a mike from her, and told everyone to get out as there was a gas leak in the kitchen. "Dinner on the house tomorrow," Sly added.

That tomorrow would turn out to be several weeks, but oh, how original and it worked.

Odd Job didn't move until Lady Tatiana called out, "Tsuji, let them out." The massive man moved just out of the way allowing all to exit, and those who were scared shitless of the big man to ask him to move themselves. Within ten minutes, the club had cleared even with the few that grumbled about having to leave with full plates of food still on the tables.

Sly ordered the waitstaff to clear the tables and make sure the dishes were all cleaned. He also ordered the security guys to lock it down and not leave until the kitchen staff was done.

After an hour or so of the staff bustling around to clean up, the place was finally all theirs and Sly dismissed his security staff. "Follow me, and Brit Baby, come on, you need to see this too," Sly commanded. "Lady Tatiana, have that mountain man come with us."

"Tsuji, come here," ordered Lady.

"Does he understand sit, stay, and heel too?" I jokingly asked.

Lady was about to laugh but defended her bodyguard stating, "That is so rude," but she couldn't help a slight smile. "He only understands a few words of English, at least I think he does, and I have no patience to learn Japanese, but he came highly recommended." I was beginning to realize that patience was not one of her virtues.

Sly pushed a concealed button on the wall and with that a seamless section of the floor lifted up exposing a stairway leading to the basement level. The marble spiral stairs—yep, I said marble—were lit along the edges with built-in lights and Sly gestured with his hand to proceed and said, "After you, ladies."

As the girls began to descend, other lights obviously set on motion sensors began to light up a spacious room. Now I'm not talking some dank, musty basement room. I'm talking penthouse quality that those with cash would have paid plenty to own if it were on top of a large skyscraper.

More lighting came on as we all moved about the room and several flat-screen monitors turned on, monitoring different news and sports stations or surveillance cameras. Of course, the room was wired for surround sound with the best of Bose systems. Sly even had a waterfall along one wall, which emptied into a pool filled with aquatic plants and Koi fish. For those of you not familiar with Koi fish, they are nothing more than decorative carp but attractive, nonetheless.

Tsuji seemed to appreciate the display.

The floors were all polished exotic hardwoods and the walls were all hand-cut stone and set in place by expert stonemasons. Sly also had a computer bank set up with laptops along one of the other walls monitoring activity in and around the entire strip plaza where the club was located. They were set up so they could also project onto the flat-screen monitors mounted on the walls. Talk about a man cave—this was the top of top end.

Off the "living room" was a fully equipped commercial kitchen with the best stainless-steel appliances money could buy.

Being the nosy one I found that all three refrigerators were full as was the walk-in freezer, all of which stored food for the restaurant also. At least we're not going to starve.

Sly continued with the tour and showed us six bedrooms, three with king beds and three with two queens, with pricey Persian rugs decorating the floors. Each room had its own ornate bathroom with marble sinks, showers equipped with seats, and separate tubs with gold inlaid fixtures.

"Sly, what the fuck?" I couldn't help myself.

Sly, still with that shit-eating grin on his face replied, "Gotta have some secrets, bro!"

"Yeah, I'll say. Dude, how did you get all this done?"

"Well, I know people," Sly responded.

I asked, "Who knows about this?"

"Nobody that's around now. And we ain't done yet. I have a couple more surprises for you." With that Sly hit yet another secret button and another wall panel slid open and we entered an eight-car garage. Sly stated that the entrance was hidden from view disguised as an exterior wall and monitored by high-definition motion-detecting surveillance cameras that could find a pimple on a fly's ass. The exterior wall would descend into the ground when Sly activated a remote from inside or out. "Lady Tatiana, have 'Jumbo' bring the Rolls around back and I'll drop the hatch and he can pull it in here," Sly suggested. Sly also had several classic cars in here that I also was not aware he owned. One was a '63 Corvette Split Window Coupe complete with an optional 327-cubic inch fuel-injected 360 horsepower engine in pristine original condition. God, I hated him!

"Sly, man, you just full of surprises today. And here I thought I had your security all sewn up!"

"You did, Carlo, for the club, but it's all tied in down here," responded Sly. We both busted out laughing and the ladies were still in awe at the lavish surroundings, yes, even Lady Tatiana.

Lady sent Tsuji for the car and Sly and I waited for him to pull it in.

Obviously, this all took up much more room than what was beneath the club above. Apparently, Sly had obtained exclusive property rights to the ground under the other three buildings that comprised the strip plaza where the club stood. Again, WTF!

Sly told the girls to each choose a room as all were stocked with men's and women's bed attire, other casual wear and such, all still with tags attached. Sly even had stuff to fit Tsuji. Brit and Lady chose to stay in the same room and Odd Job took one of the king rooms.

"Pick a room, my friend, because you're staying also until we get this mess cleaned up. Anything you or the girls need I can send out for but as of now no one leaves. Now, when are you going to tell me what this is all about?"

I couldn't help myself and replied like Master Po, "Patience, Grasshopper." I then agreed that that was a plan, at least a start. Besides, how bad could it be bunkered up with Lady?

CHAPTER SIX

THE THUNDERBOLT

I KNEW IF WE WERE TO DEFEAT THESE *PORCO DI MAIALE* ("PIG fuckers" for those not up on their Italian), we had to know as much as possible as to how they operated and who they were. I spent the remainder of the night and into the wee hours of the morning on one of the computers pulling up as much data as I could find, all the while nursing a Booker's, okay several, straight up. I forgot to mention earlier that the bar in the bunker was very well stocked. What I found online about the Albanians only disturbed me more.

Most of the lights had dimmed, as there was no activity in the great room. It was sometime past midnight when I heard a door open to one of the bedrooms. As the lights came back up when the motion sensors caught the movement, I saw Lady Tatiana make her way to the kitchen in nothing but French-cut panties and a matching lacy bra.

"Lady Tatiana, you do know I am sitting here."

"Ah, no, Carlo, I didn't know anyone was out here. But I am sure this is not the first time you've ever seen a woman in her underwear, is it?"

"Ah, no, Lady, but not someone like you, and I usually know the woman a little more intimately before I see her like you are." I turned my head to look away, but I caught an amusing smile on her face and she just had to make me more uncomfortable.

Lady came over to where I was seated, spun my chair around, and commanded me to look at her as she placed her hands on the arms of the desk chair. Not many people commanded me to do anything, but I tried ever so hard—yeah, *hard* being the operative word—to keep eye contact, but her perky D girls were right up in my face.

"And what do you mean by a woman like me?" she said making me squirm even more. What kind of game was she playing and why with me?

I managed to stammer, "Just...just someone so stunningly beautiful that she has the ability to take a man's breath away... and from your walk of life." And I don't stammer easily but she had caught me off guard which is not something I like.

"Do I take your breath away, Carlo?" she cooed in her intoxicatingly cool voice.

In response all I could do was nod my head nearly brushing my chin against the "girls," and yes, I was breathless and yes, that is how close she was to me.

"Carlo, I appreciate you being a gentleman. It is so sweet and different from what I'm used to. Men usually just want to get with me, if you know what I mean, and could care less about the woman I am. Don't change, Carlo."

With that she leaned over more and kissed me on the forehead with the "girls" lightly grazing me. Then she said good night and went back to her room as if nothing happened.

She smelled so incredibly sexy, I did want to get with her for all the right reasons, and I think she knew it. If there was ever a time I thought I could lose control, it was when she kissed me. I wanted to desperately and fiercely pull her to me, kiss her long and deeply on those full sensual lips, rip off the remainder of her clothes, and make love to this astoundingly beautiful woman. But I couldn't, I was frozen.

I couldn't move, I was hit head-on by a rushing avalanche of emotion. Just as Carlo and Fabrizio claim Michael Corleone had been hit by what Sicilians call the "thunderbolt," a powerful, almost dangerous longing in a man for a particular woman, I too had been struck. My smoldering had now turned to a flame. All I could do was sit there for a while. I couldn't concentrate on the work I was doing on the computer and occasionally I would take a sip of my Booker's trying to figure out what had just hit me. What the hell did I say at the end of the last chapter?

CHAPTER SEVEN

THE ALBANIANS: "WHO ARE THOSE GUYS?"

YES, READERS, YOU'RE RIGHT. I BORROWED THAT LINE FROM *Butch Cassidy and the Sundance Kid*, when they were being pursued by the Pinkertons. And like the Pinkertons, they would not stop until they got what they were after. When the Lady's intoxicating scent had cleared from my head, I poured another Booker's before documenting the following on the Albanian mob. We would need this later in the morning when I would tell Sly everything.

Though the Albanian Mafia has strongholds in all of Europe and North America, I concentrated my research on North America and particularly New York City, where Lady told me the people who approached her were from. Wikipedia had some of the best information and along with some other sites, this is what I found:

Rudaj Organization

The most famous Albanian criminal organization was the Rudaj Organization. The Rudaj Organization, also called The Corporation, was a well-known Albanian criminal organization operating in the New York City metro area.

In October 2004, the FBI arrested twenty-two men who worked for the Rudaj Organization. This included its leader Alex Rudaj, and effectively ended the criminal organization.

"But," I said talking to myself, "that was seven long years ago and I am sure they had secretly rebuilt by now."

They had entered in the territory of the Lucchese crime family in Astoria, Queens, New York, and are said to have even beaten up two made men in the Lucchese family. The name Rudaj comes from the boss of the organization. According to The New York Times, published on January 2006, "Beginning in the 1990s, the Corporation, led by a man named Alex Rudaj, established ties with organized crime figures including members of the Gambino crime family, the authorities say. Then, through negotiations or in armed showdowns, the Albanians struck out on their own, daring to battle the Lucchese and Gambino families for territory in Queens, the Bronx, and Westchester County. What we have here might be considered a sixth crime family, after the five Mafia organizations— Bonanno, Colombo, Gambino, Genovese, and Lucchese—said Fred Snelling, head of the FBI's criminal division in New York.

I continued with this from Wikipedia:

On the streets where the Italian mob once ruled, a new syndicate was taking over, run by tough, ambitious Albanian immigrants, who still cling to a code of silence. "We're still trying to learn about their culture and figure out what makes them tick," James Farley, FBI supervisory special agent and expert on organized crime, says of the Albanians. "They're difficult to infiltrate. We're just now catching up with Albanian organized crime." While Italian gangsters may be three or four generations removed from the Old Country, the Albanians grew up under brutal communist regimes, engaging in protracted blood feuds with rival clans, and subscribing to a strict code of silence that makes the Italian credo of omertà seem playful. "The first-generation Albanians have a tendency to be more violent than American-born syndicates," claims Hall.

In the United States, Albanian gangs started to be active in the mid-80s, mostly participating in low-level crimes such as burglaries and robberies. Later, they would become affiliated with Cosa Nostra crime families before eventually growing strong enough to operate their own organizations under the Iliazi family name.

Speaking anonymously for Philadelphia's City Paper, a member of the Kielbasa Posse, an ethnic Polish mob group, declared in 2002 that Poles are willing to do business with "just about anybody— Dominicans, Blacks, Italians, Asian street gangs, and Russians. But they won't go near the Albanian mob. The Albanians are too violent and too unpredictable." The Polish mob has told its associates that the Albanians are like the early Sicilian Mafia—clannish, secretive, hypersensitive to any kind of insult, and too quick to use violence for the sake of vengeance.

The more I read, the worse it got. New York City has the largest Albanian population in the United States. For twenty-five years, a small number of them have been popping up in spectacular ways on the blotter: shooting up Scores strip club, putting a hit out on Giuliani and his prosecutor, employing an active-duty cop for crime jobs (nothing new especially in Boston), muscling in on and pulling guns on the Gambino family during a sit-down at a gas station (allegedly), demanding John Gotti's old table at Raos (allegedly). Plaurent "Lenti" Dervishaj, the most-wanted fugitive in his native Albania, the alleged head of an organized crime syndicate, is on the federal authorities' most-wanted list for New York City. (Among other things, he had rocket launchers.) *Cazzo*! Figure it out, it's Italian.

Albania is a prime transit zone for heroin, situated on the way from Afghanistan, where all dope comes from, and Europe, considered to be the most lucrative market in the world. The product goes from Afghanistan to Iran to Turkey and then to the Balkans where "interception efficiency drops significantly…the route is exceedingly well organized and lubricated with corruption," according to *The World Drug Report*, 2010, produced by the United Nations Office on Drugs and Crime. The report also notes that "…important networks have clan-based and hierarchically organized structures. Albanian groups in particular have such structures making them particularly hard to infiltrate." There is an old Albanian tradition of families and clans (*fins*, *fares*) and a code of honor (*besa*) that criminals appropriate and corrupt.

Albania also has been a very significant corridor for human trafficking (sex work) and smuggling of migrants. Ethnic Albanians are also heavily involved in the fake passport industry. Yeah, no shit. These guys are a bad bunch of *scopa della madre*. Yep, go find an Italian slang dictionary. From a private source, an ex-DEA agent, who had dealings with an Albanian national in the past, told me this person stated that he fled Albania fearing for his life. The AOC had killed many of his friends and family using car bombs as the preferred method of terminating with extreme prejudice. He would say nothing further. And that is straight from the horse's mouth.

Well, now I knew what we were dealing with, and none of it pretty. It was time to get a few hours' sleep, get with Sly, and plot out our next step. I definitely did not like where this was headed.

CHAPTER EIGHT

PLANNING FOR WAR

I AWOKE LATER THAT MORNING, AROUND 8:30, TO THE scent of bacon sizzling in a fry pan and the aroma of fresh-brewed coffee. Next to strong coffee, bacon was my second favorite breakfast food. It smelled strong and that was exactly what I needed to help clear my head from the long night and "other" distractions I encountered. I thought for sure Sly had gotten up before me and he was the one at the stove. But when I entered the kitchen area and saw Lady Tatiana busy at the stove and yes, dressed more appropriately, I couldn't help but say, "Dang, woman, you cook too?"

"Oh, so you think just because I'm successful and have staff that I can't cook? My momma taught me a long time ago to be able to take care of myself, and cooking is one thing she taught me well. Wait until you taste these buttermilk pancakes with real maple syrup, Carlo, you just might propose to me."

Where did that come from?

She gently brushed against me in such a subtle way while I was pouring coffee, which I nearly dropped, that she was either the biggest tease trying to make me more uncomfortable or she was actually attempting to flirt. She certainly knew how to get what she wanted, and I certainly hoped it was an attempt at flirtation, but I couldn't find a lot of reasons she would want someone as old as me when she could have her choice of any man. Things like this just don't happen to guys like me unless we had *beaucoup* bucks. I sure as hell was no sugar daddy, not that she needed one.

"Carlo, take a seat, breakfast is done. Let me know if there is anything else you need, and I'll get it," she stated as she placed platters of food on the table.

"Let me wake up Sly so he can get out here while the food is hot," I responded.

"Already done, hun, you eat up and they will be out."

Hun, did she just call me hun? I'm just going to stop thinking for a few minutes and eat. Sly, Tsuji, and Britiney all came into the kitchen and took seats as if on cue. Everyone was famished from the long night before, and forks and knifes were flying so fast I thought I saw sparks. Lady was right, the pancakes were worth a proposal, but I wasn't going there. Not now or anytime soon, so I say. Nope, no way, that was one pony I wasn't looking to ride again, and just to be clear, I mean the marriage pony.

After we had finished, I said, "Sly, let's go in the other room, we have some talking to do."

Lady replied, "I will be right in also. Brit and Tsuji can clean up." I started to protest but Lady shot me this look that pretty much froze me in my tracks. How the frigging hell does she do that?

I relented, "Okay, come on in with us and try not to interrupt too much. And thanks for breakfast. That was the first home-cooked meal I've had in a while, at least by a woman." She just smiled. Oh yeah, she knew exactly what she was doing.

"Sly, we have a major problem on our hands. These guys are Albanian Mafia and there is a good chance they have heavy-duty firepower like RPGs, and they are adept with car bombs. Here's the stuff I printed out last night. These guys will all play for keeps. They have pushed the Italian mob out of strongholds in NYC and are absolutely ruthless. Where are we going to get the kind of artillery we need to take a war to them?"

"Damn straight we'll take the war to them. This whole city is our turf, Carlo. Don't worry about the hardware, I think I have that covered too. What I wonder is where we will get enough men we can trust? I know that most of my guys will do what I need them to do so I figure eight men there."

"That is all fine and good when they're tossing people out of the club, but do they have shooting skills?" I inquired.

"Trust me, they know how to get dirty when it's time to throw down. What about you?"

"All I need to do is reach out and touch a few people and I think I can get another dozen or so. If you know you can arm them then just maybe we might stand a chance."

"Tsuji will stand with you and so will I," Lady chimed in. In the background we could all hear Tsuji and Brit trying to communicate and laughing as neither understood the other, or so we thought. A bit of comic relief in light of the dire situation.

Sly and I simultaneously responded, "Hell, no!"

"Look," Lady said, "if we lose, I'm a dead woman anyway so I would rather fight and die with you all if it comes to that." Nothing either Sly or I could say would change her mind.

"Do you even know how to shoot a gun, let alone kill someone, Lady?" I asked.

Lady replied, "Just how hard can it be? Besides, Carlo, you can teach me, can't you?" Again, she spoke in that cooing tone that could melt icebergs and getting her own way again! Damn her!

"Not a bad idea if we had a range," I said.

"Uh, Carlo, I got it," Sly piped in.

"Sly, what the hell don't you have covered?"

"The guys you said you could get," Sly answered letting out a big belly laugh. "So, who are you going to get?"

"Years ago, I did some work with the DEA before I was a cop and I'm still in touch with this guy. He recently retired as director and I'm sure he knows a few party crashers who have retired and are dying for some action. All you need to know is his name is J3 and we will leave it at that.

"My second guy has Special Ops training, has done some high-level protection work in the Middle East, and his guys are all shooters and looters. All have had sniper training and are very hard-core. He goes by Jake Magnum, and no jokes about condoms or dick size, please." But it got a few laughs anyway, as I knew it would.

"Now, as I said before, the AOC has been giving the Italian mob a lot of problems and there is no love lost between them. I know a guy who's a friend of a friend of mine in the North End, or In Town, and he may just jump at the chance to fall in with us.

"Lastly, I know a retired cop friend who would not have any qualms about joining us. He has always had my back. That's my list for better or worse, but you never know who might show up."

CHAPTER NINE

THE BAD GUYS

ALBAN TOLE WAS A MEAN-ASS, DANGEROUS, LETHAL MAN. He was as smart—street-smart—as he was big, and he had a head and body like a bull. He stood 6'4" and was 310 pounds of steroid-induced muscle. His criminal skills were honed in the Russian prison, Lubyanka, and after the fall of the Soviet Union it continued in the streets of Shkodra as part of the Xhakja Klan. He bore the tattoos of where he had been and who he was and now he was so mad he could barely speak. Spittle flew from his mouth as he screamed at the Mezini brothers, Astrit and Kastriot.

"You stupid, ignorant fucks, how do you lose a Rolls Royce in a shit part of town? How does this happen? Don't even make an excuse!"

As tough as they were, the brothers knew better than to try to answer Alban when he was in a rage. It was a good way to get dead fast. They had seen Tole kill a man who happened to look at him funny. Tole no doubt was the meanest, but all of them were way beyond violent.

"All of you get the fuck out of my sight and find that black-ass bitch. Put some money out on the street, all of it if you have to, and find her. Do I have to do everything myself?" That was a question that better not get an answer. "Kill the gook if you have to but leave her to me. I'll take great pleasure in making her sign the paperwork and then dispose of her." Tole had brought a substantial stash of cash and could easily get more if needed. Getting people to talk for a few dollars wasn't difficult and if they did meet a stubborn source then their means to get what they wanted resulted in pain that one would not want to endure.

The brothers, along with Koli, Zeni, Luli, and Shpati, left the two-story warehouse they were holed up in the Southampton area. A couple of the crew came up a few days before to get it all set up and to scout the area. Ironically, not far from the South Bay House of Correction and a Boston Transit Police substation. But Tole didn't think much more of them than overpaid security guards. And the overhead doors had too much glass in them for Tole's taste. But it was better than nothing. Toti, short for Kastriot, was the first to speak and second in command. "Astrit and I will take the South End, Shpati and Luli take Dorchester, and Zeni and Koli take Roxbury and Mattapan. No stone unturned, do what it takes to find her, use all our connections and make more by any means necessary. Call me when you find something and don't come back here until you do, *kuptoj* (understand)?"

They didn't have to say a word, they all understood quite clearly. As good as Tole was to them, the rewards they received in the form of money, women, and status in the organization, they didn't let it fool them that if they screwed up, they would be just as dead as someone who tried to cross Tole.

CHAPTER TEN

A Long, Long Time Ago in a Continent Far...Okay, you get the Picture!

Let me digress a couple of hundred years to the time of the real, original OGs—Original Gangsters for those living in 1950. That's right, the Italian gangs, and possibly part of my family heritage. Whether they were called the Mafia, Camorra, Apulian Sacra Corona Unita, 'Ndrangheta (possibly the most powerful and richest crime family in the present-day world), or the Cosa Nostra, many give Garibaldi and the Sicilian Mafia credit for uniting Italy. If I may take a page from Joseph Bonnano's autobiography and with all due respect:

"In my grandfather's time, Sicily was under the influence of the Bourdon Dynasty, a royal family of Spanish and French ancestry. Italy itself was like a jigsaw puzzle with the pieces owned by various powers. Because of the patchwork of foreign domination and internal weaknesses, Italy was the last major country in Europe to be unified

*under a native ruler. The unification was spearheaded by King
Victor Emmanuel II and his brilliant Prime Minister, Cavour. It
could not have been accomplished, however, without the leadership
and inspiration of the patriot Guisseppi Garibaldi. Garibaldi
catalyzed the unification movement by enlisting a volunteer army to
liberate Sicily. These volunteers, a motley crew of idealists and
zealots, wore a distinctive garb and became known as the Red
Shirts."*

Now back to my words. My great, great grandfather was part
of the Red Shirts and hence possibly mafia. Since that time, my
family has in some way been connected with those of this closed
society whether by direct association or part of it.

My great grandfather and grandmother came to this country
in 1911 when my grandfather was seven years old. On his
eighteenth birthday he declared his independence from his
parents who had since settled in Connecticut and he moved to
Buffalo, New York. This was around 1922 and Italians were
treated like dirt by the Irish, Germans, and Jews. He hated being
Italian at the time and even tried to change his name but in his
later years he embraced his heritage. My uncle, Ricardo,
embraced it and I looked up to him for guidance and inspiration.
I heard stories from him about a certain "family" in the Buffalo
area and as I grew older, I ended up having personal contact with
many of the characters in this family. My personal attorney, his
father, was consigliere to Don Stefano Magadino. But their
names will remain undisclosed. So, my dear readers, it was time
for me to get down and dirty and start my own little motley crew
as fierce and deadly as those we faced.

CHAPTER ELEVEN

THE SISTAS

BRITINEY AND LADY TATIANNA WERE IN THE BUNKER sitting at the table with their morning coffee. They sat reminiscing about the past and their childhood and how rough it had been. Both had grown up in the South End of Boston not far from where they were now. While Lady had become successful despite the neighborhood and the hood rats trying to keep everyone pulled down, Brit had had issues and went from job to job, in and out of college and occasionally getting into a little trouble. That's when she had encountered me. But, y'all know that.

"So, Brit, what's been going on since we last saw one another? I know it's been a long time and I know the shit has hit the proverbial fan, so to speak, but let's forget that for a while and catch up. You knew I'd bring you onboard in some way, so you didn't have to work here…"

"Actually, I am pretty good here," Brit cut in. "Sly is good to me, it pays well with tips, I'm safe, and I have a nice place. Small but nice. I like the vibe here and Carlo is always keeping an eye out too. He's a sweet guy but I think you're finding that out for yourself!"

"And why would you say that?" asked Lady with a bemused look on her face.

"Come on, do you think I'm blind? I see the looks you give one another and when you look at him in a certain way he can hardly speak. For him to be speechless...well, let's say it just doesn't happen. And you have never, ever let anyone talk to you the way he did. Even Dad, when the rat bastard was around, couldn't talk to you that way. You kept all four of us safe from his rages. But, Carlo, dear Sis, has caught your eye. I have never seen him so mesmerized by a woman. You know he has a soft spot for us colored girls!"

"Oh, really, he does, huh?" Lady Tatiana said laughing. "So why isn't he married or have a lady? Seems like there was plenty of chocolate when I came in here last night."

Brit replied, "His ex-late wife was murdered, and he never could seem to get close to another woman. At least that I know of. He always comes in here alone, and let's face it, these hoochies are not what he wants. He does have class and cleans up real nice. And let's face it, Sis, all the men around you are yes men and might as well have a pussy."

"So, you think you got me all figured out?" Brit's last comment got a laugh out of Lady as she spoke.

"At least that part, and I see that look in your eye," Brit said with a radiant smile.

"He wouldn't want to put up with my work schedule, ugh! Some days I don't even want to. And he is so much older, not that I mind his maturity. I like mature men, but why would he want me?"

"Oh, really now? You're gonna use that line with me?"

"I jus'…I just don't know…"

Brit retorted, "Have you looked at yourself in the mirror lately? Where is that tougher-than-nails, confident, strong woman that walked in here? He would be honored to have you on his arm as would any man with a temperature, and that man's is running 103! Call the paramedics already, the man is overheatin'."

Lady smiled and then said, "I don't know why we're even talking about all this with this other big mess going on. We could all be dead by tomorrow."

"Yeah, you're right, Sis, but not if Carlo has anything to say about it," Brit said again with that knowing little smile.

And those, my dear readers, were the operative words, damn skippy straight!

CHAPTER TWELVE

Traitor in the Midst

As instructed, Tole's men had fanned out across the city spreading cash, asking questions, kicking some ass, and takin' names as he knew they would. It was "do as he said or get a bullet in the head." He didn't need nor would he accept contradiction to his orders. These guys didn't worry about the neighborhoods because some of them looked like the lap of luxury compared to some of the shitholes they had come from and been to. Yeah, they got some evil looks from the brothers, but they didn't give a fuck and gave it right back. They walked with purpose and could not—would not—be deterred. Just picture two badasses doing the slow walk like in the movies, leather jackets flapping in the breeze, days' growth of beard and slicked-back hair. How European, but that's them. The few that challenged them ended up with an expensive trip to the emergency room and after that everyone seemed willing to talk even if they knew jack shit. Word got around the hood quickly. That was exactly what they got for the most part until Luli called Toti who was with his brother Astrit in the South End.

"Yeah, what you got?" asked Toti a little more than impatient.

"I think I have something. I ran into a guy on Ashmont Street near the train station and he said he knows a guy who might know where the bitch is or at least a way to find her. He said this guy he knows works at a club called Chez Rendezvous in the South End. The guy that owns the place has his finger in a lot of stuff in the city. He gave it up for a couple of hundred."

Toti barked back, "Enough already. Where do we find him?"

"The guy told me our dude's name is De'Londo and he might be found at Slades, an R&B bar down on Tremont Street, when he's not running bitches or at the other club. You'll know when you see him. He looks like a front lineman."

"Good work," responded Toti. "Keep on looking in case this is a dead end."

"Will do, Boss."

Like Luli said, Slades was an R&B soul bar that had been open for years at its location in South Boston. It had once been owned by renowned Celtics player, Bill Russell. The place had even been frequented by Muhammed Ali, along with many other noted celebrities, and their pictures adorned the walls. It currently had three new owners and now had the flavor of a supper club with live soul and R&B. It had been quite the spot for many years and was still going strong regardless of ownership.

Toti and Astrit parked their bad boy black BMW 740 I X-drive in front of the club regardless of the *No Parking* sign clearly posted, and they entered the club. There was a pretty, light-brown-skinned girl with a head full of braids standing behind the hostess podium and her looks were not lost on the two brothers. Regardless of their prejudice, they still admired a hot little young thing. To them it was another body to make money. The hotter the better. Her nametag read, "Ashantee," and she asked, "How may I help you gentlemen?" Yes, the quality of the club had come up a notch or two.

Astrit asked, "Do you know a guy by the name of De'Londo? And please, do not look in his direction, just tell us if he's here." He handed her a $100 bill.

She answered, "That's him over at the bar in the red and black Polo jacket. And that's not necessary."

"Keep it anyways," Toti said sliding the money to her. Astrit and Toti looked in his direction and noted, yeah, he was as big as a front lineman, but they knew how to deal with that shit. They walked up to him and had him flanked and Toti asked, "You know this black whore?"

With that De'Londo answered, "Who the fuck are you two clowns and why do you want to know?"

Of course, dear readers, that was obviously the wrong answer and with a sharp, swift, adept flick of his wrist that went unnoticed by the other patrons, Astrit deployed a Canadian Special Forces Karambit knife in De'Londo's groin area. It did not go unnoticed by De'Londo, which got a rise out of him and not the kind he wanted.

"Listen, you cocksucking black bastard, you can make a little money, or you can lose your balls. The choice is yours. So you want to try again?"

De'Londo really didn't have to think long before he replied, "Yeah, I might know her, I mean, I've seen the bitch. She came into Chez Rendezvous two nights ago with some big-ass gook. I think her sister works at the bar. She is a hot little sista named Britiney. They had a talk with the owner, Sly, and some other motherfucker of a white guy and they shut the club down. Big sign on the door, *Closed for Renovation*. But the place isn't closed for shit. They're all hiding out in the place underground."

Astrit said, "Now see, was that so hard? And what do you mean, underground?"

"It's all hid below the club. I have no idea what he has down there except supplies for the restaurant. No one is allowed down there, ever, not even that honky. I don't know how Sly gets down there either. All a big secret," he said as sweat broke out on De'Londo's forehead.

Toti asked, "Who the fuck is the white guy? And be careful who you call honky, asshole."

De'Londo answered with beads of perspiration now running down his forehead, shaking slightly, scared shitless for the first time in his badass life. "All I know is he's really tight with the owner, used to be a cop and now does PI work. He thinks he's someone special, but I can't stand his white motherfuckin' ass. He thinks he's VIP or something. Now can you please get that knife outta my junk?"

Astrit backed off on the pressure and said, "You should be glad we didn't cut your balls off anyway, but here's $500. Make sure we can find you, give us your cell number now. Call this number if you have anything else. If this pans out there may be more for you, but keep your nigger mouth shut, *kuptoj*?" Yeah, he understood loud and clear and gave them his number, and Astrit handed him a business card with just a number on it. No white man had ever spoken to him the way they did, and it left him chilled.

"Yeah, yeah, man, I got you, Sly would kill me himself if he knew I talked to you." With that, Toti and Astrit backed away and left the club not failing to give Ashantee another leering look on the way out. They discarded the parking ticket on the Beemer that was on the windshield in the street and left the curb with a cloud of smoke.

CHAPTER THIRTEEN

A Hint of Doubt

SLY HAD LOCKED UP THE RESTAURANT TWO NIGHTS BEFORE and placed a *Closed* sign on the front door under the pretense of renovation. Sly was in a meeting with his guys and said, "Y'all are on duty until this is over so no one isn't gonna lose any money. You guys are all like family and I need you, as does Carlo and the ladies. Stay close to your phone, no bullshit out on the street, as if I need to say that, and if anyone hears anything, report back to me. All right, get out of here and keep an ear to the ground. We can't fuck this up. Be back here by 2:00 PM tomorrow."

De'Londo couldn't look Sly in the eye or any of the other guys he worked with. He had a bad feeling that they were all going to die, and he wasn't about to be one of them. So, he slinked out like the traitor he was, got his Ninja ZX-10X SE, sped off, and wasn't coming back, ever. He'd take his chances with the Albanians.

Back inside, Sly couldn't quite put his finger on it. He felt something was wrong, very wrong, but decided to keep it to himself until he was sure. He trusted his guys but still, it ate at him.

The feeling ate at Sly all that night and he tossed and turned. The next morning, still looking groggy, he exited his room in the bunker and briefly spoke to the ladies before checking with me who, as usual, was glued to the computer screen. Sly had a VPN network setup and used the Tor browser to protect our privacy and location. Between the two it would be hard to find us even using a NSA computer. The signal would be bounced all over the world and our IP address could be from several dozen countries of our choice.

"Carlo, did you get something to eat, or you been at that all morning?"

"I'm good, bro, the ladies took good care of me when I got up. But, my God, you look like shit, and those bags under your eyes, what's up with that?"

"I bet they did, and thanks for the compliment," he said looking a little in a haze.

"Sly, you know you look like shit, couldn't sleep, big boy?"

"I don't know, something's just naggin' at me, can't put my finger on it."

"Wanna talk about it, or should I call a shrink?"

"Nah, I'm good, but if I figure it out, you'll be the first to know. By the way, how's the list coming for your guys? Mine are on call with full pay."

I answered, "Well, that was mighty white of you, and yes, I have all the party invitations sent out and I expect responses to start rolling in shortly. I contacted Jake, J3, Dave from NY, the old cop buddy. Couldn't get the friend of a friend of mine, as he's *away*, nah mean?"

"Yeah," Sly said half-chuckling at my comment. "That would make it a bit hard but I'm sure we will make it work. Just need to find out how many we are up against."

"Whatta you thinkin', Sly? Maybe fifteen, twenty guys? Don't think that should be a problem. I think we will be better prepared and armed but ya never know. We will be better armed, right?" I asked with apprehension.

"Yeah, Carlo, when I show you what I have stocked I think you'll like it. As far as the Albanians, with all that research you did, you are the in-house expert."

"I'm a far cry from that, big man, but I'm sure J3 will have more info."

After I said that, Lady walked in from her living quarters and asked, "What are you two talking about?"

"Nothin,'" we both replied at the same time looking like two cats that caught the canary.

"Yeah, I'm sure," she answered. "Who knows what you two are cooking up." All the while she stared at us with that look of, *I'm not buying that.*

"Just guy talk," Sly responded.

"Right, but I'm sure you'll tell me when you're both good and ready." Lady sauntered away not looking pleased with the answer.

CHAPTER FOURTEEN

THE BAD NEWS BEARS

LATER THAT EVENING, I CHECKED MY EMAILS ON THE secured server and found that the "boys" I had contacted had all responded and were on the way with reinforcements. They all wanted to know if they should gun up and I advised them that it was all covered. There would be something for everyone whatever their taste may be. They were all shooters and looters, as famed Navy Seal Dick Marcinko would say, and I would not want them coming to look for me, well, except maybe to save my ass!

J3 had headed up some of the biggest investigations and had been agent in charge of several plum posts in the US before becoming the head honcho. He and the two guys coming with him had hunted Pablo Escobar in South America, Amando Carrillo in Mexico, Khun Sa in Burma, and Griselda Blanco aka the Cocaine Grandmother, right here in the good ole' USA. These guys were no joke.

Back in the day when J3 was still in Buffalo, we worked a case that ended up in El Paso. But by the time it moved to trial and the jury, it went sideways. We had suspected that the attorney for the defense, a Lebanese man by the name of Lee Chagra, who had emigrated to the US through Mexico, had his fingers in the pie. To make a long story short and some years later, he and his brother Jimmy, also an attorney, were responsible for hiring a well-known actor's father to do the hit on the federal judge, Maximum John Wood, that heard our case. The hit man got life and eventually flipped but not until he served a long time. It was even suspected that he was on the grassy knoll in Dallas on November 22, 1963, when Kennedy was killed. A few years after this happened, he, Chagra, was found shot to death in his office on December 23, 1978, and $500,000 missing from a floor safe. Sounds like wet work does pay. Oh, well.

Now, Jake Magnum was a whole different creature, a badass Spec Ops guy with lots of history, as were the three guys he had headed our way. All had sniper training and had many successful hunts in the dry arid lands known as Afghanistan and Iraq. Not the guys you would want on your "six" at one thousand yards as they were collecting souls and stacking bones. They had made piles of money as independent contractors, which was well deserved, not like the measly pay that good old Uncle Sam paid them. Shaking Jake's hand was like grabbing a vise that was closing on you very rapidly. When it came to bad guys I would rather he use that hand to crush our enemies' scrawny chicken necks.

My team couldn't be—wouldn't be—complete without my old buddy Dave. We had gone to the police academy together in the winter of 1977. We both worked for different departments but dished out the same kind of law. Dave and I were kindred spirits, loving bikes, guns, and girls, perhaps a little too much at times and not necessarily in that order. I remember a bike trip we took one fall to Vermont and we froze our asses off. But I digress again. He was the type of guy that wouldn't back down from anyone, never, regardless of their size or who they were. Once when I had locked up a corrupt city official from his city for DWI, oddly enough she was a big campaigner for making drunk driving arrests due to her son being hit by one. Dave and some of the guys got me a case of beer. It never tasted better.

Last but not least was Ritchie. Ritch was as Italian as they came with the classic charming good looks, dark hair and skin, and a firm square jaw. Though not a shooter and looter, he could still handle a gun, but better than that, he was one hell of a driver. Just think of the movie *Baby Driver* or *Transporter* but on steroids, and you'll get the pic. I had seen him do things with a vehicle that even the best personal protection guys couldn't do. Ritch could drive anything, anytime, anywhere, and his favorite phrase while driving was, "Don't look at me!" Yes, it's an insider joke.

So, dear readers, with Sly's guys we're up to nineteen for the home team and no telling who else might want to play. All I know is that Tole's guys better come fast, hard, and armed to the teeth cuz we weren't backing down. Now if I could just get the Lady and Brit to stand down, I'd feel a lot better, but I don't think it will happen.

CHAPTER FIFTEEN

MERCHANT OF DOUBT

DE'LONDO WAS UP EARLY AS HE HAD A HARD TIME SLEEPING that night. *No wonder*, he said to himself. He had betrayed his boss and the only man that had cared enough to pick him up off the streets. His mother had been a junkie whore and had died when she was in her thirties from an overdose by her pimp-boyfriend and who was also De'Londo's father. He had beat De'Londo every chance he had as he was usually high or drunk, and De'Londo couldn't wait to get away from him. De'Londo knew he had a lot of potential. He was smart, fast, and big, and probably could have gone pro in the NFL if he had only taken the time to apply himself. He dropped out of school his sophomore year to live on the street and seek an income there.

That was where Sly found him about a year later and made him an offer—a place to stay and some odd jobs around the club until he was old enough to be security. De'Londo caught on fast and couldn't wait to wear the security tux. He knew he would attract the girls, as he was a handsome young man. But even after all that Sly had done for him, he became disgruntled. He didn't think he was advancing fast enough, not for him, not by a long shot. As Master Po said, "Patience, Grasshopper," but the meaning eluded De'Londo.

As he would, he got dressed, ate, and hopped on the Ninja. He knew where he was headed, and it was to find the Albanians. He called the number Toti had given him and said, "We need to talk."

Toti replied, "Half hour at Victoria's Diner." Toti disconnected and told Tole where he and Astrit were going. Tole just gave his massive head a nod and brushed them away.

Toti and Astrit set up surveillance across the street from the diner and waited for the Ninja to pull up. They wanted to make sure no one was following their rat. De'Londo pulled up and parked on Massachusetts Avenue at Newmarket Square. It was no coincidence it was around the corner from the warehouse. They let him go in and get seated to make sure there was no tail and there wasn't. They exited the Beemer, went in, and Astrit sat next to De'Londo and Toti sat across from him, all in a booth in the back.

After the waitress had taken their orders, Astrit said, "What you got?"

De'Londo was sweating even though it was a cool day, but with the heat of deception upon him, he couldn't do anything else. "Sly has all the guys on duty with full pay and I think that white motherfucker has a bunch of guys coming in. I hope you got more than a few guys."

Toti snapped back, "You're not giving the orders, we tell *you* what to do, got it, *nëna qij*?" That is "motherfucker," for those of you not fluent in Albanian.

De'Londo knew to keep his mouth shut at that moment, as he feared reprisal from Toti. He just nodded his head.

"Now get out of here and call us when you hear more," said Astrit.

"I can't go back there, I'm done. Can't do anything else. It's over for me."

"Too bad, *nëna qij*, you got your thirty pieces of silver, and remember we know where you hole up," Toti growled with pieces of food coming out of his mouth. Astrit let him out of the booth and with a nod from Toti followed him outside.

CHAPTER SIXTEEN

I Smell a Rat

Reshaun and Khaseem were on the way back to the club for the 2:00 p.m. meeting when they saw the top end Ninja sitting at the curb. Reshaun told Khaseem, he pulled over and watched to see what De'Londo was up to and whom he might be having lunch with. They had never much cared for him as they thought he was too ambitious, but out of respect for Sly, they tolerated him. They cut through the lot and noticed the 7 Series BMW parked with New York State plates. It wasn't uncommon to see a car from New York State due to the close proximity to New York, but this felt different. They both knew that the badasses were from New York and this was too much of a coincidence to not be strange or out of place, especially with De'Londo's bike outside. They parked further down on Newmarket and just waited. To the untrained eye this would have meant nothing, but this was exactly how Sly and Carlo had taught them—to look for the not so obvious. So they sat and waited.

They didn't have to wait long before De'Londo came out. Reshaun nudged Khaseem as he was playing a game on his phone and pointed to De'Londo. What really took them back was the Eastern European guy following behind.

Astrit grabbed De'Londo by the leather jacket and pulled him close, didn't say a word, and then pushed the big man back.

"Damn, man, I knew, I knew that sack of shit was no good! Khaseem, look at that dude with De'Londo."

"Awww, shit man, did you see what that dude just did to our boy?" said Reshaun.

"Yeah," said Khaseem. "That shit is off the hook! He's got that boy completely intimidated and about to shit his pants! We gotta tell Sly."

"Sho'nuff, looks like our boy done gone and got hisself in a mess."

"Shit, man, Sly will have a meltdown and no telling what Carlo may do. Sly say he's not another one to put a hair across his ass but I like the dude. Far as I'm concerned, he's solid. Come on, we gotta ride!"

Khaseem put the big Town Car in gear and followed De'Londo at a discrete distance.

CHAPTER SEVENTEEN

BACK IN THE BUNKER

SLY GOT A PHONE CALL FROM RESHAUN AND AFTER SLY hung up he said to me, "That little fuck De'Londo was seen by Reshaun and Khaseem at Victoria's Diner. They think he was talking to one of the Albanians. They saw a high-end Beemer in the lot with New York plates on it and De'Londo's bike. They put two and two together and figured something was shakin'. I told them to not report here until they knew what was up with him. This really fries my ass. I probably gave more to him than any of the others and look how he does us. That's okay, we'll get the last word out of him yet. They're going to stay on him."

I replied, "I'm sorry to hear that, Sly, I know how much you've given to these guys. You think we can get to him?"

"If any of my guys can get to him it will be those two. They'll get him and drag his sorry ass back here and then we'll ask him a few questions old school, know what I mean?"

I knew exactly how Sly wanted to do it and I was all in.

"Hey, Tat, what are you up to?" I asked. She was seated in the big room and using a computer and phone.

"Calling the office and trying to keep things afloat while I am dealing with this hot mess. Not much else I can do. I had my staff move back all my appointments and clear the rest of my schedule but proceed with the recording plans that were made before all this happened." Lady was visibly upset not being able to handle her business. She was the type of woman that was always on top of her game and this was not the game she liked playing.

"Tatiana, I know something that might take your mind off things for a bit..."

"Carlo, I am not in that mood!" she responded adamantly and with some attitude.

"What the hell were you thinking anyway? That's not where I was going but..."

"Sorry, Carlo, just stressed. What did you have in mind?" Her tone mellowed out.

"I thought a little one-on-one session on the range would be the perfect cure for that stress."

That broke out a smile on that beautiful face of hers and she enthusiastically said, "Hell, yes. Let's do it!" Shooting had that effect on women. They started out sweating with anticipation then ended up feeling like a badass.

"Sly, where the hell did you hide the range? You haven't shown that to me yet. The Lady wants to kill some paper."

"Now's just as good a time as any, so follow me. It's off the garage. I suppose you will need a few weapons too, right?"

"Yes, Sly, that would be an affirmative."

"Not a problem, the armory is there also."

Now this I gotta see, dear readers, as ole Sly had been bragging his behind off about what he had. The three of us walked out into the garage and Sly opened a panel on the back of the garage to reveal yet another hidden area. When the lights came up, inside was a fully equipped armory (more on the toys later), and a twenty-five-yard range with electronic controls to bring the targets to and away and also to blade the targets.

"Sly," I said, "I am just amazed. I won't even ask, man, but give me a Glock 19, if you got one," I said smirking. "And an AR-15 with a box of ammo for each." Sly showed me where everything was in case I wanted more ammo or guns and handed us a couple of sets of ear protection. His collection, or should I say *armory*, was beyond impressive, but stay tuned for more on that.

"Thanks, bro, I got it from here."

He just nodded with that knowing look in his eye.

CHAPTER EIGHTEEN

A Rat in a Trap

De'Londo didn't go far. He took a surreptitious route to where he was going just to make sure he wasn't being followed, but Khaseem was a bit better at the game than De'Londo. Reshaun saw him pull up to the Park Lane Seaport Apartments, something neither he nor Khaseem could afford even as generous as Sly was. Rents here started at close to or more than $4,000 a month and there was no way De'Londo could afford that on a bouncer's pay. Sly paid good but not that good. De'Londo parked the Ninja under the overhead drop-off pick-up area and walked into the office. Khaseem drove past going down Harborview Lane and parked in a spot at a meter on Congress Street.

Reshaun said to Khaseem, "Wait a minute or so, then drive through where he's parked and see if he's in the lobby. If he isn't,

I'm going in to talk to the security guard. Call Sly and let him know where we are."

Khaseem called Sly and filled him in and Sly was wondering the same thing that his two men were—why and how the hell was he there at those apartments? By the time Khaseem got off the phone Reshaun said, "I'll walk through, let's see where the rat is."

"Okay, got ya, and just so you know, Sly said he doesn't care how, but we need to bring him back to the club still breathing."

"No problem, brother," replied Reshaun.

Both of them were a bit bigger than De'Londo and there was little doubt in their minds that that is exactly what they were going to do.

Reshaun walked past the front doors and didn't see De'Londo so he walked into the lobby. He was greeted half-assed by a security officer who still looked wet behind the ears. A gawky kid barely out of his teens, if that. The security officer got out of his chair and looked like he was inconvenienced by being pulled away from the game he was playing on his I-Pad.

Reshaun asked, "You seen this dude, did he come in here?" He held up his phone with a picture on it.

"Well," the young boy said with a seeming Texas drawl, "I'm not supposed to give out information about the tenants." He was about 6'3" and 180 pounds, skinny but with a spare tire growing around his waist. Evidently from the junk food and Dr. Peppers that he seemed to be consuming while on duty.

"So, he is a resident then, right?"

"I didn't say that, now did I?" the boy stated with a goofy-ass redneck grin on his face.

"Well, ya, you did, sort of." Reshaun wanted to reach out and touch someone and not with a cell phone. "Maybe this will help you refresh your recollection." Reshaun slid a hundred-dollar bill over the desk.

The young man's hand slid out and tried to cover the bill and hide it from the four cameras that were in each corner of the lobby. But it was already too late as the bill had been placed on the counter of the security desk.

"What do you want to know?" he asked.

"He does live here, right?"

"Yeah, he does, up on the seventh floor. Couple young girls up there with him if that's a help," he said as his hand slid out palm up.

Well, Reshaun mused, *maybe this kid does have some skill.* Reshaun peeled another fifty off the roll of bills and placed it in the boy's hand. "I bet those girls are pretty hot, right? Are they black?"

The boy answered, "They're right pretty now and yes, one is black and the other is Hispanic and blonde, but I tend to be partial to blondes, that's why I took a little extra notice."

Like I really needed to know his preference...and I really doubt he could handle a black woman or Hispanic for that matter, Reshaun thought shaking his head.

"And what else do you know?"

"Well, I usually work nights and there seem to be a lot of people going up to that apartment for an hour or so. The dude that rents the place takes the girls out on the weekends. Where they go, I don't know."

"And you don't think that is a bit strange? All those people? I bet they're mostly men."

"Come to think of it..." the boy replied, "yeah, they are. But they're all real polite-like and say howdy. Dressed real nice too."

Boy, Reshaun almost said out loud. *This boy has no clue.*

"How would you like to be my secret spy? Could mean some more money for you?"

"That would be cool! Should I take notes?" he asked with his face lighting up like a Christmas tree.

"If that's what you think you need to do, just as long as you can tell me who comes and who goes to that apartment. Here's my number, use it with discretion. And what's your name, boy?" Reshaun ordered.

"It's Duncan, sir!"

Now he's catchin' on, Reshaun thought as he turned and walked out the door.

CHAPTER NINETEEN

Home, Home on the Range, Gun Range That Is

I HAD SET THE TARGET BACK AT THE THREE-YARD MARK AND told Lady that we would start at this distance. I had placed a silhouette type target on the clips. The range had good circulation and had AC and heat. Nice touch, Sly!

"What's the matter? Don't you think I can hit the target a little further back?" she questioned.

"I want you to get used to the gun, and it's not quite as easy as it looks. We can always move it back if you need a challenge."

"Oh, really? Okay, so how do I hold it, like this?" She held it like every bad guy gangbanger in the movies, that's right, dumbass sideways. I just prayed this was not some bad genetic trait!

I corrected, "Not unless you want hot casings popping down that shirt of yours and burning the girls!" I stood behind her with my arms around her shoulders, my hands on hers. I rotated the Glock so it was aligned properly and told her how to line up the sights.

"Place both thumbs along the frame like this and just below the slide so you don't have the slide catching your fingers when it slams back. Do not put that finger on the trigger until you are ready to shoot, that's how accidents happen, and keep it pointed that way."

"Yes, dear!" she replied with just the right amount of sarcasm.

"Now take the magazine and put it into the bottom of the gun. That's right, make sure you hear it lock in. Now pull the slide back nice and hard and let it go." She did as I instructed, and I told her the gun was hot.

"What do you mean hot? It doesn't feel hot!" she said with a naughty smile. Beginners, ugh!

"I mean, it is ready to fire and if you pull the trigger the gun will go bang. Now line up the sights, use the tip of your trigger finger and place it on the trigger, take a deep breath, and exhale halfway. That's it, now gently squeeze the trigger."

With that she let the first round go and actually hit just on the outer edge of center mass. "Not bad, Tat! Okay, go again doing the same thing until the gun is empty." With each shot she kept closing in on center mass. She shot like a natural.

"Carlo, I think it's empty and this is so hot!" And she didn't mean the gun either. I got up close to her and I noticed the faint scent of a sexual musk arising from her skin. Yep, it had aroused her and that can never be a bad thing.

"Okay, you did good. Now load another magazine and go again."

She leaned over, kissed me on the cheek, and said, "Thank you. This is just what I needed."

We shot until the box of shells was just about gone and as she shot, I moved the target back further and further. She still managed to keep the rounds going where they should with little effort.

"Nice shooting, Lady! Now one more thing. In a close quarters combat situation, we do things a little differently. Load another magazine." I brought the target in close to about five yards as she loaded the magazine. I explained that at close distance we don't want the gun at arm's length but in close so an enemy can't grab it. I demonstrated the proper form for her and told her to watch where her rounds hit. Then it was just a matter of moving the gun up or down or to either side.

"Try to place two in the body and one in the head," I encouraged. With that she shot three round bursts and nearly nailed it every time.

"Damn, baby girl, that is nice shooting. And you never did this before, right?"

"Now, Carlo, don't even suggest I might not be tellin' the truth, and yes, this is a first for me." Some part of me realized that she just might do well under pressure.

After letting her shoot the AR with as much success, we left the range and Lady took my arm as we walked out. Of course, Sly mysteriously appeared and said, "We gotta talk, bro. Besides, it's 2:00 p.m. and my guys are all here. Let's go topside."

CHAPTER TWENTY

UH HUH, HUH, THOUGHT WE DIDN'T SEE THEM NOW

YES, I GRABBED SOME JOE TEX LYRICS FOR THAT CHAPTER title, but go ahead, sue me.

Sly addressed the two of us as we made our way upstairs. "We found De'Londo, Carlo. My boys Khaseem and Reshaun think he was talkin' to some guys from New York City. They said he looked like he was ready to shit his pants while the guy was talking to him and then took off on his bike. They followed him to the Park Lane Seafront Apartments. How the hell does that asswipe even afford to walk in there is beyond me." *I knew I had a bad feeling,* thought Sly.

"I got a couple of my boys upstairs lookin' out for the Beemer that Khaseem and Reshaun spotted as I'm sure they are going to come by here to check things out. If it was me, I'd do it."

"You're probably right on, I said. A soft surveillance would be the thing to do. Cameras are on, right?"

"You know they are, they run 24/7."

"All right, have your guys keep a close watch. No sense in them getting one up on us."

———

Outside Victoria's Diner, Toti said to Astrit, "Come on, let's give the place a drive-by when it gets dark and see if we can find any weakness."

With that, Astrit pulled out of the lot and headed to Centerfolds Strip Club on LaGrange to await darkness. While they waited in the club, they got a private room, got a couple of lap dances, and probably a little more. Yeah, it's not legal but it's the way the game is played. Don't ask, don't tell. Arkansas Billy would be right at home here.

As the sun began to set, they left the club with a few less dollars and on the drive over to Chez Rendezvous Astrit said to Toti, "Looks like a lot of these businesses have alleys that run behind them. Probably for deliveries I would guess."

Toti replied, "That would make sense and keep trucks from jamming up traffic. Here it is up here on your side."

"It's got a *Closed* sign on the door, Toti, just like the nigger told us. Let's see if there's an alley."

Astrit took the Beemer around the block and as they came up the side street, they did indeed see an alley.

"Turn here, down the alley." Astrit did as ordered.

Toti noted not one single overhead door but just a one-man door for the entire length of the strip. "Astrit, did you notice anything unusual?"

"If you mean the lack of doors, yeah. What's up with that?"

"Dear brother, if you were trying to hide something in plain sight, I think that would be the way to go. The front door looks like it's a reinforced steel door and all the windows are dark. He probably has cameras too. For what, I don't know, but this guy is sly as a fox."

No pun intended, readers. Okay, maybe just a little. Alban Tole did not just recruit these guys for their brutality but for their smarts also. Both Toti and Astrit had done some time in the Albanian BOS, or Special Operations Battalion.

As Toti said that to Astrit, Cedric, one of Sly's guys, said, "Sly, Carlo, out front, black Beemer 740 with New York plates just did a slow roll. Could be them. I'll check the cameras and see if they did the same in the back."

"Good idea, Ced."

And as the night is black so was the Beemer that did a slow roll down the alley.

"Confirmed, Boss, they rode through the back too."

"All right, as we're all here anyway, Cedric, you're in charge of surveillance. Keep one guy on the cameras in the office and one guy on the front. Rotate everyone every hour."

"What about Khaseem and Reshaun, Sly?" asked Cedric.

"They are on a mission and we just might have a visitor very soon. Stay sharp and alert. Coffee's on. From now on two of you will be here at all times to monitor the cameras."

CHAPTER TWENTY-ONE

The Boys are Back in Town

By now, dear readers, I assume you have come to realize that I have a penchant for using song and movie titles. But if the shoe fits, I say wear it!

The next day I had received several calls and my guys had all checked in at their hotels or were soon to arrive at the restaurant. Sly had made reservations ahead of time at the Westin Waterfront, got them all suites, and it wasn't a far drive from Chez Rendezvous. Sly also made sure those that flew in had rentals awaiting them at the Avis Preferred counter. Of course, readers, they were black SUVs with blacked-out windows. Sly was laying out some serious cash but who was I to question.

I told Sly that Ritchie could hole up with us as we still had a room he could share with Dave. He thought that was cool, as we would need a driver. Ritchie arrived at the front door of the club and had his Mercedes-Maybach S-560 4matic with a biturbo 463-horse V-8 capable of zero to sixty in 4.8 seconds and 20s to grab the road. Gotta say that boy traveled in style. At first Cedric didn't want to let him in and he had Tsuji backing him up. All Ritch said was, "Just tell Carlo I'm here and don't look at me!"

Cedric paused but a second and then thought better of it and said, "Welcome to our shit-storm!"

Sly and I greeted Ritchie, we had a few laughs, and Sly said, "It would be best if you park in the garage around back alongside Lady Tatiana's Rolls."

"Sounds like I'm hangin' in very select company," Ritchie said grinning.

"Only the very best, my man," Sly answered. "Roll it on around to the alley and I'll meet you there."

Sly headed into the bunker's garage, and as he watched the monitor and saw the high-end car come down the alley, he dropped the door down and it recessed neatly into the pavement.

"Now that is a nice touch, never would have seen it. You've got some slick vintage stuff in here," Ritch said, eyeing the cars Sly had lined up. "I would love to drive some of this stuff if you would allow it."

"Just one of the perks of knowing the Sly Man! If you hang around long enough, I have no problem with you taking a few for a drive."

They both came back into the club after Sly had shown Ritchie his room and Ritchie said laughing, "I feel sorry for the guys who gotta stay in the hotel. This shit is off the hook!"

"Don't feel too sorry cuz you're bunking with my crazy cop buddy Dave," I advised. "He'll be riding in by dinnertime. Come meet the girls. This is Lady Tatiana, the reason we are all here, and this is her sister Britiney, she works for Sly." Hellos were exchanged along with some small talk. But did I catch a little extra eye contact with Brit and Ritchie? I better keep an eye on those two.

Around 1800 hours, I heard a rumbling on the street and Marcus, the guy watching the front, said, "Harley Dresser just pulled up front. Older guy, bald, coming to the door."

"Hey, now, watch who you callin' old, and bald, Marcus," I shot back.

Marcus just laughed and went to get the door while saying, "You know I'm just playin'!"

Dave walked in after flashing his ID, looked around at those assembled, and queried, "Jesus Christ, Carlo, you couldn't find any bigger guys than these?"

"Ha, ha, bro, always the joker," I said as I gave him a bear hug.

I introduced him to Sly and in turn Sly introduced his crew.

"Make yourself at home, this is Ritchie, and you'll be rooming together downstairs," Sly informed him. "And this, Dave, is Lady Tatiana and her sister Britney. Brit works for me and Lady is the reason Carlo dragged your ass all the way from Buffalo."

Dave had the same initial reaction to Lady that I did—speechless. I nudged Dave, "You okay, man?" Nothing, just a dead stare.

Sly continued, "Ah, Dave…" causing Dave to snap out of it. "That mountain over there is Tsuji, Lady's bodyguard. Don't know how much English he knows but he knows his shit. The others are on the way here and then we'll eat. Ritch can show you where you'll be bunking. Feel free to use anything, but don't look at Ritch." With that, laughter erupted in the club easing a little tension. Ritch explained it was a thing he and Carlo had going on and it was nothing personal.

"Sly, I talked to both J3 and Jake and they are headed this way with their crews. We can eat, go over some plans, and then let them check out the armory. Ritch and Dave, you will like what you see."

Sly poured Booker's for the six of us and we headed back

down. Ritchie and Dave had gotten familiar with Sly's crew, so everyone was acquainted.

CHAPTER TWENTY-TWO

Gina, Lady of Death

"With that she touches my temple and I tremble, I can't breathe, and I fall to my knees. My eyes are wide and projecting out on the street like a movie screen but with every scene I feel the grief and all the pain of every death, of every final thought that left a brain. I feel the weight of everyone. Of all the sorrow, all the people who were never loved. And she asks me, 'How does it feel?'"

— LYRICS FROM "LADY OF DEATH" BY I
THE MIGHTY

EVERYONE HAD ARRIVED, AND WE WERE SEATED AROUND the table enjoying a dinner that Sly, Brit, and Lady had prepared for us. Steak, baked potatoes, and grilled broccoli were heaped on our plates along with baskets of buttered garlic bread. Sly had opened some of his best Malbec a little earlier to let it breathe, a 96 Bodega Catena Zapata 2005 Argentino that retailed for $123 per bottle. Leave it to Sly to leave no stone unturned.

The Lady made sure that when all were seated there was a seat empty next to me. Of course, that drew looks from every one of the guys and a little knowing smile. What could I do?

My phone rang with a restricted number and as usual I let it go to voice mail. But the caller didn't leave a message. A few seconds later my phone buzzed again with a text, again from a restricted number, that read, *Answer your fucking phone!*

Lady said, "Someone really wants to talk to you, hun. Maybe you should answer."

"I don't answer my phone if it doesn't show a number," I tried to say to her discretely.

"But obviously they know you, maybe it's your mama," she said with a little touch of ice in her voice. Come on now, jealousy? Really?

The phone rang again, and I answered, "Who is this?"

"What's the matter, Carlo, don't want to talk to me?" the voice on the other end said chidingly.

I knew in an instant who it was, and I excused myself before resuming the conversation.

"Gina, how good of you to call. How are you?" Tatiana heard that female name and shot a glance over at me.

"Cut the bullshit, Carlo, you know why I'm calling, I want in."

"In on what?"

"You know damn well what I'm talking about. Those Eastern European pigs!"

"How the hell you know about that?"

"Come on, Carlo, you know better than to play stupid. I hear things and I want in, I want to play."

Readers, Gina is a cold-blooded assassin who enjoys her work

74

way too much. I met her back in 2008 when I was working a case and we had formed an uneasy though trustworthy alliance. Did I approve of some of the things she did? No, but she took a lot of scum off the streets and with each kill leaving a grotesque message for others as a warning. Gina was about 32 years old, tall, trim, and ripped, Polish girl with long blonde hair with model good looks. Her specialty were blades and small arms. Even her fingernails were overlaid with ultra-thin stainless steel that came to a point, and the edges were as sharp as any razor. Her manicurist must make a fortune. I had once seen her slice a thug's throat with those nails, then grab him by the hair and look into his eyes just inches from his face until he bled out like a pig. She was cold, sub-zero cold, and had a special hatred for predators.

"Okay, all right, come on, we both know we can use you, but play nice with the boys and the Lady and her sister."

"Oh, Carlo, so many demands, but for you I'll do it, and a chance to kill some of those pigs."

"You know where we are?"

"Who do you think you're talking to, Carlo? Besides, I'm already in town so just expect me." With that, she hung up and all I could do was await her arrival.

"Sly, we'll be needing another place setting at the table." I just let it go at that.

Not only is there a lot of testosterone up in here but the estrogen is gonna flow too! I thought to myself. This could get interesting.

CHAPTER TWENTY-THREE

TAGGED AND BAGGED

RESHAUN'S PHONE RANG ABOUT 2100 HOURS THE NEXT night and it was the security guard, Duncan.

"Sir, he's on the way out and he's alone. What do you want me to do?"

"Nothin', this call was perfect," replied Reshaun, stroking the boy's ego a bit.

"Okay, we're up. He's leaving the apartment."

Khaseem and Reshaun had the placed staked out on and off since the night before and fortunately they were near the apartment. It didn't take long and Reshaun said, "Here he comes, getting on the bike now. Wait until he gets where there's no traffic before we take him out."

It had started to get dark about a half hour ago and with no moon, the lighting would be perfect if they could catch him on a dark side street.

De'Londo piloted the big bike over to D Street, hung a left to hit Fargo, and then banged a right onto E Street. After he took a right onto Broadway, Khaseem said, "Looks like he's headed to the West Broadway Housing Apartments. We should be able to trap him in there."

"Just give him enough space so he doesn't get jumpy. He can outrun us easily on that."

"I got it, 'Re', he's taking the left on Casimir. He passed Costello and is turning on Crowley Rogers."

Reshaun ordered, "Take the left off Costello and catch him on Crowley Rogers."

Khaseem hit the gas and as they rounded the bend on Costello, they heard the bike.

"Khaseem, take him at the corner, knock him off."

With adept skill, Khaseem hit the bike catching De'Londo on the lower left leg and taking him down. The impact threw De'Londo off the Ninja onto the street. Khaseem and Reshaun jumped out of the Town Car and Khaseem popped the trunk as he exited the driver's side.

Reshaun landed on top of De'Londo who was dazed and began to cry out in pain. "Give me the tape!" Reshaun shouted and Khaseem tossed him a roll of duct tape. Reshaun bound De'Londo's mouth and hands as Khaseem held the rat down. Reshaun pulled a black hood out of his pocket and placed it over De'Londo's head.

De'Londo's eyes were bugged out in fear as the hood went on and they both heaved him into the big trunk of the Town Car. De'Londo tried to scream out as they grabbed his feet, apparently his left ankle had been crushed in the crash. *Too bad, bitch,* Reshaun thought to himself.

Reshaun pulled out his cell, dialed Sly's number, and when Sly answered said, "One tagged and bagged. We're on the way there. By the way, he's been running two ho's out of the club when he's working."

"Excellent, see you in a few. Pull into the alley when you come in. I don't want anyone seeing him get out of the car." *That fuckin' bastard,* Sly thought.

"You got it, Boss," and Reshaun ended the call.

CHAPTER TWENTY-FOUR

EENY MEENY MINY MOE

NO ONE SAW HER APPROACH OR WALK THROUGH THE DOOR but when Sly's guys realized she had gotten in, it got really quiet, very fast. Gina stood just past the door and looked over at the shocked faces of those that had the responsibility of watching the front door.

"Hello, everyone, am I late to the party?" Gina announced. She stood there in a tight white, sleeveless, fitted blouse revealing muscular but feminine arms and shoulders, among other things. To complete her attire, she wore a fairly short plaid skirt and thick-soled lace-up shoes with three-inch heels. Those soles hid lethal weapons that could be deployed very quickly. I expect those weren't the only weapons she had on her person. Yeah, she had the schoolgirl look but as I said before, don't let it fool you. Along with her other skills she had a third-degree black belt in a very efficient, deadly style called Krav Maga.

I took my cue and said, "Everyone, this is Gina, a dear friend and colleague. Guys, you'd be wise to treat her with the utmost respect." Everyone was upstairs having finished dinner and they all received the message loud and clear.

"Oh, thank you, dear," she said and planted a kiss on my cheek, maybe lingering a bit too long to see if it caused a reaction in Lady. And it did. Gina got the evil eye and walked over to Lady and said, "Don't get your weave in a knot, he's all yours but maybe…I might want to play with you!" She flashed that evil smile running her finger down Lady's sternum to her cleavage.

Everyone in the club couldn't help letting out a hoot thinking a girl fight was to ensue, but Brit stepped between them and said, "Girls, play nice, we are all here for the same thing. Right, sis, right, Gina?" They both stood down and Gina walked away smirking, knowing she had gotten to Lady. But man, that weave comment was edgy.

Marcus, who had been monitoring the security cams, called out, "Khaseem just pulled into the alley, Sly."

"Great, I'll make sure he gets in," Sly said. He left topside to handle the package that would soon be in the garage.

They popped the trunk and the three of them pulled De'Londo's sorry, hurtin' ass out. They dragged him to the elevator and threw him in. Sly hit the up button and sent the elevator to club level. The three then came back up and had Cedric and Marcus drag him out and bind him to a chair on the dance floor. This just might be De'Londo's last tango.

Sly ordered, "Marcus, keep an eye on him."

"Everyone else, conference," I stated. We had a lot of talent in the room and most if not all had interrogation experience. "We're gonna break him, and if any of you don't want to be party to that, I'm cool with it, but it will not go under any set code of conduct. Know what I mean?"

Jake spoke up, "As far as the rest of us are concerned, none of this is happening. J3, you and your guys good?"

J3 answered with a shit-eating grin, "Don't have any idea what you're talking about, and who's Miranda?"

Gina chimed in, "You boys handle it for now and when you really want to get to the truth, just let me know. He won't know whether to shit or go blind, but I guarantee he will do one if not both. I'll be at the bar, call me…oh, can someone get me something to eat?" One of Sly's men checked with her and got her exactly what she wanted.

J3 side-barred me and asked, "Is that who I think it is? And if it is, are you freaking crazy?"

I smiled, looked J3 in the eye, and said, "Brother, I have no idea what you're talking about. Besides, would you rather have who you think it is with us or them? I bet you choose the former and I'll take allies where I can find them."

That was all J3 needed to confirm what he already suspected —that Gina was the deadly killer every law enforcement agency in the world had tried to catch and failed.

"All right, here's what *we* need to know if *he* knows: how many guys they have, what he told them, and where they're holed up. We all have different 'techniques' so we can mix it up, keep him off balance. Nothing is off limits."

Dave jumped in. "That's good, let's do what we came here to do. I want first crack."

I poured another Booker's and raised my glass. "Here's to interrogation! And Dave, have at it."

Glasses clinked and all had no problem with letting Dave go first.

CHAPTER TWENTY-FIVE

ANOTHER ONE BITES THE DUST

DAVE STRUTTED OVER TO DE'LONDO, WHO WAS STILL covered with the hood. He had no way of knowing who was coming at him. Dave ripped off the hood and put pressure on the broken ankle with his foot. De'Londo let out a shriek.

"What's a matter, can't take a little pain? Get used to it, it's just the start," Dave said as he pressed his foot onto the broken ankle again a little harder.

De'Londo felt a lightning bolt of pain shoot through his leg and howled, gasping for breath, as he tried to maintain. Dave stared right into his eyes. "Where are they?" De'Londo still tried to put forth a hard guy image and looked right back at Dave and said, "You cut your fucking hair with a beer bottle? Cuz it's the worst haircut I've ever seen!"

The rest of the guys couldn't help but break out laughing and then Dave hit De'Londo so hard upside the head that he knocked him over backward in the chair. De'Londo spit out a mouthful of blood before Sly's guys picked his ass back upright.

"Plenty more where that came from. Now answer the question," Dave demanded. The side of De'Londo's face began to swell and his left eye was getting puffy.

"I don't know what you're talkin' about."

This time Dave caught him square in the mouth and De'Londo lost two front teeth. "Wrong answer. Try again. You were seen talking to one of those Albanian pricks."

"Albanian who?"

Sly walked over to De'Londo from behind and put his hands on the big guy's shoulders.

"After all I've done for you, this is how you repay? You betray me? Boy, you got a lot of pain getting ready to come down on you if you don't talk, but in the end, you will talk, you worthless piece of shit! Do this the easy way and save us all some time and grief cuz I ain't stoppin' it."

"Go to hell, you and everyone else, I ain't sayin' nothin'!" De'Londo yelled.

Jake finally stepped up and pushed him back onto the floor. "Get me a bucket of water. Time for some water sports."

Marcus brought over a pail of water and Jake took the hood and placed it over De'Londo's face. De'Londo started to shake as he knew what was coming and had a profound fear of water, deep or not.

"No, no, not that, I'll talk."

"Too late, you had your chance, pig." One of Jake's men held De'Londo's head so he couldn't move it. Jake slowly started pouring the water over his mouth and nose and all De'Londo could do was gag and gasp for breath, but when he breathed in all he got was water.

Jake finished the first bucket, removed the hood, and said, "Got something to say, boy?"

"There were just two, that's all I know, that's the truth, just two is all I saw. Please, no more!" De'Londo begged.

"How did you meet them?" Jake replaced the hood and poured more water.

Again, De'Londo thought he was going to drown and when Jake was done De'Londo sputtered out, "They found me at Slades, I don't know how; they paid me five hundred dollars. Stop, please, that's it, that's all of it!" he said shuddering and sobbing.

Gina stepped up. "He's still not telling it all. Sit him up. I will have the truth in a few minutes." By now the interrogation had lasted close to an hour.

Marcus and Jake set him upright and removed the hood.

"Are you having fun? Because so far they've been going easy on you and that stops now," Gina softly said in his ear. She pulled a concealed blade out of the top of her boot with her right hand as she straddled his lap.

"No more, please, I told you all I know!"

"Yes, yes, I get it, it's all you know. Poor baby, but you must talk to Mama or she will hurt you so good!" she said grabbing his hair and pulling his head back.

The blade was pressed against his now swollen shut eye. De'Londo could feel the pressure of the blade and Gina punctured the swollen area around his eye and blood spewed from it. "The next one goes deeper. You want to leave here with one eye? Because you'll never see anything this good again," she said as she moved her hand down her torso.

"They're in the South End somewhere, I think in a warehouse. That's it, please! Are you all crazy?"

"I don't think so, little boy, but I see you need a little more persuasion. And yes, I am very crazy." With that Gina loosened his pants, revealed his man parts, and placed the blade under his balls.

"No, no, what? No, not that, no, no, please, I'll say whatever you want me too!" he screamed.

"You do have some balls, I'll say that, but not for long."

The next thing we knew, we saw a spray of blood and De'Londo's testicles securely in her hand.

"Jesus Christ," J3 muttered and no one disagreed all shaking our heads.

"That was cold!" one of J3's guys said while holding his groin. I looked around the room, more than a few of the guys were doing the same, and a couple blew chunks. So much for tough guys.

Gina gave De'Londo a minute to let the pain subside and said, "At least you won't be breeding any more ghetto rats that don't know their daddies." She grasped hold of his penis and again placed the blade firmly against it with enough pressure to draw blood. "You want that gone too, little boy?"

"I got a number, please don't, please, Jesus, please don't do it. I got a number for them, no more, please, I told you everything!" De'Londo was now shrieking like a little girl and crying. "It's in my phone, jus, just look, please, man, I'm telling you it's all I know!"

J3 found the phone in his jeans pocket, scrolled through the contacts until he saw one with a New York City area code.

"I think I got it, is this it? 212-555-4372?"

"Yes, yes, that's it. It's all I got, please, no more, please don't cut me, please!" De'Londo begged.

Gina increased the pressure and De'Londo screamed, "They know she's here and they'll come for her!" De'Londo's voice got three octaves higher. Tears streamed down his face from pain and shame as Gina pulled the knife completely through his manhood.

Regina stood up and said, "That's it, he told everything he knows. No use keeping him around."

Sly looked at everyone in the room and we all wore the same

hard expression. Shock and disbelief at the cold brutality she employed. We were all glad she was on our side today.

Finally, Sly broke the silence, "Khaseem and Reshaun, you know what to do. Marcus, help them if they need it."

The three of them nodded and Reshaun stuffed the bloody hood into De'Londo's mouth and took him away still alive.

As for the rest of us, Lady was the first to speak, "Thank you, Gina."

CHAPTER TWENTY-SIX

THE FOX WILL CATCH YOU WITH CUNNING, AND THE WOLF WITH COURAGE

TOLE AND HIS MEN WERE BOTH CUNNING AND HAD courage, but Tole knew that may not be enough to defeat the men he knew they were up against. Alban picked up his phone and placed a call to New York, a call that he was well aware could change the balance of power to his favor.

Tole called Aleksander, a Captain like himself. He and Tole had grown up together, their families were close, and they had come up through the ranks at the same time. They often did "jobs" together and shared in the profits of those ventures. They were big earners for the New York family and with that came a lot of power and respect.

The phone rang three times before it was answered, and a voice as rough and deep as Tole's answered, "*Përshëndetje, shoku im si je?*" (Hello, my friend, how are you?)

"To get right to the point, I need some more men for that situation up here. I have my crew, but I need about another ten, and weapons."

"How soon do you need them and is that for that bitch with the recording company?"

"Yes, it's just turned into a clusterfuck. Somehow this bitch has connections up here and they've put together a small army. I don't know who they are, but I got some info from one of their guys. Astrit and Toti 'convinced' him it was in his better interest."

Aleksander asked, "You in a secure spot?"

Tole answered, "We're in a warehouse, overhead doors in front, plus a man-door front and rear. If they come, we'll see them. We've done a soft surveillance on their location but if we attack there could be too many civilian casualties."

"Is it worth all that bloodshed, my friend?"

"To get what I want, yes, it is. It will help us both become richer."

"You shall have what you need, brother, I hope you succeed. I look forward to the rewards. *Fat mund të jetë me ju*!" (May luck be with you!) "They will be there by tomorrow afternoon or evening."

"*Faleminderit vëllai i Allahut mund të shikojë mbi ju.*" (Thank you, my brother, may Allah watch over you).

Tole disconnected the call and waited.

CHAPTER TWENTY-SEVEN

CLEAN THE HOUSE BECAUSE YOU NEVER KNOW WHO'S COMING OVER

SLY TURNED TO THE REST OF US AND SAID, "WE NEED TO get this placed cleaned up. All this has to disappear so there's no DNA. Cedric, get some buckets and mops, hot water and bleach. That should do the trick." Those of us that had crime scene experience knew that was the only way to make sure nothing blew back on any of us. Bleach destroyed DNA. It was always the little shit that got the bad guys caught, and we weren't the bad guys or the stupid guys for that matter.

"Gina, you need to burn those bloody clothes," Sly continued.

"Already on it, Sly, not my first rodeo," she responded and dropped the stained clothes where she stood. No one dared to cast a furtive glance in her direction, but damn! "I'll be downstairs in the shower." She hefted her bag and headed down into the bunker.

Before Khaseem and Reshaun left they had wrapped De'Londo still alive in plastic sheets, then duct-taped it tightly so he couldn't move and dumped him in the trunk of the Town Car with Marcus's help. I almost felt sorry for him. His death would be slow and tortured through suffocation, and panic would course through every cell in his body as the air supply became less and less. He would try to claw his way out as suffocation victims did, their last futile attempts at survival.

Within the hour we had the place clean and hopefully there would be no trace of anything that anyone could tie to us. Dave spoke up, "I don't know about the rest of you, but I could use another drink or three."

No one disagreed and we all went over to the bar. Britney had since come upstairs, glad to be with the rest of us, went behind the bar, and did her usual job of pouring drinks.

I asked her, "Baby girl, you okay?"

"Yeah, and I'm glad I went downstairs after stepping in between Gina and my sis. Did she really do what they said? And by the way, I showed Gina her room."

"She sure did, couldn't believe it myself, no one could. And thanks for the other."

"Carlo, not to change the subject…but is Ritchie attached? I know there's a lot going on but he seein' anyone? I mean, I'm just sayin! Those Italian good looks of his…" She flashed that beautiful smile of hers and even looked a little embarrassed.

"Oh, really, I thought I saw a little eye contact going on there when he came in. Between you and me, he could use a good woman."

"You think I'm a good woman?"

"If you weren't, I wouldn't have bet on you."

With that, there was a loud rap on the door and as everyone was on edge, about a dozen guns were pointed at the door. With the adrenaline, the Booker's and guns, this was not the time for someone to come knocking.

J3 peeked out the front window and said, "Guys, beat cop at the door. We all cool?"

Jake said, "We're just a bunch of guys drinkin', right, Sly?"

"I'll get rid of him," Sly said as he went to the front door.

"Hey, Buck, what's going on?"

"I saw the lights on and the sign on the door and it looked a little unusual. You all good?"

"Well it's always good to see a friendly face down here. But yeah, just a private party. Me and Brit are here, and my guests. You need anything, something to eat? You know I been cookin'."

"Naw, man, not since the lap band surgery. Weight's coming off and all this walking helps." Buck had gone through a rough divorce and had taken it out on food, a lot of food. He blew up to three hundred and fifty pounds on a five foot eleven frame. But he was a great cop, well liked, and knew everyone on his beat.

"Okay, brah, I got you if you need anything."

"Thanks, Sly, and be careful, I heard there was a bad crew of Albanians up here from New York."

"Thanks, that's good to know." With a fist bump, Buck walked away and Sly locked up the front door wondering how Buck had heard so quick.

CHAPTER TWENTY-EIGHT

"Take Out the Paper and the Trash, Yakety Yak, Don't Talk Back"

Reshaun and Khaseem had a good idea where the Albanians were holed up. Khaseem pointed the Town Car, with De'Londo in the trunk, toward the Waterfront and the warehouses in the South End along Topeka and Atkinson Streets.

They made small talk on the way over mostly about what had just occurred. Reshaun said, "You see how cold she was, what she did to De'Londo? Man, that was just out and out cold. That bitch is bad!"

"I hear ya, bro. She can keep the fuck away from me. My baby momma wants what I gots in one piece, not filleted like a piece of fish. That woman is beyond cold, she is the freezer queen."

"Khaseem, see that one with the lights on? Bit unusual for

this time of day, don't you think?" Reshaun said getting back to business.

"You right on, brah. We'll go up to that parking lot at the end of the street. It's all dark up there and we'll get the body out and in the back seat, and you get in the back too. Then push him out when we go by. Make sure you have the gloves on."

Neither one had qualms about what they were to do as they would do anything for Sly including dumping this body. There was no room for traitors in their lives and this they considered a minor inconvenience. Being downright cold was one thing, but a rat was an entirely different category. Snitches got more than stitches.

"Like I'm an idiot. Who you think you talkin' to, nigga?" Reshaun was half laughing and shaking his head. He smacked Khaseem in the back of the head just for the fun of it. "I got this." Reshaun and Khaseem were like brothers and always rode one another but it was all good.

They pulled the body from the trunk after making sure no one was around and there wasn't any traffic. With the body in the back driver's side, Reshaun climbed in. Khaseem rolled down Topeka Street and in front of 71-95 Topeka, Khaseem slowed enough for Reshaun to push the body out. They watched it bounce once and it came to rest just off the side of the road. The boys sped away.

"Let's go, let's go, I need to get home and take a shower. Man, I'm creepin'! Dead bodies aren't my thang'."

"I hear ya, I'm gonna get my old lady and get some stress relief, nah mean?"

Reshaun nodded his head knowingly and said, "You better clean up first, man, you don't want dead body stank on you!"

CHAPTER TWENTY-NINE

Late Night News

Sly told his guys they were good for the night but to keep close to their phones. "All y'all be back here tomorrow at 1800 hours unless you hear otherwise." They knew it was not a request but an order, and none of them had any trouble following Sly's orders. To many of them he was like a dad.

Sly locked the door behind them, turned to face the rest of us, and said, "You know the shit will hit the fan tomorrow when the body gets found. We sent a message to the Albanians tonight. We let them know that we know they had a snitch, and they will know what we do to snitches. And as you Spec Op guys are so fond of saying, 'The only easy day was yesterday.' J3 and Jake, you and your guys be back for breakfast. Take a couple of bottles back with you, I'm sure you all could use it. Again, thanks for coming, it means a lot to me and Carlo."

"We're just glad we could be here. I know all my guys and I'm sure Jake's guys are glad to get some action. Retirement can suck. Besides, you have great booze."

Everyone raised their glass and drained them. "Here, here. Kill them all and let God sort 'em out."

Yep, my kind of guys. I was ready for bed and knew I would sleep without a guilty conscience.

The rest of us followed Sly downstairs. Some of us cleaned up and others poured another drink and watched TV. Gina came out to the main living area looking refreshed, wearing an expensive silk robe that was nearly see-through, but no one complained, and why would they? She poured a drink from the open bottle, took a seat on the large top grain cowhide sectional sofa, and said, "Like the boys said, at least you have good liquor, Sly." That got a laugh out of all of us.

Lady came out of the room that she and Brit shared and took a seat next to me, a very close seat, and complained, "What I would give to get my hair done and a great massage." She looked at me with a knowing look.

"I don't do hair, sorry about that."

"I was thinking more of a massage, if you aren't too tired."

"Doesn't that fall in Tsuji's job description?"

"Carlo, are you just thick or being funny cuz after today I'm not so sure."

"So, you're serious, huh? Better be careful what you wish for," I replied with a naughty grin and started asking Sly for some oil. "Sly, you got massage—"

"In the room, Carlo."

"Thank you, Sly!" I trailed off behind Lady. Guess I wouldn't get to sleep as soon as I thought I would be.

Gina, not being able to help herself said, "Now isn't that touching."

Yes, that got a look from everyone.

"Speaking of a massage, my shoulders are killing me," Ritchie complained. "Gina, want to reach out and touch someone?"

"Please, boy, you are so out of my league." Another sarcastic smile crossed her face and she laughed a little before she took a large sip of her drink.

Before she could finish the sentence, Ritchie felt two hands kneading his shoulders from behind him. "Is this hard enough and in the right spot, baby?" cooed Brit.

Ritch taking it all in stride said, "Oh, Jesus, yes, I'll let you know when to stop."

"No problem, baby." Brit had no problem stepping up to take something or someone she wanted. And she saw something good about Ritchie.

The delicious aroma of estrogen and testosterone filled the room until the news came on.

"This just in and first on WHDH Channel 7 News," Kim Khazei chimed in. *"A body was found in the warehouse area on Topeka Street in South Boston. Now to our reporter at the scene Amaka Ubaka. Amaka, what have the police told you?"*

"Well, Kim, police state that a motorist saw a large mass wrapped in plastic and when he got out of his car to check he discovered it was the body of a black male. They further state that it appears this may be gang related and the man may have been killed vendetta-style. He was badly beaten about the face, appears to have a broken ankle, and his genitals were dismembered according to the officer with whom I spoke."

"Amaka, did we hear that correctly?"

"Yes, Kim. They will not let us near the body, and they state that the victim had no identification. They are hoping a witness may come forward to shed light on this ghastly incident. Back to you, Kim."

"We will keep you updated on this story and others as we gather more information."

I had waited until Lady had disrobed and covered with an extra-large bath towel before I entered the room. I straddled over her and began massaging her back when I heard everyone call out my name. Damn, why did that have to come on now?

CHAPTER THIRTY

BACK AT THE WAREHOUSE

"BOSS, LOOK OUTSIDE, THE PLACE IS CRAWLING WITH COPS," Koli called out. "They're all over the place out front, looks like they're looking at something. Could be a body."

Toti and Astrit peered out and Toti whispered, "Shit, that looks like the guy we talked to. This is not good." He peered out the window with field glasses. "Turn off the lights, last thing we need is for them to come knocking wondering what we're doing here."

"Zeni, change the channel to the news and see if they say anything. Channel 7, I see their truck out there," Tole said while peering out the window alongside Toti and Astrit. He listened to the news and that was all Tole needed to hear, the absolute last thing. He picked up the 50" Vizio flat screen and threw it over the rail from the second level in the warehouse along with all the cables and box. The Mezini brothers and the other four in the crew sat in silence as Alban continued with his rage. "We can't catch a break with this black whore. First, she disappears only to be discovered holed up with a crew of guys we know little if anything about, and then this nigger asshole gets himself killed. And dumped right in front of us. How dare they! I will kill them all."

Toti broke the other's silence, "Alban, maybe it is a blessing. This may be the best thing that they killed him. We don't need anything coming back to us. After all, just how much did he know? *Allahu mund të qeshë me ne.*" (Allah may be smiling on us)

This caused another immediate and angrier outburst from Tole, "Fuck Allah, fuck everyone. I am my own god." Every vein in Tole's massive head and neck stood out and looked like they would pop. "I make the rules, I play by my game, not anyone or any deities' rules. I run this shit." Tole withdrew his Kimber 45cal from his waistband and pointed it at his lieutenant's head. "Do you understand? Do all of you understand?" he said now waving the gun at all of them as they flinched and ducked. Tole grabbed a bottle of Stoli off the table and chugged nearly half of it. "Somebody get off their ass and get another TV. And while you're at it, clean up the mess." Tole started to calm down after his outburst with the help of the alcohol.

Shpati and Luli didn't wait for Toti to tell anyone to go. They wanted to get away from Tole for a minute and breathe some fresh air. They jumped into Shpati's BMW 3 Series Sport Wagon and headed to Best Buy, which was right down the street in the South Bay Plaza.

Toti, Astrit, along with Zeni and Koli, obediently went downstairs and cleaned up the mess Tole had made, muttering to themselves and one another but not loud enough for their boss to hear.

When they got back to the warehouse, Tole had calmed down quite a bit and had Shpati and Luli set up the TV. It was getting late and they all needed sleep. While they were gone, Tole had popped a handful of tranquilizers—Xanax—and with the Stoli it almost had him in a good mood. It took the edge off his steroid-induced rages, if you believe those exist.

"All right, let's get some sleep. Aleksander's guys will be here sometime tomorrow. Let's try not to look like a bunch of fools and fuck-ups, *kuptoj*?" He knew he had a good crew but tended to lose it when things didn't fall into place and take it out on his men.

CHAPTER THIRTY-ONE

The Sixth Day

ALL THE GUYS WERE PRESENT AND ACCOUNTED FOR AT breakfast and Sly and the two girls, minus Gina (she just didn't cook for strangers, at least not yet), made steak and eggs, home fries, bacon, grits, and lots of toast. Sly had made his regular strong coffee using freshly ground extra dark roasted expresso beans imported from Italy. Coffee never tasted so good. The food was awesome, and all the guys had a chance to talk and swap stories.

J3 shared one about me and him regarding a case at RIT, that is, Rochester Institute of Technology. We had this deal set up to buy fifty pounds of weed. The contact I had was not supposed to come out, as he was an up-and-rising tech star and a high school friend of mine but not a druggie. J3 and I had a deal—as long as the contact stayed in he would not get popped. But he just had to do it. His guy, who had the weed, showed me and J3 the stuff in the dorm basement and then slung the bag over his shoulder, looking like Santa Claus on Christmas night. He exited the building to get the money from us as I told him it was in the car. But as Gomer Pyle would say, "Surprise, Surprise!" The rest of the DEA boys were waiting outside. Yep, it was a buy/bust. We all got cuffed, including tech boy, and off we went. It ruined tech boy's future, but he avoided jail time. Both he and the dealer were expelled, but the dealer did time.

Jake asked Sly, "When do we get a chance to see the armory? We'd like to get acquainted with the toys."

"If we're finished eating, we can go check it out now," Sly responded.

"Don't worry, guys," I said, "you won't be disappointed. I saw it the other day. While you guys do that, I'm going to check the news for any updates."

J3 said, "Not a bad idea. No rush to see the guns."

I changed the channel in the living area to Channel 7. Kim Khazei and Ryan Shulteis had just started the morning broadcast.

"Here is the breaking news on last night's gruesome homicide," Khazei started off. *"We know now that the deceased is De'Londo Williams. The Boston Police crime lab was able to match prints from a previous arrest for larceny when he was sixteen."*

With that, Reshaun's phone rang as he sat up in bed. It was the security guard from the Park Lane Apartments.

"Yeah, what up?" Reshaun asked.

Duncan said, "The cops just got here and are serving a search warrant."

"You know enough to keep your mouth shut, don't you? You can tell them when he last came in and left but nothing further, understand?"

"Loud and clear."

"All right, I might have something for you later. Good job. Keep your head down."

"I know," Duncan said and disconnected.

Reshaun called Sly from his crib and told him what he had heard. "All right, thanks, the news is breaking the story now."

"We know that the police have obtained a search warrant for his residence at the Park Lane Seaport Apartments," Khazei reported.

"Kim, isn't that a little high end for someone like that?" Shulteis asked.

"It is, but our source within the Boston Police Department has told us that a large quantity of heroine was found along with two teenage girls."

"Kim, do we know if they are part of a human trafficking network?"

"Ryan, at this time we do not know but we can only assume the worst."

"Is the deceased part of a gang or drug network?"

"Our source would only say that they have not uncovered any known gang affiliation. For now, we can only speculate. We will keep viewers updated."

CHAPTER THIRTY-TWO

Cold Blue Steel

Sly addressed the assembled group. "As you can all see, the shit is hitting the fan. The Albanians must be going nuts especially with the body dumped on their front doorstep. So, as soon as you all are ready, I will open the play store."

Everyone had eaten their fill, thanked the girls for breakfast, and headed out to the garage. Sly hit the button and I stood back and watched. It was like kids in a candy store.

Jake spoke first, "My God, Sly, this is all military grade shit. How? How did you get all this?"

I answered the question for Sly. "I'll tell you what he told me. It fell off the back of a truck." Everyone got a bit of a chuckle out of it.

Beside the array of Glock and H&K pistols there were M-16s, AR-15s, Russian-made AK47s, M4 CQBRs, HK 416s, HK MP 5&7s, Mossberg and Remington tactical shotguns, and one minigun—an electronic Gatling gun capable of firing 6,000 rounds per minute. Last, but not least were the sniper rifles, which Jake's guys were drooling over. All were fitted with the best of optics. Sly had XM2010s, MK 13 mod 5s, and finally the big daddy of them all, the Barrett M82a1. Sly also had breaching equipment, spools of detcord, and C4 to round out the artillery.

"Sly, my guys got erections! Nice collection. J3, what do you say?"

"I'm just speechless. Damn. I mean, how is this possible?"

"Anything's possible for the right price, right, Sly?" I asked but didn't expect an answer.

"There's a small range just on the other side of this door if you want to use it. It's only 25 yards but better than nothing. Take as much ammo and magazines as you need. There are gear bags over here and there are BDUs to fit all of you. Try the vests on and take what works for you. Like the guns, they're all military grade. There are also comms like Seal Team 6 uses, and there should be enough for everybody. On the other wall are the Ground Panoramic Night Vision Goggles but no need to explain it all to you, you all know what they are."

The team just stood there amazed at the collection Sly had put together. He definitely moved in mysterious ways.

Jake and J3's guys all took M16s and a mix of close combat and long-range weapons. Dave and Ritchie grabbed 9mm Glock 19s and Dave grabbed an M16 while Ritchie took an MP7.

Ritch said, "The length of this is just right. I can drive and shoot, won't get it caught in the steering wheel like I usually do."

"That's why they made them," Jake informed him.

"Gina, dear, what about you, what do you like?" I asked.

"I like working close and personal. I have my knives, but I'll take an MP7 also."

My choice, readers, was another Glock 21 and an MP7 along with mags and ammo. I also grabbed an M16 for the Lady along with another Glock 19. I hope she didn't and wouldn't need to use them but better armed than not.

By the time I left the armory area, rounds were popping off on the range as everyone checked out their weapons of choice. They were all like kids on Christmas but consummate professionals, nonetheless.

CHAPTER THIRTY-THREE

COVERUP

As the teams were shooting, I found Sly in his room just chillin'.

"Never thought life would come to this, did you, Sly?"

"Not in my wildest imagination, my brother. I knew it was trouble, the minute Lady walked through the door. That is, after I was able to think clearly again. Brit's a good kid, she doesn't deserve this, but it's her sister and we're in this for good or bad," he replied.

"I have other concerns. I believe you may be thinking the same things. Once all the shooting starts, there's no turning back. The cops will be all over us in no time even if we create diversion. The other guys don't need to get jammed up over this, but they also knew what they were buying into."

For the first time during this past week, Sly could not honestly say that he had this. "You know I have connections, but you and I both know those kinds of people do not want to stick their political necks out. They all have elections to worry about and kissing ass and sucking up, they're just typical politicians. But before we go out that door, I think I can at least keep us from going to jail. People owe me—owe me big time—even if this is an all-out gun battle, which we both know it will be. I think I might have this."

"You certainly have greased enough palms from the police commissioner, mayor, and councilmen, and ladies on down, and their chit is due too, Sly. You've been good to the people in this neighborhood and you look out for those that don't have a thing. The people around here love you, almost like a Godfather. Not like a neighborhood is going to get shot up. We can try to minimize the damage as much as possible, do surveillance beforehand, and put that drone to good use. Might as well use everything at our disposal. J3's and Jake's guys are the ones cut out for that kinda thing and are some of the best at it. You let whoever has the need to know that we will make this as clean as possible. It's not like we're going to shoot up a neighborhood and get a lot of collateral damage because we have minimized that. As far as I'm concerned, De'Londo was the only one and he put his own self in play."

The Godfather comment was not lost on Sly and he continued, "Even with me greasing palms this is still going to take more cash. I'll meet with some people on the DL. They will need to spread a lot of misinformation and delay first responders. Any of them get hurt and all bets will be off. So, what do you say, Carlo?"

"Go for it, I'm all in," I said. "You know Lady plans on picking up the tab. She ain't gonna leave you hangin', she ain't like that." I slip in and out of proper grammar depending on the folks I'm talkin' too.

"I know just the spot to soften them up. I won't be at dinner here tonight. I will have them meet me at Strega. I'll call Phil and have him give us a private table away from the crowd. I trust him, and he will forget we were ever in there. He knows how his bread is buttered."

"You got that for sure. Phil is A-1 with me. He knows how to handle his shit. Sly, what do you think of proposing to them that the North End boys be responsible for the mess? Of course, none of them will get nailed, just maybe called in for questioning. One other major problem. You know some, maybe all of us, may be hit. Even with body armor there's no guarantee we all walk away. What do we do if we take casualties? We can't leave guys lying there."

"That will have to be part of what I can negotiate," Sly said. "I can also have a doctor, one that worked for the Celtics, and support staff here and set up a mini ER. At least we can do that for guys that don't need major surgery. Be like a field hospital. He is top-notch."

"I was thinking the same thing. Ah, you aren't talking about Dr. Glen, are you? If you are, he is one of the best. If we can get the guys back here, we treat them here. All it takes at a hospital is one cop asking too many questions of one of our guys who's pumped up on morphine. Jesus, this is too much, I'm getting a killer headache. Haven't had one of these fuckers since I was a kid. Where's the ibuprofen, brah?"

"My feelings too, but it's what we have to deal with. The sun isn't over the yardarm yet so it's not beer-thirty, but the ibuprofen is over there," Sly said chuckling trying to ease the pressure.

"What I really would love right now is for Lady to give me a massage. Just thinkin' about that makes me relax, I think. You're right, alcohol would only make this worse right now."

"You really think that will happen, the massage, that is? I hope it does. I've noticed how you two have been gettin' on. I think she needs it as bad as you. I truly believe that woman is falling for you."

"You meant a massage, right?"

"What else do you think I meant?" Sly remarked with a smile.

Sly and I sat there for a moment before I broke the silence. "I want to run something by you. I know it's crazy and I know you'll tell me no, but we may be able to get some good Intel and put a hair across the Albanians collective asses."

"Aight, what you have in mind?"

"Well, you know we now have their number—at least one of them. What if I were to call them and arrange a meeting? I mean, what's the worst that can happen?"

"And you really think that's a good idea? Are you freaking crazy? What's to stop them from killing you? You saw the fear they put into De'Londo, and Gina had to cut his junk off before he told the truth."

"That's simple, we bargain with Lady. They want her, we have her, not that we will give her up by any means, but they won't know that. I can take Jake and a couple of his guys and they can cover for me from across the road. Tole won't know they're there until I want him to know. We'll need to do some work beforehand, scope out the area with the drone and some boots on the ground. I won't go until we do that."

"You really want to do this?"

"I suppose I do." I sat there hoping the pounding would go away.

CHAPTER THIRTY-FOUR

PHONE CALL FOR ALBAN TOLE, PHONE CALL FOR
ALBAN TOLE

SLY'S GUYS HAD RETURNED FOR THE NIGHT, SET UP WATCH upstairs, and the rest of the team had finished up on the range leaving enough empty brass behind to make a poor man rich. The sun was definitely over the yardarm and we had all settled in with our favorite beverages—beers, bourbon, or scotch, and anything in between. It seemed that Ritch and Brit were becoming a pair and he took some good-natured ribbing from the guys. Brit gave it right back to them and Ritch just grinned. Of course, the Lady made sure that all present (read *Gina*) knew what was up with me and her, but I didn't even know what the dilio "was" was, but it was all good. Her skin was soft, and she smelled amazing. Did I just sound presidential? Was/was-is/is what is the definition of it all?

I arose from my seat next to Lady and asked that the guys

raise their glasses for a toast, a remembrance so to speak. "Today, my friends, one of our own has lost someone near and dear to them. To him and his family I offer a salute of condolence. Sometimes we are taken too young by things that never should be. It is why we fight. *Salute!*"

"Here, here," was heard from all and we downed what we were drinking.

Sly excused himself and stated that he had some unattended business to take care of. "I'll see you all in a bit, I have a dinner date."

"Must be nice," I said sarcastically.

"Now, on another issue. I spoke with Sly earlier and as De'Londo gave up a phone number, I want to call the Albanians and set up a meet. I know it's suicidal and beyond dangerous, but that's where you all come in and I think we can get some good Intel."

After everyone had told me I was crazy and insane, not something that they didn't know already, J3 asked, "How do we do it?"

"I thought you might see it my way," I said. "Jake, I want you and a couple of your guys to get on top of the Trico building which is across from the warehouse where they are holed up. It's about 450 feet and your guys can cover me. More than an easy shot from that distance. The warehouse has a lot of windows in the overhead doors which makes them vulnerable. I am sure they will take me inside and I don't doubt that I will be in for a rough time. We'll have comms and when I give the signal you and your guys light them up with the lasers. They won't want to die without getting what they want so it's a good bet they let me walk out. Ritch, I am counting on you to drive me there and back and you'll be wired up too."

All the while I was talking, Lady sat there in disbelief and finally cut in, "I won't let you do that, they'll kill you. No, you can't go!"

I continued on ignoring her plea, "We'll send up the drone tonight and use its night vision to scope things out a bit and then drive through the area to get a firsthand feel for the area. I'm familiar with the area but you all need to be too. This isn't my first choice of things to do but I believe it will keep them off balance."

J3 said, "Pretty well thought out. You agree, Jake?"

"Sounds pretty tight. I'll take one of my guys in one car and you take one of yours in another. We can meet up at the Micky D's right near there."

"Carlo, I guess you're up, ET phone home."

I dialed the number De'Londo had given up from one of the burners. I half expected the call to go unanswered but on the eighth ring an Eastern European accented voice answered, "Who is this?"

I responded, "Put Tole on the line now!"

"How did you get this number?"

"Wrong answer," I said and hung up. "That should piss them off, let's give them a sec to reflect on what just happened and I'll call back. Tat, pour me another Booker's please."

Reluctantly, she got up, poured me a drink, and handed it to me with daggers in her eyes. I gave her the *we'll talk later* look but she wasn't buying it.

Time to call again. The phone rang three times.

"Who the fuck is this?" This time it was not Toti or Astrit. It was Tole.

"I'm assuming I am talking to Alban Tole?"

"Who is this?"

"I'm the man who is going to make your life miserable. I have something you want but you have to talk to me first."

"And why should I do that?"

"Like I said, I have something you want, *kuptoj*?"

"So you think you know me, *karin kokosh*?" Which means sucking a part of the male anatomy.

"Better than you think, *porco di maiale*."

"Be here tonight," he ordered probably not having a clue what I called him.

"No, big man, that won't happen. Tomorrow night, 2100 hours. I know where you're at and I know you know where we're at. Your two stooges weren't that discrete. No wonder Albania is close to becoming a Third World country. Tell the boys to wear their party hats and dancin' shoes cuz I'm ready to tango!" I said and then hung up the phone.

CHAPTER THIRTY-FIVE

STREGA

SLY HAD ARRANGED TO MEET THE MAYOR AND THE POLICE commissioner for a late dinner at 2000 hours in a function room at Strega. Phil, the host, had accommodated Sly, and the five-hundred-dollar tip didn't hurt. It was an unspoken courtesy between the two and was just good business. Sly noted that the commish and His Honor both had bodyguards and were probably carrying themselves. The bodyguards were dismissed by their employers and waited outside in the cars.

"So, what brings us together tonight, Sly?" the mayor said being the first to speak up.

"Business soon enough, let's enjoy our drink." Phil had brought over three special cocktails along with a very aged cheese platter reserved for special friends to whet their appetites. He chatted with us for a bit, letting us know he was at our disposal.

"Your Honor, how is the family? You have a daughter in

Harvard, right?" Sly said knowing that he had used some—no, *a lot*—of influence with a certain administrator who had gotten jammed up with a gambling issue. Sly had made it go away with a debt he had to repay to Sly. Even the elitist educators at Harvard had their weaknesses, and Sly would exploit them when and if he could.

"She's doing well and the wife, what can I say. But very nice of you to ask."

Of course, it is, you rat bastard, Sly thought to himself. Half the time he felt filthy just talking to these people.

"Commish, are the new recruits coming along well? How's my man I sent over there?"

"Actually Sly, I'm impressed. His test scores are good and physically he challenges everyone in the class including the instructors. He should make a good cop. In fact, if he keeps up the way he is, we may pull him to do some undercover work. He seems to have a knack for that, but you knew that anyway," the commish said with that knowing look on his face. Sly knew the commish knew that Sly now had another mole in the agency. But payback is a bitch.

"That's good to know," Sly said knowing he had another "in" in the Department.

Phil made sure the waitress had taken care of all our needs and our meals came out in good time. You couldn't beat the lamb, it melted in your mouth, and the scallops left you wanting more.

"Mayor, Chief, I have a huge, huge problem and I will need your utmost cooperation and discretion."

The chief spoke, "You always know you have that, Sly." *Yeah,* Sly thought, *cuz you bastards are bought and paid for.*

"This is different, very different. The shit is about to hit the fan in the South End along the waterfront. I'm talking some very bad people have come into town and are making a power play for a friend of a friend of mine. I think you both get the drift."

"Are you talking about Carlo?" the mayor asked.

"Your Honor, you know I can't divulge that. You both are going to have to trust me on this. I don't want any cops getting in the way or getting hurt. Enough of that happens already. We don't need any unnecessary casualties. You know I take care of any of the officers when they stop by." Sly meant that they drank for free and the food was free, and he kept track of it all.

"Okay, Sly, you have our attention. What do you need us to do?"

"I need you both to spread disinformation to the media and the public as to what goes down. We can spin this that the North End boys got into it with the Albanian mob. Pick up a few of them, ask some questions, and let them go."

"Jesus Christ, Sly, Albanians? Since when have they been a problem in Boston?"

"Come on, Chief, you can't be blind to the Albanian population in the city." Sly was really thinking, *Are you that fucking stupid?* "They are all over Roslindale and stick very close together and most of them are hardworking, educated people but they all pay up. But these guys are from New York City. They are part of the Rudaj organization, and they've been pushing the Italian Mafia around for the last few years in New York. And they are ruthless. It's just natural that the North End boys get the blame for the incident. Sort of a payback, you understand where I'm comin' from?"

"Why do I feel there's more?" asked the chief.

"Because we all know there's more. We, meaning me and my friends, are going to take care of the problem but we may take casualties. I hope that isn't the case, but you know in any firefight both sides lose people. As for the Albanians, hopefully all you will need is the coroner's van, but for us we may need ambulances and cover-up at the hospital if it comes to that. My guys that are injured can be spun as a first response team by the feds, military, or whoever you think best to contain the Albanian presence. We have all military grade equipment."

"My God, Sly, I don't know. That is one hell of a coverup, er…forget I said those couple of words. The news would have a field day with that if they got a whiff," opined the mayor.

Sly responded, "That's why I need you both to do what you do best. Sell it. How many times have they questioned what you told them? My guess is none. They love this administration and think you're all the best thing since JFK, Obama, and sliced bread."

"You have a point there; they have cooperated with us all along. *The Herald* has even got in step and that is unusual," the mayor added, and the chief nodded in agreement.

"Maybe because you haven't taken the usual 'tow the democratic line.' I will keep you gentlemen informed every step of the way, but it is going down soon. What I will do right now is give you a tip. You know the body that was found down on Topeka?"

The mayor and the chief both nodded that they were aware.

"That is part of the problem. As far as you two are concerned, he was a heroin dealer and was running girls out of the apartment you searched. Keep the news on that track. They don't need to know any different. Also, any of my guys that are injured and can be taken off the scene in our vehicles before your guys show up, Chief, will be treated at my place. We will have a field hospital set up. That is for your ears only. I won't give you any more details. It will be less headaches for you, the less you have to account for."

"Wait a sec," said the commish. "How did you know we searched the apartment?"

"You mean the one on Seaport? Come on, Commish, you really think I didn't know about that?"

"Sly, you should have been a cop, not a club owner."

"Yeah, but then I would be the commish and you would be...what?"

"So, gentlemen, do we have an understanding?" Sly asked.

"I think we both agree that we're onboard. Sly, just limit the damage if you can."

"You know I will. Now, let's get another drink and finish this delicious dinner. By the way, Phil took a package out to the cars for each of you, just a little sumthin' sumthin'. And yes, the boys were fed, very well at that," Sly said not wanting them to forget what he had done, and it was on their tab.

"Sly," the Chief chimed in, "we have always appreciated the generosity and what you do for our boys in blue and the community as a whole."

"Point taken. I thank you gentlemen for the chance to dine with you, and as always, the bill is all set. I must get back to the restaurant and you will be hearing from me soon. I will use your personal cells."

"Good night, Sly," both men echoed.

Sly walked out of the restaurant a little more confident that he had them between a rock and a hard place. They had his back for real, and maybe he, Carlo, and the rest of the crew could pull it all off.

CHAPTER THIRTY-SIX

ALBANIANS IN THE MIDST

AS PROMISED, THAT EVENING, ALEKSANDER'S MEN ARRIVED at the warehouse with a cache of weapons and munitions and Tole ushered them into the warehouse and had them unload.

"My brothers, it is good to see you. I hope your trip was uneventful?"

"The ride up went as expected but we got a little bit of a late start. We have everything you asked for and maybe a little more. Aleksander didn't go into detail about what's going on. Can you fill us in?" asked Valmir. Valmir was one of Aleksander's best lieutenants and was flawless in his loyalty to him.

Tole spent the better part of the next hour rehashing what had been happening and how we had dumped the body on his front doorstep, so to speak. Tole told them how I had called and had the balls to challenge him and ask for a meeting. Tole further stated that it would take place tomorrow night at the warehouse.

"They know we are here, and they also spotted Astrit and Toti when they did a drive-by."

Valmir asked, "Is he on a suicide mission? Does he know we will kill him when he gets here?"

"My dear friend," Tole continued. "He is merely a pawn but a useful one. He is the key to getting the black whore and getting her business. So, we must keep him alive but who said anything about not having a little fun with him? He knows he must come alone. Besides, we don't need any more attention from the authorities after last night." And Tole did have a point at that.

"Find somewhere to get comfortable. We have food and if you need anything, we can get it. No ordering in unless I approve it, as if I need to say that. All of you will take a shift on the second floor as lookout, two at a time. If they come snooping, we need to know."

They all understood and nodded.

CHAPTER THIRTY-SEVEN

DRONE ON AND ON...

SLY ARRIVED BACK AT THE RESTAURANT AROUND 2230 hours. J3, Jake, and I were looking at maps and satellite images on the computer. Both their crews were in attendance and scoping out the pics.

"J3, this lot over by the McDonalds would be an ideal spot to launch. Two of my guys will man the drone and the rest of us can take the SUVs and scout around. If it looks doable, we can get out on foot for a closer look-see. Sound good?" Jake asked.

J3 answered, "Sounds good to me and it should be late enough that there won't be much traffic, foot or vehicular."

"Then we're all good. Anyone have anything to add?" No one from their crews said anything but indicated they understood.

"Carlo, no real need for you to go," Sly chimed in. "You have enough on your plate with having to talk to the Albanians tomorrow. You get the humint—human intelligence for those of you uninformed with Spec Ops language—on the inside, and then we can coordinate late tomorrow."

"Presuming I am in any shape to talk. You all know what they will probably do tomorrow, but I am counting on Jake's guys to get me out when the time comes. As I said earlier, Ritchie will be wired up also and when your guys light them up that will be Ritchie's cue to ex-fil me. Ritch, make sure you're armed. Bring the MP7."

"Got you covered," Ritch said.

"All right, let's saddle up and go outside and play. Your guys set, Jake?" J3 asked.

"We're good to go. We'll get the drone and the laptop and comms. Can't wait to see how good the night vision is on it."

"I'm getting another drink and taking a chill pill. See you all when ya get back. Thanks again, I really appreciate everyone coming," I said gratefully.

They didn't have to say a word. I could read it in their faces. Going into danger and not away from it was what they were trained to do, what we were all trained to do. They were good with it and they knew what they had to get done.

On their way out the door, J3 called to Dave, "Come with me and Sal. Never hurts to have a pair of extra eyes."

Dave didn't have to be asked twice and jumped at the chance to get out. "I thought you ladies would never ask!"

The three big SUVs entered the parking lot of Micky D's around 2345 hours and Jake had two of his men set up the drone. Once it was set up, they did a test flight around the lot and the night vision was incredible.

"This fucker is sweet!" said Max who was operating the drone. Mike was monitoring the drone via the laptop and both were very satisfied with what they saw. "Jake, guys, take a look at this. The clarity is stunning."

"All right, take it out a little further," Jake ordered.

Max and Mike did as they were instructed, and all systems were go.

"Let's mount up and see what we can find," directed Jake.

Dave jumped back in with J3 and Sal while Jake took Brando with him. Mike and Max stayed with one vehicle, monitored the drone, and passed Intel along to the others.

Mike broke the silence and called out to Jake, "Looks like there is fencing around the back of the Trico building. Trico is open in the front along Atkinson Street as is the building they are in on Topeka. Trico building is long enough that we could get ladders along the east side and be out of view. The building where the Albanians are suspected to be has a fence along the back and there's a man-door on the back. The backside also backs up to Winston Flowers. On the front there are all overhead doors. Lots of lights on in the building on Topeka. Looks like an alleyway between the florist and them. Not enough room for a vehicle to get down. Sending you sat photo now. Definite activity so keep your heads down."

"Roger that," responded Jake. "J3, take Atkinson Street then swing down South Hampton and meet us on the corner of Cummings and South Hampton. We're gonna get a closer look at the back of that building."

"That's a copy. On the way."

Both crews met up at the location and exited the vehicles.

"Here's what I want to do," Jake said. "Me, Dave, and J3, we'll head down the alley and check out the back. Sal and Brando will stay with the cars. Slow and easy."

"Mike, how is the activity going?"

"No one outside, Boss, but they're still up and awake inside. Stand by. Okay, I have eyes on you. Go now."

"Copy that."

The three of them headed down the alleyway and there was little debris to hinder them or make noise to alert anyone to their presence.

"J3, cover me to the west and Dave cover to the east," Jake said in a low voice. Jake checked out the door. "We can hit this with a little detcord and it will come right off the hinges. J3, your guys know how to use detcord?"

"Yeah, Sal does. He has military training and they used it all the time so we're good."

"Awesome, place it all the way along this side, get out of the way and ignite it. It'll take the door right off, blow it inside. We'll make sure Sal is on this team. Dave, you will be back here too, you good with that?"

"Fuck yeah, I don't want to sit in the car!"

"J3, if you don't have any questions let's head out. I'll go over the demo with Sal to make sure he's up to speed."

"All right, let's head home."

Before they left, J3 tagged the back wall. "Do not fear those who kill the body but are unable to kill the soul; But rather fear Him who is able to destroy both the body and soul in Hell."

Valmir was on watch with one of his men. "Anton, black SUV just did a slow drive. Looked like it was blacked out."

"Okay, *qij* (fuck), no doubt it's them. Keep a sharp lookout. Any activity out back?"

"Nothing, Alban," Toti answered.

That, my friends, was a very, very bad answer!

CHAPTER THIRTY-EIGHT

"Knock, Knock, Knocking on Heavens Door"
Bob Dylan

When the teams left, I downed another Booker's and a Xanax and headed to my room. I was stressed and wasn't afraid to admit it, at least to myself. I took a hot shower and stood under it for what seemed like an eternity. The muscles in my neck started to loosen and I didn't care what it was from—the hot water, bourbon, the tranq, or a combination of all three. I got out, turned on the TV, and scanned the channels for a movie that I hadn't watched or at least one that I hadn't seen in a long time. Finally, I said to myself, *screw it*, and turned on a Classic Soul station. The music was rhythmic, smooth, and relaxing, taking me back to when I was a much younger man. Damn, those young girls with those Afros looked so good back then. I remember watching the movie, *A Bronx Tale*, and the young

Italian boy fell in love with a black girl played by Taral Hicks. Yep, that would have been me back in the day, but in my community, it was all Italian, Polish, Lebanese, and Syrian. Even then, some of us suffered discrimination because we were from the wrong part of Europe. But there I was standing with a towel wrapped around me and about to lay down on the bed when I heard a knock on the door.

Five minutes prior to the knock on my door, Lady and Brit were talking in their room. "I am so livid at that man, what the hell does he think he's doing. I am so afraid, for him and for us, Brit."

"He's fallen for you, sis, don't you get it? He would walk on fire for you. He's doing what he's doing because he cares about you. Cut the man some slack. Tsuji is probably the only other man that would put himself in harm's way for you. None of those little bitch boys that work for you would. He is probably stressed as hell. Go talk to him, be there for him, and if you don't come back tonight, it's all good. He's a good man. Besides, I might want a little company!"

"Brit, you are such a little thot!" Lady said laughing and Brit did too. "So, you like that Italian boy, do you?"

"What's not to like? Besides, he's a real gentleman and I think he likes me."

"He just about melted when you rubbed his shoulders, sister girl. We both need to be careful, Brit. These are dangerous times, we're all under a lot of stress, and we might not be thinkin' clearly. But you're right, they both seem like good men. If we get through this, maybe it can go somewhere. You don't think I should worry about Gina?"

"Hell no, he doesn't want her, and she doesn't want him. That would be no life for him, you know what she does. She's just playin' with your mind. Don't fall for it, you're too smart for that, besides, Carlo likes chocolate!"

"All right, I'm going, I'll go talk to him," Lady said with a smile. "If he kicks me out, I'll just sleep on the couch."

"Yeah, uh huh, I'm sure that will happen. Now go get your groove back."

CHAPTER THIRTY-NINE

Lay Lady Lay

But there is only one thing that has power completely, and this is love. Because when a man loves, he seeks no power, and therefore he has power.

"Just a minute, Sly," I said in response to the knock.

"If you want Sly, I can go get him, but I think you would rather have me come in," a sexy female voice replied.

"Hold on a minute, I'm in just a towel, give me a moment to get decent."

"Don't give me a reason to step off, Carlo. I want to talk. The towel is fine, and I know you are being a gentleman but open this damn door, boy! Besides, I have goodies."

Okay, Carlo, this is what you've been waiting for, admit it or not. Let the Lady in and I bet she does have goodies!

I opened the door and Lady had two rocks glasses filled to about four fingers. I was gonna either pass out from the Booker's and the pills or have a very interesting night. She was also dressed in a silk kimono tied just tight enough, but I could still see her cleavage and the outline of her voluptuous body. She had nary a stitch of clothing under it. "I guess you do have goodies, and I've been sippin' pretty good already tonight but nothing wrong with another. But, please come in," I said at the same time begging my body not to pass out. I could be such a junkie at times.

"Thank you, hun," she said as she handed me a glass and took a seat on the bed. She continued, "I need to get something off my chest, can we talk for a minute?"

At this point in time I didn't know what to think. Between the tranq and the Booker's I wasn't sure what reality was.

"Sure, what's on your mind?" I hoped I remember this in the morning.

"Carlo, it's you on my mind. I don't know what's come over me. Ever since you put me in check on the first day, my emotions have been a mad mess. I-I-I mean, what I am trying to say is I believe I have feelings for you, and I know this is the worst possible situation to start feelin' someone. And I know if we get through this, I would like to give us a shot. I know you're older, I run a business, don't have much time, but you seem the type of man to take it all in stride. I could be falling for you, I mean really falling in love, and I hope that doesn't scare you. You doing what you're doing, no man has ever done anything like that for me before. And would you just freakin' kiss me and make me stop talking?" Her voice pleaded and her eyes had misted up.

My dear readers, she did not have to ask twice.

My right hand reached behind her neck and I pulled her close to me, I could feel the heat coming off her body, her scent intoxicated me further and deeper than the bourbon could ever have. My lips met hers, so full and sensual, and I slowly kissed her softly and gently at first, pulled away and looked into her beautiful, shimmering, chocolate eyes losing myself and then kissed her deeper, like there was no bottom to the depth of our kiss.

Her hand loosened the sash of her kimono and pulled away the towel wrapped around me. I kissed the entire length of her body. She wanted me, and I wanted her so badly, and we soon fell into a rhythmic motion of ecstasy. I don't know how long our lovemaking lasted but during the night I looked at her face and saw a smile of contentment that told me she was not going anywhere. She shook me all night long and she knocked me out with those African thighs. She was the best damn woman I had ever been with. A smart man would stay where he was, and I was no dummy, but then again, I was about to walk into the lion's den.

CHAPTER FORTY

ITALIAN BOYS, THEY KNOW ROMANCE!

BRIT WALKED DOWN THE HALLWAY AND KNOCKED AT Ritchie and Dave's room. She waited a moment before leaving, no one answered her knock, so she walked into the living area.

"Hey Ritchie, what you watchin'?"

"*Mad Max*, I was a little too young to appreciate it when it first ran so I was just catching up. He reminds me of Carlo," he said with a laugh.

"Oh, no doubt about that. Carlo can be a real wrecking machine at times. And you are both the same. Mind if I join you?"

"Not at all, sweetness, I'd appreciate the company. Everyone else is out doing their thing."

She sat down next to him, pulled her feet up on the couch, and put her arm under his and said, "You nervous about tomorrow?"

"It's just another day at the office for me, not to say I don't get one huge adrenaline rush from it…but nervous, no way."

"That must feel pretty awesome, huh? You really like living on the edge like that?"

"Like going on a very high, very fast roller-coaster for the first time. I wouldn't want to do anything else. There's nothing else for me that can produce that kind of high. Maybe if you're a good little girl I might give you some lessons."

"I would love that, but I want to ask you something."

"Okay, but hold on one sec, this is a good part."

"Boy, you better put that on pause cuz I won't say this again! Don't make me snatch that remote from you!"

Ritchie placed the movie on pause, turned and look at her and said, "I'm all ears."

"Um, my sister won't be coming back to the room tonight."

"Why, she did go somewhere?"

"Ritchie, you are as bad as Carlo. You know damn well what I meant!"

"Okay, so you need someone to tuck you in, right?" Ritchie said with a big grin on his face.

"Are you dense, just jerking my chain, or is that an Italian trait? Cuz I'm about to smack that white off you."

Ritchie began laughing and said, "Look, I don't know you all that well and I try not to get attached in my line of work, but I kinda like you and if you can deal with that, then I'm all good. Look, you're a stunning young lady and I don't take advantage of women, but if you want to have something, I wouldn't mind having something with you."

Brit realized that that was Ritchie's way of saying *I'm into you.*

"I'm not looking to tie you down, walk you down the aisle, have a fam, or be my baby daddy, but…"

"I get it, I do, let's just chill with one another tonight and see where it goes. I'm a free man, no ties."

And with this, Britiney leaned over and gave Ritch a kiss that said *come with me.* "Come on, the rest of the guys will be back soon. I don't want them knowing our business. God knows they'll know soon enough."

The lock clicked into place and there was no one to bother them. Jake and J3 dropped Dave off at the restaurant and they headed back to their hotel. We had a meeting set for the morning after breakfast. We were going to draw the line in the sand and if the Albanians wanted to cross it, may God bless their souls because we wouldn't.

CHAPTER FORTY-ONE

UNDER PRESSURE

"Insanity laughs under pressure we're breaking"…

— COURTESY OF QUEEN

THE NIGHT DRAGGED FOR THE ALBANIANS AND WE SLEPT peacefully in our designated rooms whether it was the hotel or at the bunker. Sly's guys had kept a diligent watch on things and nothing unusual was reported. At 0200 hours Dorchester had become a ghost town and not much if anything was moving. It was almost peaceful in a way.

The subways and buses had stopped service several hours before and wouldn't resume for several more. Vagrants wandered the streets digging through trash bins in hope of finding something edible or redeemable bottles to turn into cash, or for a somewhat sheltered place to sleep. There were those who couldn't find a place to sleep in the shelters dotted around Boston. Thankfully, the weather was warm and accommodating for those that remained outside. In the colder months, they would try to stay hidden in the subway tunnels that at least stayed above freezing and try to avoid the police patrols that would throw them out. Even the clubs closed early here at 0100 or 0200 hours. Sure wasn't like Buffalo where they stayed open to 0400 hours and drained every last cent they could from paying customers. Even then, in both cities the hardcore knew where the after-hours places were.

By 0530 the sun began to break the horizon and shed light on a new day. Clouds previously stained gray by the night were now streaked with red, crimson, pink, and orange, beckoning the day to begin. Streaks of deep azure blazed across other parts of the sky not occupied by the clouds, and if the lighting was just right you could see a full-color spectrum not unlike a rainbow. People began to stir from their slumber and prepare for another day at work. Breakfasts were cooking, lunches were being packed for kids or themselves, and clothes were chosen for another day at the old grind.

Tole was awake, having had an uneasy night. He wouldn't admit his weakness, but anxiety plagued the man partly due to the massive amounts of steroids, amphetamines, and downers he took. Tole was a true freak of nature and any boy in the gym would have killed for his build but no one, no, not one, dared mock or ridicule him about his size. Tole walked along the second-floor balcony and kicked at the mattresses that his men and Aleksander's men laid on.

"Get up, *ju lindi dembelët e nënës*, you lazy mother fuckers, someone start breakfast. Toti and Astrit, go make a patrol around the building and for Christ's sake keep the weapons out of view!"

No one dared countermand his order and everyone was up in

seconds. One of Aleksander's men suggested they go out to eat and Tole actually conceded to that point, as there were so many of them.

Toti and Astrit had finished their tour and reported in. "Boss, they were here last night. I took a picture of what they wrote on the back wall."

Toti showed the picture of the words that were inscribed on the wall and the veins in Tole's neck bulged to the point of exploding. He was a man that did not enjoy surprises.

"How is this possible? How could they get close enough to do this and we not notice? What are you telling me, that we're a bunch of incompetent fools?"

No one was quite sure how to answer until Astrit stated," That's our blindside, Boss. We can only see so much from the windows. I suggest we get cameras on the corners of the building."

"Finally, someone who has half a brain. Get it done, now! Wait, get the cameras after we eat," Tole barked. Food was always a precedent with Tole.

Two of Aleksander's men said they were on their way to Best Buy and would meet them all at the restaurant, Victoria's Diner.

Zeni and Luli, two of Tole's men, stayed behind for security and the rest headed out to the diner. At this early morning hour, the restaurant was packed with commuters getting their grub on. Tole slipped the waitress, a young girl maybe still in her teens, an extra twenty to seat them in the back room away from prying eyes. Tole's façade was beginning to show signs of cracking as hard as he tried to hide what was happening. No one, not even him, liked his outbursts. The waitress seated them at a table for fifteen but with their size it was still a little crowded.

"After you bring the food, bring a couple of pots of coffee and leave it here and don't bother us any further. Here is something for your trouble, *pëllumbin tim të vogël* (my little dove)." Tole pushed a fifty-dollar bill inside the open top two buttons of her uniform shirt.

After she had set the last plate on the table and had brought the coffee, Tole couldn't resist reaching out his hand and giving her ass a squeeze. She jumped and gave him a dirty look and received dirty laughs from the horde at the table.

CHAPTER FORTY-TWO

THE SOUND OF AWAKENING

"Do you feel my heartbeat quickening
  In between the bated breaths before the turning of the page
  The sense that everything's about to change?"

— SOUND OF AWAKENING BY WALK THE
MOON

I FELT HER GENTLE BREATH ON MY SHOULDER AS THE FIRST light of morning were turned on in the bunker. What more could a man ask for than to wake up next to this heavenly goddess? I wasn't looking forward to the day that was about to be as I knew it would not be an easy one. I settled back into a sedated slumber, one evinced by her love, though not yet totally professed. I knew that today was a day I did not want to die; no day was a good day to die, not now, not ever.

I wanted to lay there wrapped in her arms for an eternity if God so willed it.

"Could she feel my heart quickening in between the bated breaths before the turning of the page? She could not make me leave this heavenly place if I kicked and screamed. I was cradled in her arms and I knew then and there that I loved her. It was the sound of awakening, psychotropical symphony washing over me." (Courtesy of Walk the Moon).

I couldn't ask for more nor could she give more than she had. She had given her all. It was just an illusion in our differences and an illusion that made us one.

I could hear voices in the living area, and I decided as much as I wanted to stay in bed I needed to get up and find out what the guys had learned the night before. As usual, the smell of cooking food was in the air, hickory-smoked bacon, eggs, and a mass of home fries. At this rate I was gonna weigh three hundred pounds before this op was over. I was able to leave Lady nestled in the bed with blankets wrapped around her as my arms would have been. I pulled up a chair at the table and asked if everyone had a good night and they all laughed before J3 said, "I'm guessing not as good as the night you had."

Do these guys have ESP? I mean what the…okay, you know what I mean.

"What, you have my roomed bugged?" I asked sarcastically.

"Would you suspect anything less?"

"You're such a dick! But can I get a copy of the video?" which got a round of laughs. I was unable to take offense at anything these guys said. These guys were the best and I loved them all. In the short time we had all been together, we gelled into a cohesive unit that felt like we had worked together for years.

Lady came out about twenty minutes later into the kitchen area wearing the same kimono as the night before and her hair had that freshly copulated look. If y'all don't know what that means, ask a woman. Yeah, it was a mess, but she tried to hide it as best as she could as the night before left her starving. On her worst day she looked better than most women did on a good day. Of course, I got the looks that said, *you lucky bastard*. What can I say? I just got game!

"Good morning, boys, everyone sleep well?" she asked.

Of course, this cracked the guys up being the children they were, and Lady asked, "What is it you all think is so funny? Never mind, little boys never change."

Of course, that got another round of raucous laughs.

CHAPTER FORTY-THREE

WAR PIGS
Black Sabbath

WHILE TOLE AND HIS MEN STUFFED THEMSELVES AT THE diner, Valmir and another of Aleksander's men were busy securing the equipment. They had gotten several security cameras, lights, motion sensors, and several monitors. Hopefully this would make Tole happy. They headed to the diner, then joined Tole and the others in the back room and ordered food. Regardless of the fact that they were Muslim, there was enough bacon and ham steaks on the table to choke a horse. Tole's thoughts on it were, "When in Rome do as the Romans do." He knew that alleged devout Muslims such as Princes, Kings, Emirs, and Sheiks all indulged in the worldly pleasures of food, booze, and babes when they visited this land of infidels, especially in Vegas, because what happens in Vegas, stays in Vegas, or at least it's supposed to.

"So, Valmir, what did you get us?" Tole asked.

"Cameras, lights, motion sensors, and six two-way radios. That should give us enough time to beat them to the punch," Valmir said. "The back area should be all secure. We'll see them coming."

"That had better be a fact and not an opinion, my friend. We cannot afford mistakes."

"We may need some tools to get through the walls and we have the mounts for the cameras and such. At least a drill, Sawzall, sledgehammer, and some drill bits."

"What we don't have we can buy," answered Tole. "It's not a big deal. When we get back, we'll make a list of tools and accessories and I'll send someone to get the stuff. Let's go so the others can eat. Two of you take watch when we get back."

When they had arrived back at the warehouse, Valmir went through all the equipment and made a list of tools: a cordless drill, masonry screws, and a pack of drill bits varying in size, Sawzall, a sledgehammer, and a spool of coax cable.

Valmir ordered two of his men to go get the needed tools and get back ASAP. While they were gone, he set up the monitors and installed the necessary software to operate all the surveillance toys. Those not on watch were loading empty magazines and cleaning all the weapons. There was no telling how soon they would need them and better sooner than later. Not that AKs needed much maintenance because you could bury then in a pile of dogshit and they would still fire flawlessly.

Valmir's men did not waste any time getting back with the needed items and Valmir put them to work.

"Drill several holes in the wall about a foot from the corners. Then knock it out with the sledgehammer. One of you get on the roof with the drill and mount the brackets. Put a motion sensor, light, and camera on each side of the corner. Connect the cables and feed it down to me. I'll hook it up and run a check."

A couple of hours later Valmir called Tole over and showed

him what they had set up. "All the blind spots are covered, and if they get near the building the motion sensors will set off the lights and the cameras. I have two guys outside and they will test it."

Valmir called out to the two men and when they approached the buildings' back corners Tole observed everything was in working order.

"Very good, at least something is going our way," Tole ventured. "The PI is coming at nine tonight. No telling how many people he will bring with him but at least they won't get around the back unnoticed. Remember, it's not what we see, it's what we don't see that bothers me, so I hope your system works when it is supposed to."

"We'll check it again as it starts to get dark," Valmir said.

"Good idea."

CHAPTER FORTY-FOUR

Modern-Day Warriors

Mean, Mean Stride
Rush

After we all had our fill, once again we headed back into the living area. For those of us unaware of the results of the surveillance last night, Jake gave us a rundown. He had sat images on the large-screen monitors for all to see.

"We put the drone up and everything was pretty much as Carlo had said. It's almost four hundred and fifty feet to the inch from the back of the roof of Trico to the front door on Topeka. There is an alleyway behind their building and no sign of any type of surveillance equipment or foot patrols. We did a couple of slow drive-bys and signs of activity were noted. There is one single man-door on the back that can be blown with a little detcord. If it comes down to a final assault, we should easily be able to take them down. Any of the long guns we use will be capable of penetrating the doors and the cinder block. Any questions so far?"

"Yeah." Sal asked, "Who's all playing tonight?"

"Good question. As of now, Ritchie will drive Carlo and Tsuji will ride shotgun. Both Ritchie and Tsuji will be armed with MP7s and of course Carlo will be unarmed. They will probably come out and get him and I'm sure they will come out armed. Ritchie, you don't pull away until Carlo is inside. Both you and Tsuji have your windows down, so they can see we aren't defenseless. You both got that?"

Ritchie nodded and when Jake looked over at Tsuji he said, "*Hai*."

So, he does understand what we are saying...

"I want to be in the car with Carlo," Dave chimed in. "I'm not gonna sit around."

"Okay you got it," Jake said.

J3 asked, "Where will the rest of us be? I know we're not going to need everyone."

"Me and my guys will be on the Trico rooftop as we will need to red-dot the bad guys when the time comes. Your guys can take up positions just west of the building on Topeka. See this heavy machinery? This should be good cover for two of you. Place the other two at the east side of the Trico building where the overgrowth is. This way we should have a good field of fire if need be. The two guys on the corner of the Trico building—make sure you have lasers on your weapons. You'll be able to light up a couple of them too."

"Roger that, we'll go wherever we're needed most."

Lady spoke up. "Y'all aren't leaving here without me. The cars got room, I'm going."

She had that look on her face that said she was not going to be denied, and no one spoke up to try to stop her.

"Fine, whatever," Jake conceded.

Whatever? Did he just whatever the Lady?

"Sly, other than Ritchie, I want two of your guys to drive. We will have enough boots on the ground, and we don't want to be tripping all over one another. You good with that? In fact, if your guys do that, we would appreciate the assistance. That would be a big help. That way we don't have to worry about the vehicles."

With that Reshaun, Khaseem, and Cedric almost said in unison, "Hell, yeah!"

"Okay, it's all set then. Nothing fancy, guys, just be where we need you when we need you and be armed."

"Yes, sir," Khaseem said.

"Gina, you ride shotgun with the boys. Won't be any assassinating anyone tonight but another gun never hurts."

"I thought you'd never ask!" was her response with a touch of her own brand of sarcasm.

"Carlo, no one's asked you how you doin'. You're the one going into this shit-storm and unarmed at that. I know you got a lot on that big plate of yours, but you good?" Sly asked.

"As prepared as I'll ever be. No dinner for me tonight, I ain't puking in front of those fucks if they beat me. I'll take a couple of Vics and a Booker's or two, that should numb me a little. Besides, the Vicodin will keep me awake so I won't miss any of the fun," I said with a smile.

Of course, Lady thought none of this funny.

"What time we roll, Jake?" I asked.

"2030 hours—should be dark by then."

"Roger that, zero dark thirty."

There wasn't much for me to do other than chill but that was hard to do knowing what was coming. The rest of the guys were checking, double and triple checking, so Mr. Murphy did not show up and present us with a FUBAR. For those uneducated in military speak, that is Fucked Up Beyond All Repair. New batteries were put in all the electronics, and the drone's Li-SOCl$_2$

(Lithium-Thionyl-chloride) state-of-the-art batteries were also charged.

"Sly," Jake asked, "where did you get this drone with these batteries? These are impossible to get."

I was close by and said, "Don't ask, they just fell off a truck," which got a good laugh from Sly and the rest of the guys.

"Okay, man, it's your show but glad we got 'em."

Finally, the guys took a break and piled into the kitchen and threw together some grub. I sat around and chatted for a while enjoying the guys' and ladies' company—enjoying their special brand of humor that only guys that had seen action could interpret as funny. People like us thought we were funny, but common folk tended to think us a tad morbid. Whatever keeps the boogeyman away I say. I managed to slip away and headed to my room. I kept a bottle of my friend in the drawer and I intended on having a chat with him—my dear friend Booker Noe. I know, sounds like a George Thorogood song, that, or I was an alcoholic, but that wasn't likely either. And then came the inevitable knock on the door, again! Good Lord, could I just rest in peace? But no, I had to open my mouth and say, "Come in, Sly," knowing damn well it probably wasn't him.

"You know damn well it ain't Sly, now I'm comin' in. Jeez, gonna start thinkin' you gay for him."

"You're too funny, I knew it was you!" Actually, glad you came. Come on, snuggle up to Big Daddy!"

She curled up to me and I felt her hands run over my back. "You're knotted up, take that shirt off. Time you got some TLC."

"What was last night?"

"You know damn well what that was," she responded as she slapped the back of my bald shaved head. "But right now, you're as tight as a wound-up alarm clock. You can't go saving the world like that."

"You sound awfully calm about all this and just to correct

you, it's *your* world I'm saving, not everyone else's, just yours, got that?"

"You know I'm not calm, and I know it's me you're putting yourself out there for, I'm scared as hell but touching you gives me some strength."

It didn't take much longer, and she made us both more relaxed.

CHAPTER FORTY-FIVE

"Pleased to meet you, hope you guess my name"

— ROLLING STONES

WE HAD SLEPT FOR SEVERAL HOURS BEFORE LADY AROSE and went out into the main living area. She saw that everyone had finished eating before the night's mission and she came back to the room and gently woke me.

"Hey, hun, everybody's in the dining room. I know they would like your company."

"Roger that, babe, I'll get up." We both had slipped into an easy comfort zone and the pet names seemed to roll off our tongues with ease. I was getting way too comfortable with her calling me *hun*.

She handed me a black tee and my jeans (standard uniform). I pulled them on and we headed out. Sly, Brit, and Tsuji made a big stir-fry with chicken for everyone just before I went to my room, which I am guessing was the big man's idea. I did succumb to my stomach and took a small plate, and Tsuji turned out to be quite the cook. Everyone had complimented him on the food and when I did, surprisingly he said, "Thank you."

We all looked at him and of course Lady jumped in. "You do understand."

He answered by smiling.

"Almost time to roll out. All y'all ready?" I asked.

"We were born ready, my friend," J3 chimed in. "The question is, are *you* ready?"

"Ready as I'll ever be. Let's go play with the Ali Babas."

"Fuck yeah," Dave said. Everyone nodded and echoed his sentiments.

We all had out car assignments, everyone was locked and loaded, and nothing had been left to chance. I say screw Mr. Murphy should he rear his ugly head, I'll let Gina deal with him. And I would feel sorry for him.

I climbed into the back of the spacious Maybach along with Dave and Lady who of course sat next to me. Tsuji sat up front with Ritch because it was the only place he would fit. As our convoy headed out onto Dorchester Avenue, I told Ritchie, "Play some Zeppelin, that always gets me amped up especially in the gym." I laid back in the seat and let the music overtake me.

We all pulled into the parking lot next to the Micky D's and the usual traffic was in and out of there. Max and Mike put the drone up and did a flyover to check for anything out of the ordinary before we moved in. No one paid us any mind as they were all too engaged with buying junk food.

Max remarked, "Hey guys, looks like they have installed some security measures. Looks like cameras, lights, and sensors. That shouldn't be a problem for tonight. We should be good to go."

Jake said to Sly's guys, "Park the SUVs down on South Bay and wait for us to call you to make an extraction. Don't waste any time getting to us."

Sly's guys let us know very clearly that they would not play around when that time came. "We won't leave you hanging when you give the word."

Max called out to Jake, "When we hit this place, we can knock out the power and they will be blind."

"We're counting on that," Jake said.

"All right, my crew and the guys I need from J3, let's get set up on Atkinson Street. We need to be on the roof before Carlo goes in. J3, two of your men need to be over by the construction equipment on the west side of the Topeka building. Your other guys can cover the area with the overgrowth next to the Trico building."

"Roger that."

"Ritchie, when we are all set and have doped our scopes, you roll in with Carlo, not before. Let them sweat a while before you roll in." For the uninitiated, "doping the scope" means taking calculations and making sure the scope is set for the range, wind, and atmospheric conditions. Not that at this distance it was a problem as they could shoot a pimple off a fly's ass at a thousand yards, but it still needed to be done.

"Everyone good, everyone ready?" Jake asked. Affirmatives were given all around and Jake said, "Let's roll."

Everyone moved out while Ritchie and those in the Maybach stayed behind until they had secured their positions.

It wasn't long before these trained operators were in place and zeroed in on the targets across the roadway. The others also had taken up their posts at their designated points by the machinery and foliage.

Jake got on the comms. "Okay, Ritchie, you are clear to go."

"That's a go." Ritchie lit the tires up, peeled across South Hampton, and then backed off the gas taking a slow stroll down Topeka Street. "We are onsite," Ritchie said.

"We have you, you are clear to make the call."

I picked up the phone and dialed the number. Tole answered. "Who is this?"

I answered, "That's a good question, but call me Lucifer cuz I'm in need of restraint."

"I'm sure you are, and we have lots of it."

"Getting out of the car. They will not leave until I am inside." I told the Lady to stay down so they did not see her to give them any reason to open fire. With this, Tole sent out Toti and Astrit to retrieve me. They were armed with AK 47s and Dave and Tsuji put down the windows to show that they had their own firepower. There was a tense moment or two as both sides were unsure what the other was going to do.

As I exited the car with my hands behind my head I called out, "Don't shoot, coming out," and I approached Toti and Astrit. Again, my tongue went into overdrive and I said, "Pleased to meet you, boys. Let's all play nice now."

They pushed me through the door, and I was knocked to the ground with the butt of one of the AK47s between my shoulder blades, and it knocked the wind out of me. I got up half on my own power and half them dragging me up, and I was frisked thoroughly before being allowed to go any further. I looked around and tried to get a body count and note any weak spots in the building. They thoroughly searched me but didn't find the small transmitter secreted on my shirt that looked like a button. It didn't take long to identify Tole as he was the biggest motherfucker in the building.

Tole approached me and demanded, "Where is she?"

"Not quite sure who you mean. I know a lot of women."

That earned me my first punch to the head, but I managed to stay on my feet.

"That all you got, bitch?"

"Put him in the chair and secure him well," barked Tole. "I will enjoy breaking him. He'll be the bitch before this night is over."

His boys slammed me into a wooden chair and duct-taped

my arms and feet to it. Yes, duct tape does have a million and one uses.

"I'll ask you again, where is that black whore?"

"Excuse me, I don't think you get the gist of this meeting," my mouth rambled on. "This is not a negotiation, the line is drawn, and you have two options—leave now alive or all y'all die, and Allah will not save your goat-screwing asses, and besides, I'm not sure what black whore you mean. I know a lot of them too..."

Tole did not appreciate my brand of anti-Islamic humor. He caught me with another hard blow landing near my left eye and the swelling started almost immediately. I heard a slight crunch and figured he cracked my orbital rim socket. It took a minute for the fog to clear and my mouth went into overtime again. You know that little thing that keeps you from saying things you shouldn't? Yeah, well, I don't have one of those and this was one of the nights I wish I did!

"Come on, Tole, really, that all the harder you can hit? I thought you were tougher than that. Must just be rumors...yeah, big man, you just growl mean and people get scared? Heard your man parts shrunk up from your obvious steroid use. Your daughter hit me harder than that last night when I took her."

My eye was beginning to shut so I couldn't see much coming from the left side. His sledgehammer-sized fist caught me dead center, my nose broke, and blood poured out. Tole followed that with several punches to the body and I swear I felt something give. I spat out a large glob of blood—not unusual considering the blows that were landed.

"I'll kill you here and now, you worthless greaseball Dago!"

Tole was close enough that I could smell his fetid ass-smelling breath and I said, "Jesus, Tole, you're hurting my feelings and that is so old-school. Couldn't you think of anything more up-to-date? Dago, really? Don't stop with that. Try goombah, Guido, wop, now those will really hurt my feelings.

But, my God, don't you brush or use mouthwash? Because your breath reeks of camel cock." I managed a laugh. "You just don't get it, big man."

"What don't I get? You're the one tied up."

"You don't get the nature of my game. I told you, you can leave now or you all will die. That is not a threat, just a sincere promise," I said kind of garbled.

That got me another belt on the right side of my head and I nearly blacked out. My head bounced around like one of those bobble-headed dolls sitting on a dashboard, and it took a minute before I could focus.

"Doesn't seem anyone is coming after you, little man. Seems to me they left your ass behind. Maybe I should kill you now and go take the woman myself."

"She's more woman than you would ever be able to handle, you limp-dick bastard. You're repeating yourself now, Tole. Maybe you should turn around and look at your chest, big man."

That was Jake's cue and Jake ordered, "Light them up!"

Tole looked down at his chest and saw four red laser dots dancing across the most vital areas of his body. It took the hostility out of him and replaced his look with a look of fear. A slight sweat broke out on his forehead.

"So, what do you say, Tole, looks like I have four of a kind and you only have what, shit? You want to die right here, right now?" I said reversing the tables on him." Tole knew this was not the time to start a shooting match and he ordered his men to cut me loose.

"Wise choice. Looks like you aren't quite as dumb as you look. Like I said, Tole, pack up and get out, or (and in my best Arnold voice) *I'll be back*!" I laughed and spewed blood out of my mouth at the same time, some of which sprayed on Tole.

I got up and was a little—no, a lot—wobbly on my feet and fell. Two of them, don't know who as my face was swollen, grabbed me and dragged me outside. They also noticed the red dots on their chests and didn't make a move for their weapons but dumped me on the asphalt.

Ritchie was already on set with the car's passenger side to the overhead doors, and Dave and Tsuji had their MP7s leveled should Tole's men make a move. Dave covered Tsuji as he grabbed me with one hand and picked me off the ground and got me (more like tossed me) into the car like a limp rag doll. He looked back at Tole and grinned, just wishing he could have a go at him. It was a match I would love to see. Dave and Tsuji jumped in and Ritch spun the car around, raising a dense cloud of burnt rubber, and headed for home. All I could say on the way back was Alpha Mike Foxtrot (military for Adios Mother Fuckers).

Ritch called to Jake, "We are clear and heading to base. Carlo is in rough shape and may need more than a Booker's when we get back."

I knew I was dripping blood on the expensive leather seats and I apologized to Ritch. "Don't worry about it; it's not the worst thing that has gotten on those seats." I tried to laugh but it hurt too much, and Tatiana could only say "Ewww!"

"Copy that, we are extracting."

Jake called to Sly's men in the cars and they picked up the rest of the teams at the designated positions.

CHAPTER FORTY-SIX

Anyone Got an Ice Pack?

By the time we got back to the bunker my face was swollen enough that I had a hard time seeing, and that was stretching the point. More accurately, I couldn't see at all as my eyes were pretty much just slits, but boy, did I piss off Tole. He thought he had it all in the bag. Tatiana was shocked at my injuries after Tsuji threw me in the car, but she did manage to staunch the blood flow coming from my now broken nose on the way back. She started to repack my nose and now that the adrenaline had started to decrease, the pain level started to increase, more like it shot off the pain meter.

"Damn, baby girl…careful, that hurts. Grab me one of my pills."

She grabbed the script bottle out of the nightstand drawer and gave me two Vics and a bottle of water. "You need a doctor and we both know it, I don't know why you have to be so stubborn. I'm worried about you, if it matters."

"Yes, it matters, you know it does, but I don't think seeing a doctor will be happenin' anytime soon," I said. "Too many questions. Besides, you're doing a fine job. You can be my nurse anytime. I think I have a couple of cracked ribs too. He hit like a train." I grabbed the 129-proof Booker's from the nightstand and took a swig trying to drown the pain while I waited for the pills to work.

"And your dumbass looks it!" she said defiantly with tears beginning to form in the corners of her eyes. "And no more booze with those pills!" She snatched the bottle from me and hid it safely away.

Sly came by the room and said, "You know the doctor I mentioned? He's on the way."

Lady blurted out, "I'm glad someone's got some sense. This hard head thinks he's all good to go, but I appreciate it and thanks, Sly."

"Anything for my man there," responded Sly.

About thirty minutes later the doctor arrived and Sly introduced him as Doc Glenn, no last name, nor did I want to know, all the less culpability. If he had worked on the Celtics, he was good enough for me. Besides, I don't think I would remember his name anyway, at least not now.

Sly asked, "So can you fix up our boy here or isn't he worth saving?"

"Fuck you, Sly," I managed to mumble, and I could feel the narcotic starting to kick in.

After a cursory exam, Doc Glenn confirmed pretty much what I already knew. "Well, even with the swelling it appears that the orbital rim is fractured, and the nose is broken but I can fix that." And with that he placed his hands on either side of my nose and snapped it back in place and I let out, "Motherfucker, that hurt..."

"You may want to see a plastic surgeon when this is all over."

"Just another battle scar, Doc."

"Any trouble breathing? Looks like you got hit pretty hard in the ribs."

"Naw, I can breathe fine except through my nose, but I think they're cracked. Felt like getting hit with a jackhammer."

"We can tape those up, be a little uncomfortable, and besides that's old technology," he said as he gently applied pressure where the largest bruises were. "I will give you a shot of morphine now and leave you a few tabs to get you through the night and tomorrow."

"Now you give me the morphine. Wish you gave that to me before you straightened my nose!"

"Will someone be with you all night tonight?" he asked unassuming.

"I'll be with him," Lady spoke up before anyone else could.

"Okay, great. Keep ice on the wounds, it should get the swelling down. Those ribs are good as they are, no need to tape. Anything else before I go, and I'll check on you tomorrow."

"Great, now I can't rip it off and all the hair with it," I said making an attempt at humor.

Doc got me all squared up, gave me the injection, and left me in the care of my comrades and Lady. Tsuji even came by the room to check on me and I thanked him for pulling my ass off the pavement and throwing me in the car. The big man just grinned and bowed. The morphine kicked in almost immediately, and combined with the Vicodin and the Booker's, I was feeling no pain. I wasn't feeling anything! If the building collapsed on top of me I would be all good.

"Tat, now is good as any to try to clean me up. Help me so I can get in the shower. You'll need to walk me over to it cuz I can barely see."

"You don't need to be moving right now, just stay in bed, but

I know you'll do as you please anyway because you're one thick-headed man!"

She offered to wash me, and I told her I just needed to stand under the water and let the filth wash off me.

"If you would please put out a clean tee and jeans for me, I think I can find my way back into the bedroom."

"You are one stubborn man. Sometimes I just want to hate you."

"Just one of my socially redeeming qualities, my dear. So, you like me?"

"I'm not even gonna answer that!" But that was just as good as an answer.

By the time I got out of the shower, dried off, and groped my way back to the bedroom and dressed, she had prepared ice packs for me and the guys took turns stopping by and checking on me before she shooed them away to allow me to rest.

"I will keep you all posted, just let him rest for now."

Lady stayed with me the rest of the evening, made sure I was comfortable and not in pain, and kept the others away when I did manage to get some sleep.

CHAPTER FORTY-SEVEN

Ask Not for Whom the Bell Tolls, It Tolls for Tole

Okay, give me some credit for being a little clever!

Tole was the fool not knowing that the entirety of his world was heading at him at breakneck speed and there was nothing he could do about it. He had no clue because in his psycho-sadistic mindset he had always gotten his way by force and intimidation and was not used to others having bigger balls than him. Sure, he was fierce and deadly, but so were my own band of marauders.

After we had all pulled away, Tole looked over at Valmir and Toti and shouted, "What the fuck just happened?"

"Alban," Valmir said, "maybe those were just lasers. We don't know if they had rifles with them or not. Or how many of them there were. They could just be playing us for stupid, trying to get us off our game."

"And you really think that? *A besoni me të vërtetë, a jeni duke u ndyrë budallenj?"* (do you really believe that, are you a stupid fuck?) Tole blasted Valmir. "I should tell Aleksander what a fool you are. Are you telling me I didn't do the right thing, that I should have gambled with my life and not let him go? I didn't see any red dots on your chest!"

"You are right, Alban, and I believe they will come for us. Toti, you agree?"

Toti hesitated to answer then Tole said, "Well what, speak up?"

"Yes, Boss, they will come for us. We had best prepare."

Tole eyed them both back and forth, his face reddened in rage. "Then let's prepare. We start now, we will beat them at their own game. Tonight, have four men on watch at all times and check the security system."

Valmir sent two of his guys out while Astrit checked the monitors, and the lights and cameras activated as the other two men came within range.

"We're all good, Boss. Everything's working as expected."

"Check them every hour, no mistakes. Someone stay glued to the monitors and watch for any foot or vehicle travel," Tole ordered and swigged from the vodka bottle before passing it to Valmir. "We're good, Valmir." That was the closest to an apology the other big man would get.

Valmir nodded and took a long hard pull on the bottle, thankful for what Tole had said. Like I said earlier, Tole hated his outbursts as much as his men.

Alban was always used to getting his way, not having people stand up to him. But neither the booze nor the pills would help Alban sleep tonight. He may have picked on the wrong woman and the wrong group of friends, but he could not let himself admit that he may have bit off more than he could chew. He went outside and smoked cigarettes, something he rarely did, drank some more—a lot more—and stayed there for what seemed like an eternity by himself. He barely noticed the patrols making rounds nor did he speak to them as he was lost deep in thought or maybe just lost. Finally, after several hours and the moon arcing its way across the late-night sky, Tole fell asleep in the chair, the booze and pills at last having some effect on the big man.

CHAPTER FORTY-EIGHT

IT'S ANOTHER VODKA SUNRISE

AS THE FIRST FLEDGLING RAYS OF DAWN BROKE INTO THE sky, two of Aleksander's men found Alban Tole passed out in front of the warehouse while doing their patrol. They awoke Toti and Astrit and the four of them managed to wrestle the three-hundred-and-ten-pound gorilla into the warehouse and put him down on a cot in the office to sleep off the night before. It would be 1100 hours before the big man awoke.

Alban's and Aleksander's men took turns going to the restaurant and they always returned with a coffee in case Tole had come out of his stupor. Once it was fully light, they ceased the exterior patrols but still manned the computer screens.

"Toti, Astrit," came a froggy-sounding bellow. "Someone get me some coffee."

No sooner had Tole spoken when Koli and two of Valmir's

men walked in from the restaurant bearing black coffee and plenty of it.

"Alban, here you go," said Koli. "We also brought you some food, but I am sure you'd rather have that *zuskë*, slut, from the restaurant serve you."

That got a small chuckle from Tole whose head was pounding. "Ah, someone who knows me. Can you get me some aspirin and thank you, Koli, and thank Aleksander's men also. It is not often that I get like that and whoever brought me in I appreciate that. This is causing much stress. I am proud to be with such good men."

Koli replied, "It was Toti and Astrit with two of Aleksander's men. They were patrolling and found you and got the other two. We understand, we know that much is on your mind, and you have our full support no matter what is ahead of us."

Tole nodded his head acknowledging Koli's statement. "Have Toti call the men together, I need to say something."

"Boss, we are all good with everything. Nothing happened as far as we are concerned."

"Koli, please do as I ask. I know I don't need to, but a good leader admits when he's wrong." Koli did as ordered and the men gathered in front of the office.

"Comrades, my friends, I know that I can be difficult at times, but you always obey my every order without question. For this I respect you. I also know that each and every one of you is prepared to lay their life on the line to complete our task. Last night I became overwhelmed. I am ashamed that you all had to see me like that, but even leaders have their times. Thank you for this morning and thank you for all you do for me." With that, Tole ended his apology. But deep inside of this beast he knew the men feared him, thus causing them to respect him just as he had feared his boss when he was only a soldier. Someday he would be challenged for his power and status and his share of the money that was generated, but that someday would not be today.

"Now to attend to matters at hand. I want someone to go to a paint store and get some black paint. We are going to black-out the windows. They already know too much about us and that doesn't sit well with me. Whatever we can hide from them the better. Does anyone have any ideas on how to reinforce these flimsy overheads?"

Ari, one of Aleksander's men, was the first to speak, "Alban, if we get some steel angle iron, we can weld crosspieces on the doors. It will not only reinforce them but make it harder to get in if they do breech."

"Do you know how to weld?" Tole questioned.

"I learned the trade in school and worked several years before construction tanked. Then I came to America to hook up with Aleksander. It's been a while, but I can do it. Do you want the overheads welded shut?"

"Good thinking, Ari, good thinking. Yes, do that. Leave one overhead so we can get the cars in and out but reinforce it. Then there are only two ways in and out...the two doors going into the office area, can we reinforce them also? Where can you get a welder?"

"Let me check online. I am sure there are several welding supply stores in the area, and they should rent equipment. We can get all we need to get done in one night. I will also see about getting a torch to cut the steel."

Shpati spoke up, "I also have welding experience and I will help Ari. I'll go with him to the supply store."

"Okay, make it so. I think we should place guns all around the warehouse for easy access and all of you keep a handgun strapped on even if you're taking a shit."

By the time they finished talking and discussing their plans to reinforce their location it had started to get late. Tole suggested that it was time to get dinner and they would leave in an hour. That gave the men enough time to get cleaned up and into clean clothes. Tomorrow they would get the supplies and the equipment and get to work. Shpati had already made calls to rent a pickup truck and the welding supplies so they didn't have to bother with it in the morning. Two of Aleksander's men left and headed out to Home Depot in the South Bay Plaza and bought a couple of gallons of black paint and brushes.

CHAPTER FORTY-NINE

No Pain, No Gain

In this instance, that wasn't quite correct. I awoke that morning and lingered a moment before trying to get up. No lie, it hurt. The Lady was already up and assisting her sister and Ritchie and Sly were making up a mess of food. Dave and the rest of the guys were either watching TV or catching up with email on the secured server.

During the night Tatiana kept rotating ice bags around my nose and eyes and the swelling had subsided, and I could see without running into things. I couldn't help but check the mirror on the dressing table and I was really surprised to not see my head the size of a basketball, but the bruises on my face covered the full spectrum of the rainbow. The packing in my nose had been removed during the night and I was somewhat able to breathe through my nose, which had been taped into place. Doc Glenn had left a few morphine tabs and I swallowed one before exiting the room. I could feel the warm tingle of the drug starting to work and decided I was good to go.

"I'm hungry, what's for breakfast?" Of course, the jokes started fast and furious.

"Oh my God, what did you run into?"

"I just lost my appetite."

"Dude, put a bag over that head, you look nasty!"

"I think I'm gonna puke!"

"You are one ugly-looking dude, bro!"

"Hey, Carlo, want me to lance those swollen eyelids?" asked Gina as she flicked open a blade.

"You stay away from me with that knife, I saw what you did the other night and I want to stay intact a while longer and fuck you to all the rest of you!" I knew they all cared and had they not busted my chops I would have thought something wrong. We laughed it off and like you all know, it only hurt when I laughed.

"Thank you all for your kind remarks, now let's eat!"

Another spread was put out before us, fried pork chops, home fries, grits, bacon, scrambled eggs, and of course Sly's great coffee, and that coffee was the highlight of every morning. My morning ritual was having a cup of coffee before starting in on the food. Besides, the caffeine offset the dulled feeling of the morphine.

"Maybe we should send some pork chops and bacon over to the boys in the warehouse," said J3. That got a laugh all around.

"Stop making me laugh, my God it hurts," I said as I kept laughing.

"Might as well have them *hajis* get coronary artery disease along with us," cracked Dave.

Yep, we should all be doing stand-up. After the usual banter Jake broke in, "We need to do a debrief and see what we come up with. Everyone did a great job last night and Carlo, I wish you could have seen the close-up look on Tole's face when we lit him up with the lasers. We thought he was gonna explode." The other guys that were scoped in last night all got a laugh out of that. "He didn't know whether to shit or go blind."

"I'm sure he would have done all three if you hit him with that 50cal. That man is a psychopath and I was poking him like a sleeping bear. But I'm glad you guys were out there, had my back. No way I would have done it otherwise. Ritchie, you did a great job driving. Tsuji and Dave, thanks for the cover and getting my beat-down ass in the car."

Dave said, "That was payback for a long time ago except last night you got your ass kicked first." I knew exactly what he was talking about. He laughed, and I couldn't help laughing too. The morphine took the worst of the pain away.

"Okay, Carlo, what did you see from the inside?" J3 asked.

"There's about fifteen or a few more, from what I could quick see. All of them looked well armed and they don't look the type to back down. The man-doors you already know about. They are front and rear, close to the east side of the building, both of which go into an office, and one door leading out from that into the warehouse. That is too much of a gauntlet, so I think taking out an overhead would be best to get our guys in. Not all the doors house truck bays but are set up with two levels. They set up in there with beds and a kitchen looks like. Walkway all around the inside so they can look out. Somewhat defensible I would say but I can do a rough sketch for you. They will have high ground with that second level, but I am counting on us having the element of surprise. There are barrels, crates, their cars, and a few pieces of old machinery that they can use to hide behind. Other than that, it's about all I can remember."

Jake and J3 agreed that taking out the overhead door was the best option and I drew them up a schematic of the interior.

"S'cuse me, guys, I gotta take a call," Sly said.

CHAPTER FIFTY

MCI-Norfolk Prison Blues

John Bottolini, aka Johnny Botts, was pacing his cell that morning. He had heard the rumors regarding a well-armed Albanian crew that had slipped into the city and were asking questions. Prison was not a place where secrets were kept and the information from the streets flowed freely.

Many "things" could be arranged from the inside of a prison cell and if anyone watched shows about prison, they would know that. Johnny was by no means a virgin when it came to that or for that matter much of anything else. As a career criminal, raised up in the life by his father, he had seen and done it all but luckily for him, not caught for all or even a small portion of it.

Earlier in the week one of his crew had visited and informed him that the Albanians had been roughing up a few people in the Dorchester and Mattapan areas in their search for a woman, a media producer. Not that he cared, they weren't his people, but he knew it was only a matter of time before they stuck their noses in the North End, and that was one place he didn't want them, not in In Town, not while he was in here or anytime.

He knew what they had done in New York and he didn't want it to happen here. No way these pigs were going to push him off his spot, the place he did business. A lot of his business was conducted in the office of the pizzeria he owned, and he was able to launder money through here. All the "made" guys had a little something extra to give them an air of legitimacy and a way to show Uncle Sam they were hard-working stiffs.

Botts had to make a phone call and he knew the one person that could tell him what was going on was the one and only Sly Greene. He had Sly's personal cell number as they had communicated in the past about some of the more nefarious things that Sly had his fingers in. There was a mutual respect for one another, and they tried not to step on one another's toes. They always tried to settle their differences without shedding blood, and so far it was an arrangement they both could live by and prosper.

After morning chow, Botts slipped one of the guards a hundred dollars to use the phone right then and there—grease the hand that feeds you so to speak. He dialed Sly's number and on the third ring Sly answered. Sly took the collect call from Botts.

"I have a collect call from the Norfolk Correctional Facility, will you accept the charge?" the operator asked.

"Yes, operator, I will accept the charge. Johnny, is it you?"

"Sure is, we need to talk. Can you make the trip?"

"Let me clear my schedule and I will be there this afternoon. I was thinkin' about you and I need to talk to you too."

"Thanks, Sly, see you then," said Botts then he disconnected the call.

———

Sly arrived at the facility just as the visiting hours were starting. He endured the process of registering and being searched, frisked, just short of a cavity search before being escorted into the visiting room. Johnny came in shortly and sat down at the table that Sly had chosen.

"How they treatin' you in here? You good?"

"As best as can be expected but money gets a few extra creature comforts, like that phone call."

"I hear ya, bro. So, what's up, why the need to talk? I have an idea, but you tell me."

"One of my crew came in earlier this week and told me there was some shit going down in your neck of the woods. Maybe involving some Albanians looking for someone and roughing up a few people. Do I need to worry?" Johnny asked.

"What you heard is true. Without getting too specific, they are looking for a woman who owns a big media company in New York and they are trying to take control. Her sister works for me. This woman came into the club looking for the PI I'm friends with. You know Carlo, if not personally at least you're aware of him."

Johnny nodded his head that he was aware. He knew Carlo personally from an issue that Botts had at a parking lot partially owned by him on Cooper Street in the North End. But Botts knew from a very reliable source that he was a stand-up guy and he could respect that.

"I also know it is no secret that you don't have any love lost for the Albanians. We're going to take care of the problem for you, so they will not be coming to In Town. We both know we don't need another gang war in the city like when Whitey was around. That was a clusterfuck and he turned out to be a rat bastard. And the brothers are making a mess of things all by their lonesome so let the heat stay there."

"How do you propose to do that without getting the heat on

your ass? New York, meaning a New York crime family, tried that and look where it got them."

"We're going to kill them all, no one left to talk, and it will also send a message to the other puttanas in New York to stay out of Boston." Sly loved slinging a little bit of Italiano when he had the chance. "You might come outta this lookin' like the big man. You can have the bragging rights," Sly said matter-of-factly. "And all I need is a small favor from you."

"And the other shoe drops! *Merda*! And that would be?"

"I've already spoken to the mayor and the commissioner and they fully understand the sensitivity of the situation. Neither wants to get any officers killed or God forbid have the feds involved. So much for that protect and serve crap. As long as nothing goes sideways it will all be covered up and a spin will be put on it as gang war or another agency raided the place. By the time the news gets run around in circles, no one will be around. But what I need from you is some of your guys are going to get picked up. That will be one of the diversions, they will be released for lack of any proof and there will not be any further pressure on your guys. Just tell them to cooperate and because they won't know anything, they can't say anything. And no one wants a gang war starting over something they aren't involved in."

Johnny kept nodding his head as Sly explained things and then said, "You think that will all work? I couldn't be happier to get rid of those cocksuckers. I'll make sure my guys understand completely."

"I am fairly certain. Are you in? I can meet again with the mayor and commish and tell them we're solid. There will also be a donation to you for the guys for their inconvenience."

"I'm good with it. If I'm not on spot, I can't see trouble coming. You do what you gotta do and I'll owe you for keepin' things in check for me."

"No problem, that's why I live on the block. Keep your eyes on the news. You saw the news about the body, didn't you?"

"That was you?"

Sly just smiled, stood up, shook Johnny's hand, and walked away.

CHAPTER FIFTY-ONE

Plan, Plan Then Plan Some More

While Sly was gone, we went over several variations of the plan to hit the warehouse for the next couple of hours. None were perfect, but we tried to eliminate Mr. Murphy as much as possible. Jake, J3, and the rest of us agreed that the power had to be the first thing to be killed. We had night vision and were hoping they didn't. As the power lines ran between Trico's rear side and the Albanian's front side, the power could be knocked out without them seeing us or activating their surveillance equipment. Tonight, we would send out a two-man team to check the frequency of patrols if any.

Jake continued, "We'll have the snipers neutralize the patrols before we go in if they are out. That will be two less hostiles when we hit it. J3, Sal, Bobby, and Dave, I want you four to take the rear door, use the detcord, and immediately after you take down the door, throw in a flash bang. Sal, you're up to speed on the detcord?"

"Yes, sir, Brando covered everything with me and I am good to go."

"Okay, great. J3, after your guys hit the office area, throw flash bangs into the open warehouse area as soon as we blow the overhead. We'll use a grenade launcher on one of the shotguns to take the door down, maybe. We'll follow up with more flash bangs as we get near the door. Everyone good so far?"

Affirmatives were given all around.

"J3, your team will stay where they are and provide cover the length of the warehouse especially watching the second level. Your team will join us once we have them contained to one area. Make them keep their heads down and take out anyone near you but concentrate on the second level until we get guys up there. Me, Brando, Gina, Tsuji, and Carlo will hit the building after the door blows. I'll have Mike and Max on Trico taking out anyone they can see on the second level but once we're in they will back us up inside. That should give us plenty of cover and cause a hell of a lot of confusion."

Tsuji's face lit up like a Christmas tree. It was what he was bred to do. He loved working for the Lady, but he loved banging heads even more.

"I know myself and the other guys will be driving but where do you want us?" asked Ritch.

"Ritch, good question. You and the other drivers will be on the perimeter, which we will have nailed down after tonight. Ritchie, you will have Carlo, Lady, Tsuji, and Gina with you. Gina, Tsuji, and Carlo will be part of the assault team. The Lady will stay with you and that is not up for discussion, is that understood? Everyone will be armed with long guns and handguns, no exception. Stay on the comms and get guys that are hit into the cars. Doc will provide a medic to ride with you to treat anyone with serious wounds before we get them back. If we can avoid the hospital, we will at all costs."

"Just one thing, Alban Tole is mine. Keep him alive. I owe him big time," I demanded. After seeing what the monster did to me, no one disagreed.

Just as Jake was finishing the first of many briefings, Sly walked back in. "Good of you to join us. Where did you take off to this afternoon?" I asked.

"Something else I need to tell you. Let's go in the garage."

Everyone eyeballed us wondering what the big secret was as we left the room and headed to the garage. There weren't many secrets with all that was happening. Sly continued, "That friend of a friend of yours who is away? Well, I went to talk to him. We go way back. He spoke highly of you. He called me and asked me to visit him at Norfolk so that's where I took off to. He is concerned about our friends that came to visit. I told him we were going to take care of the problem for him, even though it wasn't his problem, and that the mayor and commish are in on this but with deniability. I told him I needed a favor from his guys, I told him what it was, and he was good. He told me he owed me a big one. This is all costing a bundle."

"I can see why you wanted to talk alone. No need for anyone else to know what you just told me. We'll let the others know that there are people looking out for us. Your guys gonna be all cool with this, Sly? I'd hate for loose lips to sink this ship. Just make sure that we're all on the same page. There is too much at stake and jail won't look good on anyone's resume. As for the cost, you know Lady will pick up the tab. I'm not taking a cent from her."

"They're here and they want to play, I guess that makes them as complicit as the rest of us. But I see your point, you're worried about someone maybe having a little too much to drink one night and getting diarrhea of the mouth. I'm not worried about the money, I know the Lady is good for it if I need it."

"My thoughts exactly. But I guess there's no turning back at this point. It's time for a cocktail and some dinner. All this talkin' made me hungry."

We both made our way into the living area, aka planning room, and everyone looked at the two of us. I knew I had to say something, so I did. Yeah, it's that nonexistent filter again. "Listen up, everyone, while we were doing what we had to do, Sly took a little trip to make sure our operation was all on the down-low and off certain people's radar. That includes the dinner he had out the other night. We have the assurances of very powerful people that we have a go. Nothing will blow back on us. With that said, the bar is open and it's time to get cooking."

Ritchie said, "I got dinner tonight but could use a couple of hands to get it done."

Brit and Tsuji offered to help, and Ritch had them get a couple of pots filled with water to boil more than a couple of pounds of fettucine. Lady brought me over a glass of my fav and sat down next to me examining my wounds and lightly touching my face. The area around the orbital rim was still very painful but she pampered me, and I loved it. She was still aghast at what Tole had done to my face, but it was nothing that a little time wouldn't heal.

The guys poured their poison of choice from the amply stocked bar and we changed the topic from work to telling tales that may have had an inkling of truth in them. We all had stories to tell and could have filled volumes with them.

About an hour later and a few drinks into it, Ritch, Brit, and Tsuji brought out several platters of seafood fettucine alfredo with baked garlic bread, and a large fresh green salad setting them all on the table. Sly brought over several varieties of wine, red and white, and we all enjoyed another great dinner.

J3 asked, "What we looking at as a time frame? The longer we wait the more time they have to get prepared."

Sly jumped in, "I have to have a talk with a couple of people tomorrow to let them know about the info I got today."

"I think the soonest we do this is late tomorrow night, early next morning," Jake added.

"Jake, the guys doing the surveillance tonight, how about having them take a couple of shots through the windows? Keep them off balance? If we harass them a bit, they may get jumpy, get no sleep, and that would be good for us."

"That is not a half-bad idea. Where did you learn all these psychological warfare tactics?"

"I read a lot, amazing what you can find in books, and I didn't get a degree in psychological interrogation for nothing," I responded, which got a few laughs.

"I'll let you know what my people, or should I say my *other* people, say tomorrow when we do a debrief," added Sly.

We finished eating and continued with our tales, and after a few after-dinner drinks, those staying at the hotel left and the rest of us retired to our rooms. Lady followed me in and at this point I didn't think she wouldn't. I went into the bathroom, turned on the water for a shower, waited until it drew hot and steamy, and I jumped in. I soon felt soapy hands washing my back and between our soapy bodies and making out, all our parts got washed. If anyone would have walked in they never would have seen us with all the steam. I was happy she had joined me, and I was content once again.

As Tsuji cleared the table he said to Brit and Ritchie, "You two look tired, go relax, I finish up here." He had that all-knowing look on his face.

CHAPTER FIFTY-TWO

Hɪ Hᴏ, Hɪ Hᴏ, Iᴛ's Oғғ ᴛᴏ Wᴏʀᴋ Wᴇ Gᴏ

Tʜᴀᴛ ᴍᴏʀɴɪɴɢ ᴛʜᴇ ᴄʀᴇᴡ ʜɪᴛ Vɪᴄᴛᴏʀɪᴀ's Dɪɴᴇʀ ᴀɴᴅ when the same waitress saw them come through the door, she immediately let the owner know to set up the back room. Apparently, the tip she received was worth the groping she was forced to endure while serving them the day before, but it was the first time a real man had grabbed her so intimately in some time. She made sure pots of coffee were on the table as expected, and she led the crew to the back room brushing against Tole somewhat provocatively in hopes of earning another sizable tip.

She felt a little dirty for doing it but hey, she was a young teen single mother, and no one was helping her financially. She wished she could speak their language as she wondered what they were saying about her. She could only imagine, and her imagination was probably not far off from the truth.

After they had finished and were leaving, Tole put his arm

around the young girl and slipped another large bill into the top pocket of her uniform. She smiled and said, "Thank you, whatever you need," and allowed him a little feel. *Why not*, she thought, he was probably better than that useless minute-man of a boyfriend she occasionally fucked.

After they left, she checked her top pocket to see what Tole had left her and wrapped in the large bill was a cell number. *So, he is interested!* She placed the hundred-dollar bill with her other tips and kept the piece of paper with the number on it in her top pocket. He was a big man and she wondered just how big he was. She had to stop thinking about him, as she was getting more than a little moist between her thighs…

———

After leaving the restaurant, Shpati and Ari found the Airgas dealer on Clapp Street in Dorchester where they rented an assortment of welding equipment and supplies including a 220-amp Lincoln arc welder, 6013 welding rods, helmets and gloves, and an acetylene torch. They had rented a U-Haul pickup truck beforehand and loaded the equipment and angle iron. The rest of the crew headed back to the warehouse and got ready to paint.

When they arrived back at the warehouse everyone except those monitoring the security systems pitched in a hand and got the welder, tanks of gas, angle iron, and the rest of the gear off the truck. They soon had a small shop set up in one area of the warehouse away from their cars.

Tole called out to Shpati, "You and Ari are in charge. You tell the rest of the men what you need them to do. Astrit, come with me, I want to go for a ride."

Shpati and Ari had the crew start on the measurements for the angle iron while others began to paint the windows. The paint knocked out all the natural light coming into the building so it was necessary to turn on all the lights. Ari began cutting the steel as the measurements were brought over to him, and Shpati set up the welder at the first overhead and began to tack the angle iron into place.

Astrit and Tole got into the seven series BMW and Tole said, "Drive by the restaurant where they are hiding."

"Do you think that is a good idea, risk being seen?"

"Just drive, *lezia ime shqetësohet*, my worry wart, your concern is noted, but I want to have some fun so please drive. You will enjoy this."

Astrit did as ordered and with the morning's traffic it took longer than usual to get to Dorchester Avenue. "Boss, it is up here on your left. What do you need me to do?"

"Go past and turn around. When you get near the restaurant make sure you have some room in front of you, so you don't get stuck in front of the place." Tole then pulled a high-power Colt 1911 A1 eight-shot air pistol from his waistband. The pellet traveled at 420 fps.

"Boss, what are you going to do with that pellet gun?" Astrit asked seeming more than a little worried and amused at the same time.

"Watch and laugh. Okay, we're here, not too slow." With that, Tole rolled down his window and rapidly shot out the front windows of the club.

When the first pane of glass broke, he and Astrit could see several of Sly's men diving for cover. Tole was right, this was hysterical.

Tole called out, "Step on it, let's get out of here." Both men almost had tears in their eyes from laughing. Tole finally calmed enough to speak and said, "I almost pissed my pants I laughed so hard. I haven't done this since I was a kid and shot out the baker's windows back home when he wouldn't give my mother credit."

They returned to the warehouse fully energized and refreshed from their little prank.

CHAPTER FIFTY-THREE

PLAYING POLITICS

SLY AROSE EARLY THAT NEXT MORNING, AND HE KNEW THE best time to get to the mayor and the commissioner was before they were both hip-deep in meetings and dealing with the day's problems. Fortunately, he reached them both as they made their way through traffic to their respective offices at One Schroeder Plaza and One City Hall Square. He placed a conference call to avoid going back and forth.

"Good morning, Mr. Mayor, Commissioner. We need to meet again briefly, tonight if possible. What time works for the both of you and where?" Both men raised the partition between them and the driver, so their driver couldn't hear what was being said.

The mayor spoke first, "Commish, may I suggest Fan Pier Park around eight tonight?"

"That works. All my meetings are done by seven, so we'll

meet you there, Mr. Greene." Both men continued to their offices and were wondering, and a little worried, about the night's meeting with Sly. If they were implicated, their walls would come tumbling down like they did in Jericho. Except in this case the trumpets would be replaced by *The Boston Globe*, *The Herald*, and for sure Howie Carr on 680 AM, the voice of Boston. Both men would rather their secrets go with them to the grave, but when two other people were involved, secrets were not so safe. Like Ben Franklin said, "Three can keep a secret, if two of them are dead."

CHAPTER FIFTY-FOUR

Just Another Day in Paradise

After Sly had finished his call he made his way out into the kitchen to get things started before anyone had stirred and the rest of the crew arrived. He found Dave and Tsuji elbow-deep in the kitchen making scrambled eggs with habanero peppers and onions and steamed rice with grilled fish—Tsuji's idea, and no self-respecting American breakfast wouldn't be complete without meat so Dave was pan-frying ham steaks in pure lard.

"Damn, you boys don't waste any time, and what a combination of food. Anything I can do to help? You all are making me feel left out!" Sly asked.

"You make the coffee, good and strong, no tea for Tsuji!"

"Where's Carlo, Ritch, and the girls, or do I need to ask?"

"Ritch didn't come home last night. I think he was a bad

little boy, so no need to tell you where the girls are," Dave said laughing. "I think Carlo, well, I know Carlo for sure, and Ritchie, they both caught a case of 'Brown Sugaritis'."

"I think they're both pussy-whipped," quipped Sly laughing hysterically, "But I never said that."

"Oh, sure, we no hear nothing," added Tsuji with a deep laugh. "Our little secret. But what's it worth to you?"

"Sounds like Tsuji is putting the screws to you, Sly," Dave added "And don't forget about me if you want me to keep quiet!"

"This is the most I've heard you talk since you've been here, big man, and you catch on quick," Sly responded. "But both of you can kiss my black ass!" That got the laughter going this morning.

"Tsuji just observe at first, don't know you people. You never asked if I understood, so I never say. I was raised in America!" He let out a huge belly laugh, and we all joined in. "My job not to talk but do," he added. And ain't that the truth, I thought. "Must make sure Lady is in good hands. But I see you look out for her and Carlo a good man. She deserves your help and I am warming up to you. Trust and honor very important to people like me, but I see you live by same code. Never see Lady act this way with a man but I think she has feeling for him. He hurt her I just kill him!" The big man gave a look like he was dead serious. After one awkward delayed second, they all burst out laughing.

"Tsuji," Dave began, "one summer night back in the early days of being on the force, I was attempting to make a drunk-driving arrest and this guy was fightin' me. I couldn't get to my radio to call for help when I see a sheriff's car pull up behind me. It was Carlo. He gets out nonchalantly and said to me, 'Dave, you need a hand?' I said, 'Yeah…get this fucker off me!' Carlo just grabbed the guy, lifted him off the ground, and slammed him onto the trunk of my patrol car, put a dent in the trunk hood and I finally was able to cuff him. Don't know what I

would have done but I was thinkin' of shooting the bastard."
That got another laugh from the other two men. "He's good
people and loyal to those he cares about. You are right, Tsuji, I
think the two of them are both falling for each other."

As food finished cooking, it was placed in the oven to stay
warm while they waited for the rest of the crew as they began to
straggle in from the bedrooms and the hotel. Lady looked
glowing and I knew it wasn't for the usual reason women glow,
thank you Jesus for that! She looked so beautiful as she walked
around the bedroom doing her morning stuff. Yeah, girls have
that—morning stuff. I dragged myself out of bed, put on my
standard uniform, and the two of us walked out together. Ritchie
and Brit weren't far behind and both sisters gave one another that
look. The look that says a million words without saying one.

Everyone grabbed coffee, grabbed a seat, and made small
talk. Tsuji brought over the platters and everyone dug in after
thanking the two for making the meal.

Sly decided to tell everyone present that he had a meeting
tonight before the team went out to do recon. "This should firm
up our plans as far as covering our asses. What is it you Spec Ops
guys say, Jake—Situation Normal All Fucked Up. We don't want
it to escalate into a fubar (fucked up beyond all repair)."

"Look at you, Sly, pickin' up the lingo," Jake said.

"But enough of that, let's eat and we'll talk shop when we're
done."

The girls cleared the table, including Gina, after we had
eaten, and Sly brought over another pot of coffee. Guys and
ladies in our line of work never get enough coffee, usually
because of the screwed-up hours we operate within. I think our
blood is composed partly of coffee. Jake brought up tonight's
agenda.

"Sly, I'll need two of your guys to drive the SUVs tonight.
Can I have Cedric and Marcus?"

"Okay, I'll let them know to be ready. I'll make sure they're equipped. I know they'll be glad to get out."

"Good. By the way, if you're back in time, I would like you to join us. You, me, and Carlo won't have to stay the entire time but get a feel for what we're dealing with. We're heading out about 0100 hours."

"Count me in."

Jake nodded affirmative and then continued, "I want everyone, and I mean everyone, on the range today. Make sure your gear is working properly and clean it." But these guys knew exactly what they had to do. "As for tonight, Max and Mike, you will conduct the surveillance. Sly and I will tag along for a while and then leave you two to do your thing. When it looks like they are nice and comfortable, put a couple of rounds through the windows. Make the shots close to a couple of them and give them something to dream about."

Almost before Jake could get the last of that sentence out they heard Sly's men upstairs shouting to get down and that they were under attack. Reshaun called out to Khaseem, "Bro, are you hit?"

"Nah, man, I'm good. Anyone else?"

Everyone else said they were good, but all had their weapons drawn as they got up off the floor pointing them at the now-shattered window openings. All of us in the bunker tried to get upstairs at the same time causing a bit of a jam, but we came up armed.

"What the hell was that?" Sly asked.

"Boss, Khaseem and I were standing here when the first window exploded, and we hit the ground. The rest of the windows were shattered within seconds. We didn't see who did it but should be on the cams."

"Who was monitoring the cams?"

"I was," Marcus answered.

"Go back and check the footage and let's see who did this. My guess is it was our new friends."

Marcus played back the video for the last fifteen minutes but didn't notice the BMW as it cruised by the first time. When it slowed to shoot, Marcus could clearly see an arm reach out the window with a gun in the hand and the passenger started firing.

"Sly, I got it," he called out. "Black BMW 7 series with New York State plates. I'm gonna play it back again." This time he did it slower and noticed the BMW on the opposite side of the road before it turned around.

"Let me see the video, maybe I can make out the shooter," I said. I watched as the arm came out the window and I noticed the tattoos. "Guys, it was Alban Tole. I recognize the tat on his forearm, a double eagle. It's not unlike the tattoos that many Albanian men get in prison or the military."

"And that is the same BMW that was in Victoria's lot the day we saw De'Londo talking to them," Reshaun filled us in.

"Let's get this mess cleaned up. I'll call a window repair company and get replaced with blast-proof glass," Sly said to no one in particular. "Next time, if there is a next time, we'll have a surprise for them." Sly got on the phone and called Fields Glass Service on Dorchester Avenue. They said they would be out in an hour.

No sooner did the glass company arrive and who comes walking down the street but Officer Buck. Sly couldn't very well not talk to him or not let him in so he had most of us go back into the bunker.

While the glass guys were doing their thing, the front door was open. Buck walked in, called out to Sly, and acknowledged his security officers. "Sly, what the hell happened? Are you remodeling or did someone do this?"

"Hey, Buck, don't have a damn clue but I think it was kids. And no, I'm not remodeling. By the time my guys got outside they couldn't get a good description. They took off north on

Dorchester. Just a pellet gun but it shattered the glass like it was nothing. Must have been one of those high-powered ones."

"You want me to make a report and see what we turn up? Your insurance cover this?" Buck asked. "And what about your cams?"

"Naw, don't waste your time. Even if we do catch them, their momma probably can't afford to pay me anyway. I'd like to take it out on their hides but can't do that anymore. They managed to stay close to the building so the cams were of no use."

"You know I'd be glad to but it's your call." Buck hung around for a while and Sly got him a cup of his good coffee and an egg-bacon-and-cheese sandwich then they chatted while the windows got fixed.

"Sly, you sure you good with all this? You seem a bit on edge. Anything you need to talk about? Who were the guys that were here the other night? They looked like a rough bunch."

"I'm good, I really am. Just a lot going on and I didn't need this. I know I can always confide in you, bro. Ah, those guys are a bunch of ex Spec Ops guys, good bunch of guys and man, could they drink. They just wanted a place to get away from a crowded club. By the way, that crew of Albanians you told me about, anything new on them?" Sly asked deftly changing the subject.

"As far as we know they are keeping their heads low. But I have a CI in the Albanian community and they aren't saying dick, scared to death. Guess these guys are no joke. But no law being broke with keepin' their heads down."

The two men continued to sip their coffee and Buck finished the sandwich as the repairmen finally sealed up all the windows and accepted a cash payment from Sly along with a little "sumthin-sumthin" for them. Sly liked to show his appreciation and it also helped to make sure he got service when he needed it. Buck got a radio call to back up a motor unit a block away on a domestic dispute and he left Sly to tend to his business.

Sly shouted down to the rest of us, "Safe to come up, he left."

"I think we will turn up the heat a little more tonight after that bullshit," Jake said. "They want to play games, we can too, but we're better at it."

"Ooo, Jake's gonna school them tonight!" I remarked.

CHAPTER FIFTY-FIVE

Paint It Black

Tole was beside himself with laughter all the way back to the warehouse. They stopped by the old liquor store previously owned by Whitey Bulger, now called Columbia Wine and Spirits. It was rumored that Stevie "The Rifleman" Flemmi, Bulger's right-hand man, made the previous owner, Steve "Stippo" Rakes, an offer he couldn't refuse. Rakes always thought he was cheated out of it and probably so, and Whitey held a lot of meetings in the back room. No talk about Whitey is complete about how he was solely responsible for uniting the Irish by taking out the top Killeen and Mullen leaders while he was under Howie Winter of the Winter Hill Gang.

But the past is the past and Alban wanted more vodka, and he didn't give a rat's ass where he got it or who had owned it. History was nice, but it was the past and vodka was the present. He sent Astrit in to get a couple of cases of Stoli, and the way his crew drank, it would only last the night. He wanted to celebrate a little over the small victory he had achieved earlier.

Astrit was glad to see his boss in a good mood for a change and maybe tonight he wouldn't shoot anyone if he got pissed. He may not shoot to kill but you might have a limp for life if he did shoot. Tole couldn't wait to tell his crew what he did and have a few swills of the alcohol, in fact, he could hardly contain himself. He popped the seal on the top and took a good long drink then passed the bottle to Astrit. They all drank like fish, but Tole was in a class all by himself.

Astrit pulled into the warehouse and parked the car away from the work area. Tole exited the car and observed the work most of which had been completed and was pleased. The windows were all painted and several of the doors had been secured and reinforced, including the two exit doors in the office area. Tole had all the guys take a break and he recounted what he had done to Chez Rendezvous. They all got quite the kick over the incident and Tole passed around a few of the vodka bottles, and all of them drank deeply.

"Enough work for now," Tole said. "It is time to relax for a bit, and someone call for some pizza. Eat now and more work later and drink more now." Like most criminal gangs drinking was a blessed pastime.

Zeni immediately called in an order to Regina Pizza just across the Charles River and ordered fifteen pizzas with cheese and pepperoni. Zeni called out to Tole, "Alban, they think it's a prank because we ordered so many. What should I tell them?"

Tole came over and took the phone from Zeni and told the employee, "Look, this isn't some prank, let me speak with your manager."

"Yes, sir, one second."

"This is the manager; how may I help you?"

"We are working in a warehouse at the address my guy gave you. We don't want to have to come there and get them and we will take good care of the driver. Wait, let me give you my credit card number." Tole rattled off a card number of a stolen account and the charge went through. Just another thing the Albanian mob did—credit card fraud.

Yeah, until tomorrow when the real owner sees the charge, but Tole had plenty of cards.

The manager said, "Sir, you are all set. I apologize for any inconvenience, the girl is new, and she was being careful. I'll take 20% off your order." Tole thought, *if you know what's good for you, you little shit.* "No problem, and tell her thank you for being diligent," Tole said. "You can never be too careful." Tole was feeling good, better than he had in several days, and he even thought they had a chance to pull this off.

CHAPTER FIFTY-SIX

But You're A Good Girl

AFTER THEY HAD ALL DRANK AND ATE THEIR FILL, TOLE WAS in a restless mood, a mood that could only be rectified by a sweet little thang. He was a horny fuck, the steroids making him more so, and he knew just where to get it if the waitress from the diner called him. Otherwise, he would get a hooker from Craigslist, a young one at that. If he did that the girl would be black because he liked degrading those black girls since it reminded him of the Lady Tatiana.

The waitress, though, she was what he liked, and in this mood, he would settle for just about anything that walked on two legs. But she was hot, the way she wore her uniform with her breasts pushed up…man, she had nice perky tits, blonde hair falling carelessly down her chest, and a short, tight uniform skirt showing well-developed thighs and a firm round butt that just got to him. Man, he was getting excited just thinking about her. He was almost old enough to be her father but that went for most of the girls he fucked. They were just a release and he would use her for as long as he needed, lead her on, and discard her like a piece of trash when he was done.

For a moment he thought he should take her back to New York, promise her a good-paying job, and then break her and put her in his stable of the other young girls he lured into the sex trade or bring her back to the warehouse and let the others have their fill of her. Who knows, maybe both. But he would see what happened after tonight. Tonight, he just needed a release. As he thought about her, he received a text. Was she a mind-reader or had they made a connection? It read, "Can you come in an hour?" So, he thought, she was willing and ready. He didn't hesitate and dialed the number.

The phone rang and just before it went to voice mail she answered, "Hello? Who's calling?"

"This is your friend from the diner, I got your text. I would love some company tonight and you are the company I want, my little dove."

"Thank you, you are so nice, my big man. I need about an hour to freshen up and look nice for you. I usually don't do this, really, but I don't know, you just got to me, my big man." She was indeed a naïve girl.

"What is your address? I can be over in an hour."

"I live at 52 Costello near West Broadway, but we need to get a room because I live with my mom and grandmother. The Element Seaport is just down the road and not too expensive; you know I'll be worth it! What would you like me to wear? Can you bring something to drink? I can't buy anything cuz I'm only nineteen. Oh, and pick me up on the corner of Costello and Crowley Rogers, please. I don't want my mother and gram in my business."

"Okay, for you my flower, but wear just jeans and a T-shirt

and panties and I will bring you something to drink…and no bra."

"Okay, okay, let me get ready. I can't wait for you to get here, big man," she said with sexual excitement in her voice.

Tole hung up the phone and called out to Toti, "Lay off the booze. I need you to take me somewhere in an hour."

"Let me know when you're ready," Toti replied and he lit up a cigarette, smoked, and sat back in a chair. He knew better than to ask where, he would just drive.

Tole motioned to Toti about an hour later, "Come on, let's go," and he grabbed a bottle of Stoli from the case.

They went out and got into the Beemer and Toti asked the boss, "Where we headed?"

"Costello and Crowley Rogers near West Broadway."

"You be okay, or do I not need to ask?"

"If I wanted you to know, I'd tell you. But just for your ears, you know that little *zuske*, slut from the restaurant, I gave her my number and she called. I need a little relief, my friend. We need to pick her up and go to a hotel just down the road on D Street."

Toti pulled up to the intersection and she was waiting dressed as Tole requested. Tole took in her entire form watching her breasts bounce under the T-shirt as she ran over to the car. Tole opened the rear door for her, and she slid over next to him. "You listen good. Like a drink?" he said as he opened the bottle and poured the vodka in two paper cups.

"Love one, you want to mix it with anything?"

"No, kitten, tonight you drink like an Albanian, drink it straight."

She obeyed after Tole poured about two shots in each cup and told her to drink up. The rush of the alcohol warmed her, she coughed after swallowing from the burn of the straight vodka, and Tole saw a flush on her pale white skin, and it aroused him. .

Within a few short minutes, Toti pulled up to the front of

the hotel and Tole and Chloe exited the car. "This looks fairly nice, we will have a good time." Tole told Toti to wait and he went in and registered for a room. Tole requested a room on the top floor and was given a nice suite. Tole couldn't wait to get to the room as he was feeling like he was about to explode.

He unlocked the door to the room and told Chloe to go sit on the couch. Tole went into the kitchen area and got two rocks glasses. Tole poured two more glasses, full this time, a little more than in the car, and told her to drink up. Chloe again downed the vodka and any inhibitions she had were gone. She got up, a tad unsteady, and straddled Tole with legs spread facing him, and kissed him. She had a moment of déjà vu but now she was on birth control and it didn't matter what she did. *Fuck Kevin and his broke denying punk ass,* she thought.

When she came up for air she whispered in the big man's ear, "I'm so ready to be bad! My mom and gram are with my daughter so no need to rush. We have all night. No condoms, I got that covered." Tole would be only the third man she was intimate with.

"I hope you like it a little rough, little girl."

"Anything would be better than that good-for-nothing cheap-ass limp-dick boyfriend of mine. Let's go to the bedroom, I can feel you are ready." All her inhibitions had been lost and locked carefully away by the vodka. Her mother would have been embarrassed by her talk, but she was no longer Mommy's little girl. She was a grown-ass woman and she was with a grown-ass man.

Tole did not have to be asked twice and snatched her up, slung her over his broad shoulder, and carried her to the spacious bedroom. She giggled like a little schoolgirl getting a ride on Daddy's shoulders and for that matter she wasn't that far removed from being a schoolgirl. He entered the bedroom, threw her down on the king-size bed, and removed his belt.

Her eyes widened, and she said, "You aren't going to spank

me with that, are you?" her breath quickening with anticipation. Her libido was rushing like a wild river and she would have welcomed the lashes with the belt as it wouldn't take much at this point to get her off.

"Only if you want me to, angel, but I am going to secure your hands to the bed." It only took Tole a few seconds to restrain her and she grew more excited. Her breathing accelerated, and she panted like a dog in heat, arching her back up in anticipation of him taking her. He grabbed her T-shirt and ripped it off with one forceful pull and she let out a moan. Tole could smell her feminine scent and then tore off her panties, breathing in her scent before throwing them to the floor noting the glistening on her pubic mound. He then divested himself of his clothes and she gasped as his pants dropped. It was what she had hoped for and then some. Could she take it all?

Over the next couple of hours Tole took her every way he wanted and everywhere he wanted. He raged on her, fiercely encouraged by her moans and whimpers and calling out to God until he fell spent and exhausted on top of her, both covered in the sweat of their passion even with the AC on high. Tole lay next to her for a short time before getting up and released her hands from the bondage of the belt.

"My God, can we come back here tomorrow night?"

"You might be a little sore, but maybe. My men would all love you, what would you say to that?"

"Is it what you want? You want me to please your men?" The vodka was talking, and she would not remember this in the morning, but Tole knew with a little lubrication from the vodka and some drugs she would be more than willing.

"Maybe, but I may just keep you to myself. I can be selfish. I must go, I have things to do."

"Can't you stay the night, it's such a nice room and I am not in the mood to sleep."

"Not really. I must get back. Things to do. I'll see you at the restaurant, and oh, this is for you and there may be much more in the future." He placed five hundred dollars on the nightstand —she had been well worth it, and he had spent far more for less —and he bent over, kissed her again not able to resist running his hand over her, probing her, that perfect young body one more time. Chloe would spend the night in the pleasant uncrowded surroundings, sleeping on a luxurious bed and she would get a cab home in the morning. Momma would understand, *should* understand, well, maybe not.

"Do you mean that, about the future?" she asked hoping it were true and willing to do whatever he said to escape the meager existence she now lived.

"I always mean what I say, my dove, now good night and you can call me Alban." With that Tole left the apartment and got back into the Beemer and told Toti, "I'm starving. All that fucking made me hungry. Go to the waterfront, I want a steak, and head to Morton's, I need something good."

————

The next morning when Chloe arose and started to get dressed, she realized that Tole had taken a souvenir from the night before —her moist panties. It brought a smile to her face that he took this small fragrant remembrance of her. She could picture Tole with her panties in hand, raising them to his nose and taking in a deep breath. Chloe also realized that she had a souvenir and that was she was sore as could be, and she smiled. No more of that limp-dicked boyfriend for her, it was over. She snatched up the money on the table and stuffed it into her jeans pocket. Chloe had to tie her T-shirt in a knot at the bottom as Tole had ripped it off her. It showed off her small waist and flat tummy and she liked the look. Kind of made her look like Daisy Duke.

CHAPTER FIFTY-SEVEN

FAN PIER PARK

SLY PULLED ONTO COURTHOUSE WAY AND PARKED THE Escalade, and as if on cue two limos pulled in behind Sly. Sly was already out of the car and in the park along the walkway by the water. He reconnoitered the area to make sure it was one hundred percent clear. The mayor and the commissioner approached, and their bodyguards were told to stay back, not because they felt safe, because they were, but the mayor and commissioner didn't want the two big police officers to hear any of the conversation they would have with Sly. More than one trusted employee had ruined the career of an upward-moving political hack and they both were determined not to be one of them. The mayor hoped one day to run for governor, or the Senate and the chief would have loved a plum job as superintendent of the State Police.

"Good evening, Sly, how's your night going?' inquired the commish.

"Things have been better. The Albanians did a drive-by and shot out my front windows using a pellet gun, but other than that all is good. I told the beat cop that it was kids, but I got the video, it was the Albanians. They're just trying to shake us, but let's talk about business."

"Okay," replied the mayor. "What do you have for us? Somethin' good I hope."

"Yeah, it is. I talked to Johnny Botts today. He has agreed to what we're doing, and his men will cooperate especially since I will have a package for them. He was very pleased that a little problem will disappear. A little consideration for him for his assistance would be greatly appreciated. Can that be arranged? He's not in on a federal rap, just a small-time gambling bit."

"Commissioner, what do you say, think we can do the man a favor? He does keep the North End calm," the mayor queried.

"That shouldn't be hard to arrange but I know he has a rap sheet. But for cooperation on a criminal enterprise"—the commish made air quotation marks—"I'm sure I can convince the DA to work some magic. The little prick does owe me. I let one of his girlfriend's go on a DUI after she had been arrested so he better ante up."

Sly said, "I know he will appreciate it. He will owe us some favors that will come in handy in the future. So, are we good? Oh, by the way, we are going to shake the hornet's nest tonight. You may need to spin it as kids with fireworks if you even hear about it. No one will get hurt. Just givin' you a heads-up."

"Call us tomorrow if there's a need, understand?"

"Loud and clear, Commish. Now I need to get back, people are waiting on me."

The three men shook hands and went back to their respective cars. It had been a nice night for the meeting as there had been a refreshing breeze off the ocean. Both of the officials headed back to their limos paid for at the expense of the taxpayers and ordered their drivers to take them home or to whatever rendezvous they had in mind.

————

A young man had been seated close to where Sly and the two officials were meeting. He was hard to see as he was dressed in security black and seated within the shadows of the trees. With the dark, he was almost impossible to see. He set his sandwich aside for a moment and listened with great intent as the three men spoke.

He was the type of young man that loved to listen in on others' conversations and this one was no exception. He filed it away as he felt it sounded very familiar with some things that had occurred at the apartments, which were just a few blocks away, and things he had heard on the news. He heard the names that were spoken, he was sure not to forget. He still had the phone number for Reshaun, and just maybe he could make a few more dollars or make a deal for something better.

CHAPTER FIFTY-EIGHT

CHANGE THE MOOD FROM GLAD TO SAD

LITTLE DID TOLE KNOW THAT HIS NIGHT OF PASSION WAS about to take a turn for the worst. He was enjoying a Porterhouse prime-cut steak cooked medium rare with a large baked potato slathered in sour cream, butter, bacon, mushrooms, and two vegetable sides. Toti was dying to ask about his night but knew better. Tole surprised him and gave a tell-all exposé of his night's gymnastic exploits. Tole was like most men and loved to tell about his conquests, and Chloe was just another of the hundreds Tole had been pleasured by. Toti was surprised when Tole pulled her panties out of his pocket and nearly rubbed them under his nose.

"She would be a good one for our business. I told her I should bring her back to have fun with all of you and she said, 'If that's what you want.' I think I'll do that, you all deserve a little fun. After that she wouldn't care if we whored her out. Maybe we will do that with that nigger bitch too."

"Sounds like a moneymaker, Boss."

They had both finished their meals, washing it down with more vodka, when Tole decided he wanted dessert. The waiter brought over the dessert menu and made a suggestion of the Tiramisu. Tole gave the waiter a nod and the dessert was brought over. It would not be the pleasurable experience he expected.

———

While Tole and Toti were busy with their night's activities, Jake had been going over plans with his two shooters making sure no stone was unturned. Sly and I were ready to go when Jake gave us the thumbs-up.

Sly called up to Cedric and Marcus and told them to get to the blacked-out SUVs. Mike and Max loaded up with Cedric and Sly, me and Jake went with Marcus. We threw a rope ladder in the back that had a grappling hook attached.

We arrived at Trico at 0045 hours and it didn't take long for the five of us to get to the roof. Max and Mike got set up, scanned the area, and didn't see anything out of the ordinary until they ran their spotting scope along the front of the warehouse.

"Jake, they blacked-out the windows. We're gonna have to scope them with our infrared. Hopefully the walls aren't too thick, and we can get at least some partial images."

"Nice, good move on their part, def on the IR. Let's try to get a body count and where they all might be."

"Jake, looks like there are about, maybe, twelve guys in there, but hard to be sure. I might be crazy, but it appears that they're welding up some shit, getting some big heat flares," Max said.

"Let me look." Jake peered through the spotting scope and realized that was exactly what they were doing. "You're right on, bro. That's my guess too, they're welding. My guess is they are reinforcing those overheads. Might need more than a grenade launcher. Sly, take a look at this."

Sly looked through the lens and was amazed at what he was able to discern. "Damn, this stuff is off the hook! Looks like someone, no, two guys are coming out."

Jake gave the scope back to Max and Max confirmed. "Must be a perimeter patrol. They are both armed with AKs."

"All right, you know what to do, keep track of the timeliness of the patrols and at your discretion put one at their feet."

"Roger that, Boss. Do you mean that literally? Mike, take a shot at the patrols right near their feet. Let's make them dance. I'll get pictures of them before you fire, maybe J3 can cash in a favor and get facial recognition."

"It's your fun time, do what you want, just no killing anyone tonight."

Mike lined up the shot with the MK 13 mod 5 .300cal WinMag sniper rifle while Max clicked away with the Nikon fitted with a 300mm zoom lens with IR capability. As the patrol walked across the face of the building there was a muted cough coming from Mike's suppressed rifle. All the patrol heard was a thwack as it hit the ground in front of them at 3,260 feet per second, which is about three times the speed of sound. It was two of Valmir's men and they didn't know whether to shit or go blind as they were sprayed by the gravel kicked up by the powerful .300mag round hitting the ground. Both men had been under fire before when the Balkans were going crazy, but they weren't expecting it tonight. They made a mad dash to the warehouse office door, chased all the while by rounds hitting the dirt just behind them. Sly and I could barely contain our laughter but managed to stifle it, so we didn't give away our position. Laughter would carry in the calm night air. When they managed to get through, a round shattered the glass in the door, and they shouted to the others that they were being shot at and out went the lights. Too bad for them because we had the infrared and could see their heat signatures.

"Give them some time to get comfortable. Make them think we've left and let a couple more rounds go through the windows. Make them close. I don't think they will send out any more patrols but if they do, make it difficult for them to get back in and then get out of here. Cedric will be there waiting for you and keep me informed."

"Got you covered, Boss."

Jake, Sly, and me climbed back down the ladder and had Marcus get us back to the club. Of course, we had to tell the rest of the crew what had happened. It was Miller Time for us. Now let's be clear. You wouldn't catch me dead drinking that piss water, and the Lady being on top of things had my usual all ready.

"So how long are Mike and Max going to stay? They going to do anything else besides watch?" asked Lady.

"They're going to take a few closer shots after they calm down a bit and then beat feet out of there," explained Jake.

———

Tole would have loved to finish his meal off with something sweet but no sooner had the waiter brought over the Tiramisu, and his phone rang.

"Yeah, what's going on that you feel the need to bother me?"

"Two of Valmir's men were doing perimeter patrol and they took fire. We couldn't pinpoint it, but they used suppressors and I would bet they have infrared. We have all the lights off and nothing else has happened."

"Son of a bitch, okay, we're on the way back. Get ready to open the door when I call you back. I don't want to be sitting outside if they're still there. We're right down the street. And stay away from the damn windows!"

"Toti, pay the bill, we gotta go. They were taking fire."

"Anyone hit?"

"No, and it wasn't because they were bad shots."

Toti put three hundred-dollar bills down on the table which included a hefty tip and left the restaurant behind Tole. Toti flew down A Street to Dorchester and right onto South Hampton, and when they passed South Bay Center Tole called Astrit back. "Open the door, three blocks away."

"Max, the overhead is going up. Car turned, coming our way. It's the Beemer, I'm gonna fuck it up, watch this." Now, readers, a little aside. Usually when I said, "watch this," it was something that after a little thought I shouldn't have done but in this case, it was very, very good.

As the car approached Mike let a round go and blew out one of the front tires. The car swerved, nearly going off the road, but regained control and kept riding on three tires and one very damaged rim. The shredded tire flew all over the narrow road and sparks arced from the rim hitting the ground. The next two rounds went into the engine block and by the time Toti got the damaged car into the garage the engine was smoking, coughing, and ready to die. Several more rounds went through the opened overhead door before they had a chance to close it with the rounds coming close to the occupants of the warehouse. Mike also took out a few of the windows just for good measure.

"Mike to Jake, over."

"Go for Jake."

"The Beemer came down the street and we fucked it up good. It was smoking by the time they got it into the garage. Before they got the overhead down, I took a few shots plus took out a few windows. They don't know which way to turn. I think the photos Max got may be good enough for facial. They still have no idea where we're at. We are disengaging and extracting. Have a cold one ready for us."

"Copy that, the bar is now open."

The rest of us standing around heard what had happened and gave out a cheer. If we didn't have something to toast with before the call, we all did now.

Tole was beyond angry, how could a night that started so well end up going down the tubes this fast. Tole and his band of not-so-merry men were suffering a real TARFU!

Max and Mike policed the rooftop taking all their empty brass, and dropped down the ladder. The last thing they wanted to do was leave behind any evidence that a CSI-type nerd could find and trace back to them. They jumped in the idling car with Cedric and headed back for that cold one that was waiting. Tonight was like taking candy from a baby, and Tole's men were in for the night.

CHAPTER FIFTY-NINE

STIRRING UP A HORNETS NEST

ON THE WAY BACK TO THE BUNKER MAX FORWARDED THE photos to Jake and got them up on the monitors. Gotta love digital photography, wi-fi, and blue tooth. J3 and Jake looked them over and both agreed that the shots were good enough to get facial recognition.

"In the morning I can send these off to a friend at the agency and see if we can ID these two. I wouldn't be surprised if we get a hit on the two of them. My guess is they are already in the system."

"I'd put money on that, J3. I doubt there's not one of them that doesn't have a record."

"That's a bet I won't put money on, my chances are better with Black Jack, and then I don't do so well with that," J3 said while shaking his head.

The boys walked in after parking the SUV in the garage and

found that there were several beers and shots lined up for them. They got a round of applause from all of us and there wasn't one of us that hadn't wished we could have been there next to them to see the expressions on the faces of the Albanians. We allowed them the simple pleasure of recounting every detail that occurred and the reaction of the mob boys.

———

Meanwhile back at the warehouse Tole was in one of his spitting mad moods and cussing everyone up and down as if it was their fault for him getting shot at.

Astrit was the first brave enough and respected enough by Tole to speak up. "Boss, had they wanted to kill you then and there they would have. They are playing with us and I expect it to continue. Look, many of us have military training so we know the game they're playing. They are trying to get us off point. In prison we played the same way, you know that. Fuck with the guards and other gangs to keep them off balance. You were a master at that if I recall. You made me second in command because you trust my judgement, and I am asking you to do that now."

"And what is it you would have me do?"

"No more patrols, it is quite obvious they have the ability to pick us off one by one. We have to play by their rules or at least try to bend them a little. They are playing their game on their turf, we can't be stupid. If we want that bitch, we have to take them down before they take us down. It's also obvious they have night vision, something we don't have. They can see us inside here. If they have a 50cal. they can shoot through this concrete like it was sheetrock and take us out one by one, but I don't think they will do that. It will make too much noise even if it's suppressed. They will kill us all at once if they do anything."

"And again, I ask what am I to do? Give me your trained military-minded opinion."

"We need to make it very difficult for them to get at us. They won't attack when we go out to eat because it will cause too much commotion, too much noise, too much traffic. They will do it in the dead of night. It's the way I would do it if I was running an op. They would figure most of us would be asleep and therefore mostly defenseless. I suggest we sleep in shifts. Half of us up at a time and on watch, and man the catwalks with caution. Maybe we can find some surplus night vision at an Army-Navy store. It's worth a try and will help us even the odds a bit. They will knock out our power first, so we will be in the dark and their night vision will be an advantage. We need to get a generator that will power everything in here."

"Astrit, you are a smart man. I like your plan. Tomorrow first thing, get a generator in here. We do not leave this place unless we are all armed. Check with those military surplus stores for NVG and don't do anything to draw the cops' attention, but do I really need to say that?"

"Boss," Astrit said, "I will make it so. Get some rest, we will take care of business. Don't let it ruin the night you had earlier. And if I may, I would like to give it back a little."

"Do as you wish, my friend. Get those other things done and I will bring that little *lavire*, whore, over here. You all deserve some fun, and then we take her back to New York ready to work."

Tole went into the office with a bottle of Stoli and opened his bottle of tranquillizers, grabbed a handful, and washed them down with the vodka. It was the only way he would sleep tonight. It was enough to stop a normal person's heart, but his system was so used to the massive doses that it only allowed him a night's sleep.

———

My guys had all headed back to their hotel except for the ones staying at the bunker and playing musical rooms. We slept peacefully not needing anything other than the satisfaction of a job well done or comforting arms around us. And if I wasn't mistaken, I didn't see Max leave. Could it be that Gina found some entertainment for the night? I didn't know if I should feel sorry for him or be happy. But either way I am sure he would get his just due and discard him as she never got close to any man. She certainly was a dominating force.

CHAPTER SIXTY

Don't Act Surprised

Astrit grabbed Toti and Valmir and they headed out to Valmir's Mercedes Benz 550.

"Where to?" asked Valmir.

"We're going to a place called payback. They can't just do that and get away with it. This has to be fast and quick." Astrit and Toti both had their AKs with thirty-round magazines. "No more pellet guns, that's bullshit." Astrit gave Valmir directions as they travelled the short distance to the club. "Maybe we give those asswipes a dose of their own medicine. We don't shoot until no one is around and then Valmir, you hit the gas and hard. We do *not* want any collateral damage. Put this in the CD player. I like a little music when I play." Valmir took the CD and popped it in, and Guns and Roses blasted from the speakers. It seemed fitting and it was just the way Astrit liked it.

As they started down Dorchester Avenue the mix CD started

playing, "Highway To Hell," and Toti said, "Good song to fuck up a few people to."

"Valmir, it'll be on your left, we need to turn around after we pass it. Don't drive past it too slowly as I am sure they have cameras." Astrit started laughing. "Now they'll have to replace the windows all over again. I hope his insurance goes through the roof."

Valmir spotted Chez Rendezvous and went a couple of blocks past before turning around in a Vietnamese grocery store that had closed several hours ago. "What is this, Little Vietnam?"

"Sure looks that way. Alban mentioned the same thing when we came down here the other day. Some nice little *zuske*, sluts, just like those old white men like. Those guys went to Nam and are still chasing that young slit. I bet we could buy them from their families for next to nothing. They can be fifteen or sixteen and still look like they are ten. With the pervs that come to us, they will love it."

"Valmir, slow it a bit. Toti you ready?"

"Let's do it." The streets were clear, and the front and rear passenger windows went down, and they opened fire, emptying the thirty-round magazines on the windows and the front of the building. I wish I could have been on the streets and watched the looks on their faces as the bullets ricocheted off the windows and chipped away some of the brick, some of the pieces flying back and hitting the car making it seem that they were being shot at also.

Astrit yelled out, "Go, go, go. Motherfucker, who would have thought they would put blast resistant security glass in. Not even a frigging crack!"

The cars parked along the street not only took hits but the noise from the gunfire activated car alarms on both sides of the roadway. They made a bit more noise and a distinctive sound from the M-16. It was like a Christmas tree lighting up with all the flashing lights from the alarms.

———

The two guys Sly had upstairs nearly shit themselves as they hit the deck. It was then they also realized that their boss had installed some pretty good—no, *damn* good—glass. But, damn, twice in one day!

Dave and Sly were up watching some late TV and glancing at the monitors, rehashing war stories. Dave gave him an account of the freeze-mobile trip, his late wife's name for the trip that he and I took with her. We rode up to Vermont one fall and it was so cold. Most of the time we were in the mountains, it was below 30 degrees or less, and his wife wanted to get on a train and go home! Couldn't say I blamed her since neither one of us had fairings or windshields or for that matter cold weather touring gear. That was before we got oh so much smarter. He told Sly that one morning when we all woke up there was frost on the bikes over an inch thick. Sly got a chuckle but then his jovial demeanor turned sour.

"What the hell was that?" Both he and Dave directed their full attention to the monitor and saw muzzle flashes coming from two automatic weapons. They both headed upstairs without waking the others and as they suspected they had come under fire, again.

"No glass breakage, Sly, what did you have put in there?"

"Blast-proof, my man. I learned a thing or two from that friend of yours. Looks like the cars parked along the curb took more damage than we did. Might as well get ready for the police to come by and the news. We're gonna make like no one is here. No one talks to anyone. I don't feel like dealing with them tonight." Sly called his guys and told them to stay out of sight and not respond if the cops came knockin'.

With all the alarms and commotion outside, people began to pour out of the building to see what was going on. It wasn't unusual for a car alarm to go off, but this was a chorus of alarms with different tones and modes. It was a cacophony of Asian languages and English, and only God knew what they were all saying. Most of them had pissed looks on their faces as they found that the cars parked on the club side had been damaged by shrapnel. There were also multiple 7.62cal casings laying about the sidewalk and street. The detectives arrived while the crime scene unit was still at the job of photographing, bagging, and tagging the spent casings. By now the area had been taped off and the detectives canvassing the crowd looked for witnesses. The Asians in particular had nothing to say and feigned that they didn't know English. It was a survival technique they had inbred in them from years of autocratic rule and police with no restraint. The patrol units that responded first tried knocking but received no response and the detectives tried the same with the same result.

As Sly and Dave went back downstairs Dave said, "I'm sure that will be the top story on the morning news."

"No doubt about it, my friend, no doubt about it."

———

On the way back to the warehouse Astrit said, "If that wasn't a fuck-up I don't know what was."

"Yeah, we go to mess with them and my car looks like a road sign in Red Neck country," Valmir replied more than a bit pissed. "It will cost a small fortune to get this fixed."

"We can put a little Bondo on the holes, sand it down, and get a can of spray paint that should do the job. Be just like new," Toti said trying to get a crack out of him.

"Fuck no, this ain't no hooptie and I ain't no hood rat!"

"That sounds a bit prejudiced, you're not down with the brothers or the gooks, now are you?" Toti said sarcastically. A second past and Valmir got the joke and they had a good laugh. After all, it was just a car.

CHAPTER SIXTY-ONE

HOW MANY MORE TIMES

EXCEPT FOR THOSE THAT SAW VALMIR'S CAR THE NIGHT before while they were pulling duty, the other half, now that they were awake, saw the damage caused when Astrit and Toti strafed the front of Chez Rendezvous. Of course, they all wanted to know what had happened, especially Tole, and Valmir said, "They installed blast-proof glass, that's what the fuck happened. Now my car is all fucked-up."

Tole, feeling a little defensive said, "You think I'm at fault for this? How was I to know?"

"No, Alban, you had no way of knowing what they would do in response to what we did. But you must admit it was very clever, although expensive. Most of the cars near the building got fucked-up too and alarms were going off like crazy."

Tole start laughing. "That must have been a scene. But it's water under the bridge. Let's go eat. Half of us must stay here, no exceptions. Maybe I might have a fun surprise for you all tonight."

———

Even before Sly could get to the bathroom to take a piss, his phone rang and by the ringtone he knew it wasn't a social call. "Good morning, Mr. Commissioner."

"Good morning? Who the hell are you kidding? You gotta be fucking out of your mind. Are you kidding me? Is this what I'm going to be waking up to over the next week because if it is, all bets are off."

"No, sir, this was completely unprovoked," Sly lied with the expertise of someone who did it for a living. "This will be all over in a couple of days. They know they can't draw any heat and we certainly don't want any either."

"Sly, do not let me nor the mayor get burned on this. We let a lot of what you do slide, and we probably don't know the half of it. We're friends as long as the stink doesn't stick to us. We've both squashed a lot of investigations on your behalf."

Sly couldn't resist pushing back a little. "So our 'friendship' is conditional? What about those times when you all had those little rendezvous with some unnamed ladies and packages being exchanged? And that is only the tip of the iceberg and you don't want a meltdown, no, sir, not from me. I have my own condition, and that is, Commish, if I may be clear, you and His Honor wouldn't want a certain set of books, photos, and thumb drives to fall into the hands of *The Herald*, now would you? Seems to me we have a stalemate."

After a few seconds of silence, the commissioner responded, "Are you threatening me?"

"Not at all, sir, it's just the price of business. You take care of your end and I will take care of mine as always. Everything stays locked away, you'll never find it, but if I go down, we all go down. There won't be any loose ends to come undone, now will there? Now go and have a nice day and stop getting your panties in a twist."

Anyone who had heard that call wouldn't have believed that Sly had dismissed the commissioner like that. But that was the way Sly played the game. He wouldn't back down when someone got in his face regardless of who they were, the mayor and the commissioner were no different. Neither could afford for Sly to let those books and photo albums see the light of day.

———

I wasn't the first awake and I really didn't care, all I knew was I smelled hot food cooking and a pair of warm arms and legs around me and I wasn't going to complain. But I dragged my raggedy, beat-up, sore ass self out of bed and headed for the kitchen. Most of us who were staying at Chez Bunker had already gotten up and I did a double take when I saw Max already there without the rest of his team. Gina was up too and was assisting with breakfast with a little knowing smile on her face that wasn't hard to read or well hidden, and for her that was a mortal sin. She had that FFL appearance that Lady had a few mornings previous and it looked good on her. Gina handed me a cup of coffee and I took a seat near Max to watch the morning news. As usual, I couldn't keep my mouth closed and I asked Max in a low voice, "Get left behind last night?"

"I wouldn't exactly say that, more like I had a better offer, or should I say I was told I was going to have one. No, wait, come to think of it, I was shanghaied, and who was I to argue?"

"Still intact?"

"I do believe so, but man, what a freak. She tied me up with knots I didn't know existed. She trussed me up like a calf at a rodeo! But, I ain't complaining!" After what seemed like five minutes of dapping and hand-slapping we returned to being adults and put the matter to rest, lest Gina see us carrying on like little boys getting their first peak at a naked woman in a *Playboy* magazine. No telling what she would have done.

"Bro," I said, "don't get comfortable with that and don't take it for granted. She won't be around next week, and she chews men up and spits them out. Be respectful and you will keep those man parts along with some very good memories. Ya never know when she might reach out."

"Yes, sir, I hear ya loud and clear."

And then it happened. Channel 7, more specifically Kim Khazei, was already addressing Amaka Ubaka who was on set and of all places to be, right in front of the club.

"Oh, damn, Sly, come get a look at this mess. Channel 7 is out front doing a spot," I called out to Sly. At the same time, Reshaun gave the same report to Sly as he had been upstairs monitoring the video.

"Last night on Dorchester Avenue in front of Chez Rendezvous there were numerous reports of fully automatic gunfire out on the street. Amaka, what have you been able to find out?"

I just get a kick out of these news people not knowing shit about guns, I thought to myself. Fully automatic? Isn't that redundant? What morons. They all need to take a class!

"Well, Kim, in the early morning hours car alarms started going off and neighbors were calling 911 reporting the sounds of rapid gunfire like that of assault weapons.

Oh really, I thought as I heard it.

Amaka continued,

"We don't know how many shots were fired, how many people were involved, or who the intended targets may have been. Surprisingly no one was injured. There are still spent casings laying on the ground that the police evidence team has yet to pick up. The restaurant behind me has some damage to the brickwork, and you can clearly see none of windows were broken which is surprising. Several cars parked in front of the club sustained some damage as of

the result of ricochets and brick breaking apart. There haven't been any reports of victims and there is no blood on the sidewalk, and as of now we don't think anyone was shot. We don't know what precipitated the events from last night, but it may all be tied to other mysterious happenings that have taken place over the last week. Fortunately, this took place when very, very few people were on the street."

"Amaka, has anyone spoken to the club owner, and aren't assault weapons illegal? Were any security cameras in the area checked?"

"At this time, no, as we tried knocking on the door but there was no answer. I asked one of the detectives on the scene and they said that although there were security cams in the area not one of them had a view of Chez Rendezvous. As for the weapons, a person can own them with the proper paperwork from ATF, but as we all know if a criminal wants a gun, they will get it regardless of the law and my guess is they didn't get the proper paperwork." Yeah, no shit I thought.

"Thank you, Amaka. We will keep you all updated as we get more information. The police at this time are not speculating as to what may have occurred except there was a lot of gunfire. Now a preview of the upcoming weather."

Now if that wasn't a fine good morning. Sly walked into the room after I called to him and I asked, "Sly, were you up late last night? You hear anything?"

"Yeah, Dave and I were up having a sip and he was looking at me like he was lonely." That got a laugh and of course a "Fuck you, Sly" from Dave. "But for real, we were just watching TV and happened to look at the monitor for the camera out front and saw flashes of light. Not much damage to the building but the glass is now blast-proof. Bet that surprised the shit outta them."

———

Tole and half the boys pulled up to Victoria's and by the time they got up to the door Chloe was setting up the back room. By now the owner had an "understanding" that that was Tole's room, or for any of his men if it was needed.

Tole sat down, and she came over putting her arm around his broad shoulders and said, "Hey, big man, how are you this morning? You look well-rested."

"Very much so, and I think your mama needs to babysit tonight. I may need some more of that stress relief that you're so good at."

"Oh really, you have plans for us tonight? This like a real date?"

"Consider it what you may, but wear something classy, something sexy tonight. Yes, call it a date, my little *zuske*!"

"Okay, lover boy, whatever you say. And what does 'zuske' mean?" she said just before she took all their orders and paid special attention to the big man.

Tole replied, "Just an Albanian term of endearment." She didn't notice the lustful looks that the others gave her and the smirks on their faces as she was too locked in on Tole. She had no idea what was in store for her later that night.

While eating, Tole went over the day's plans. He told Astrit and Toti to send guys out to Home Depot to rent a generator and the others go to the Army-Navy store to get the night vision goggles if they had them. He was going to make sure that black whore paid with everything she had. Maybe he would put her in a cage too, it was the perfect place for an animal, and he thought all blacks were gorillas.

When they were finished, Tole stuffed a wad of bills into the top of Chloe's uniform whetting her desire for later that evening. "Be ready at eight tonight," was all he said while walking out.

CHAPTER SIXTY-TWO

I REMEMBER WHEN I LOST MY MIND

TOLE HAD LOST HIS MIND. HE WAS IN A EUPHORIC MOOD from the steroids and a little Kush. He forbade his men to indulge in anything, he was the boss after all, but he needed to mellow out the insane surges of rage he endured from the steroids at times more than he liked to admit. The man could have competed competitively in the bodybuilding world if he wanted and won hands down, but bodybuilding didn't pay the bills and the other pleasures that Tole so needed. Bodybuilders were lucky if winning a competition even put a dent in their monthly steroid bills that could run just under ten grand a month.

The man spent more on worldly indulgences—very young women—than most any man he knew, and he always wanted the girls fresh and young, and sometimes that cost. He didn't care how young they were, he promised them anything and gave them nothing but pain, and after he had his fill of a girl, he would put her on the streets, and she would never see home again. Just like the *zuske* from the restaurant who would someday soon be on a milk carton, that is if anyone, meaning her mother and grandmother, cared enough, which Tole strongly doubted. Once she was hooked on the drugs and broken by his men, she would do anything he asked, including living in a cage until he needed her to work.

When Tole looked for new prospects, he scouted out the poor areas of the cities. These were his best picking grounds, along with bus terminals and shelters, as the little girls were so desperate for attention because they lacked the family structure they needed. Many if not most had no idea who their daddy was, and Tole stepped in to fill the void but in a much different way.

He played with them for a while, giving them money, buying them clothes, and talking to them like a father. But one day they never returned home, not the home they once knew. How long he had been like this was beyond what he could remember. He vaguely remembered his father, how he beat him and his mother, and his mother did what she could to survive but it was never enough. Eventually she too sold herself as well to the men that had enough to pay her something so she could buy another meal.

Tole's morality was the law of the streets by which he lived, not by any Bible or Koran. It had nothing to do with what was right or wrong but what he needed in the moment. Stealing, murder, gambling, drugs, and whores were the ways he made his money, and he paid tribute to those that held all the cards.

He rose from the ranks of the street, did some time with honor, if you would call it that, and made a name for himself, a name of honor, a man of honor. They all talked about honor when none of them actually had any. It was moral depravity and he was one not to look a gift horse in the mouth.

He ruled by fear and intimidation from his men and the people that lived in the community where he plied his trades.

Those that cooperated prospered, those that went to the cops for help, well, let's just say they didn't go twice. Some viewed him as a god, others as a demon, but either way he got the job done and those above him saw that and he was rewarded. He had lost his mind and thus was out of touch with what was real. It brings to mind the Gnarls Barkley song, *"Who do you think you are? Ha, ha, ha, bless your soul, You really think you're in control?"*

———

Tole was not in control, he was the farthest thing from it, and he showed it more and more every day. Had we wanted, we could have taken him at any time, day or night. It didn't matter. But we waited like vultures circling their prey and would only pounce when the time was right. Stephan Moffat said, "Demons run when a good man goes to war," but they ran in our presence, not Tole's. And one day very soon Tole was to know the vengeance that we would wreak upon him.

CHAPTER SIXTY-THREE

HERE KITTY, KITTY

WHILE THE MEN WERE OUT GATHERING WHAT THEY NEEDED at the various stores, Tole thought of the *zuske* that would give him and his men pleasure that night. He doubted this child was prepared for what was coming her way like a locomotive at full tilt with a broken brake. It reminded me of the Jethro Tull lyrics, *"The train it won't stop going, no way to slow down."* These men didn't care about compassion or pain or feeling, just their primal urges.

Tole had planned on taking her to a nice restaurant, just the thing to make her feel she was special. He decided on Strega as it was close by like Morton's, but he doubted on her pay that she could even afford the valet for the cost of parking a car or even the tip, let alone a meal. He called and made a reservation with the hostess and asked for a booth in the back. Tole knew that Chloe never would have a chance to set foot in a restaurant like this, and he would feed her a line that this was what life would be like with him.

Tole made sure that the men had his BMW polished so that one could see their reflection in the metal. He would have Astrit drive as he had the most finesse of his crew. Tole even went so far as to buy the little *zuske* a dozen roses, to be delivered at the restaurant, to make her feel that she meant something to him. But by the end of the night she would feel more like a side of beef hanging on a meat hook beaten by Rocky Balboa, and not a woman. Chloe's little girl would have to be raised by her mother and grandmother as Chloe would never return home again. The seduction was almost complete and all he needed to do was to place a tasteless drug in her drink at the end of the night.

CHAPTER SIXTY-FOUR

SMILE FOR THE CAMERA

AFTER WE HAD ALL BEEN FED, WATERED, AND COFFEE'D TO our hearts content, J3 and Max looked over the photos from the night before. "I can call a guy over in the DEA forensic unit and have him run the facial recognition on them." J3 made the call and got the thumbs-up from his contact and he gave Max the info to send the photos.

"This system is the FBI's and it is called NGI or Next Generation Identification. Any law enforcement agency can log into it and get a hit usually within ten minutes. It gets fifty-five thousand requests a day and will have fifty-one million plus photos within the year. It was designed by the defense contractor, Lockheed Martin, and was built by Morphotrust right here in Billerica, Massachusetts. It can pick out faces, scars, tattoos, and birthmarks and eventually be able to tell a person's identity by their stride, voice, eyes, and palm print. This was about a one-billion-dollar project."

"Very expensive toy," Jake said. "But then again the federal government never makes cheap toys."

"This sounds like the TV show, *Person of Interest*," I added. "They could find anyone."

"That just about hits the nail on the head," said J3. "But the good thing is they are not hooked into surveillance cams yet or security cams. But that shouldn't be too far behind. Hello, Big Brother."

"At what price do we give up our privacy and our right to move freely just to feel secure?" Sly asked.

"That's a good question, but just look how many cameras are on this building and in all the stores and banks. It's inevitable. It's not like they can't hack into your cell phone, see everyone within the phone's viewfinder, and hear everything you say. I mean, even we can all get that software to put on someone's phone. Anything can be hacked, TVs, camera on your computer, you name it. If it uses the web or Wi-Fi, it can be hacked."

Just as J3 finished giving us our security lesson for the day, his phone rang, and it was his connection. "Fred," for lack of a better name, told J3 that the two men whose identity he requested had a long history of criminal activity and were directly associated with the Albanian mob. It included drug trafficking, prostitution, gambling, and weapons, and though there were many arrests, most had been dropped for lack of cooperation from intimidated or paid-off witnesses. Witnesses were getting a convenient case of temporary Alzheimer's disease, that is, if they wanted to remain alive. Talk about nothing sticking to Teflon, Gotti had nothing on these guys; this was the epitome of nonstick.

Tatiana said, "Damn, I think I'm just gonna get a burner. I didn't know they could do all that. That's creepy thinking they can watch you in your home and I am sure they can record it."

"That's an easy fix as far as the camera, put a piece of duct tape over the lens then they can't see anything," J3 responded. "But with your phone, if they hacked it there's nothing short of removing the SIM card and getting a new one."

"Hell, ya, I keep tape over the camera on my computer. Bad enough it can still get hacked, but who needs someone watching you in your most sensitive and sensual moments?" I looked over at Lady. The look didn't go unnoticed by the rest of the crew, but after this last week we all had grown comfortable with who was with who. Except most did not know that Max and Gina were or were starting to have a little fling. The Lady had not hidden her affection for me even in the presence of others, which for her was a big step and a rarity. The entire group had bonded like one big diverse family especially around mealtime. It was surprising that this skilled bunch of warriors had such unique and different cooking skills, and it kept the menu refreshing.

The news crew finally left and life on the street returned to its normal hustle and bustle. Inside the guys were on the range, cleaning weapons or checking equipment. Once they had their fill of the acrid smell of the high velocity, high-powered gunpowder and gun oil, the Lady and I slipped back to the range.

———

"Tat, I am going to let you shoot a fully automatic weapon, would you like that? But a soft, gentle touch is required until you get the feel of it."

"Carlo, you know that I love the feel of a warm gun in my hand, you have me hooked, let me pull the trigger," she begged.

My God, I don't know how any man could refuse her. Readers, if you are sensing a double meaning then you are with me.

"So, you love the feel of a warm gun, do you?" I looked at

her with a knowing look on my face and I lifted her onto the counter where the weapons were stored.

"You know I do, so stop teasing me and let me have what I need."

"But what if we get caught playing with the gun?"

"Jesus, Carlo, you know I love you, why do you make me say it? Why? I know you love me too as you show it in all that you do, putting yourself out there like you did." She stopped for a second after she realized what she had said. She knew it was a slip, a Freudian slip at that, and it wasn't supposed to come out, but her lips worked faster than her mind had.

"I thought I was just a diversion for you, someone to help you get the job done, a toy to be played with and then put back on a shelf, but I began to realize it was becoming more than that as the days passed. But me, I fell in love with you the moment you walked through the door ten days ago. I thought I was a fool until now." I grasped her shirt with both hands, pulled, and popped all the buttons as I yanked it open and to my delight, she had nothing on underneath as if she had this all planned.

I caressed her firm, perky breasts and kissed them passionately and continued down the full length of her perfect body. Her figure-hugging yoga pants came down as I lifted her, and I continued my kissing between her delicious thighs. As I didn't have hair, she placed both hands behind my head and pulled me tight to her as I brought her to sensual climax over and over. I had all I could take, and I couldn't help but plunge deep inside her. We were both engulfed in a bonfire of passion, we burned as one hot intense flame, inextinguishable, and if I was to die at this moment I would be at complete peace, a happy man.

Shooting a gun now seemed anticlimactic. Now I think I lost my mind, as there was something so pleasant about this place. Does that make me crazy?

CHAPTER SIXTY-FIVE

Can You See Me Now?

Toti assigned Zeni and Ari to go to Home Depot to look for the generator, one that could run an entire home for twelve hours would be more than sufficient. Shpati and another of Valmir's men would go to the Army-Navy surplus store as they had some experience with night vision optics. Now picking out a generator is a whole lot easier than getting the night vision optics.

Night vision first began as far back as 1929 when Hungarian physicist Kalman Tihanyi invented the infrared-sensitive electronic television camera for anti-aircraft defense in the United Kingdom. The first military night vision devices were introduced by the German Army as early as 1939 and were used in World War II. Allgemeine Elektricitäts-Gesellschaft (AEG) began developing the first devices in 1935.

In mid-1943, the German Army began the first tests of

infrared night vision devices and telescopic range-finders mounted on Panther tanks, a medium-sized tank, smaller than the Panzer. From there the technology expanded, and during the Vietnam War the first generation 1-night vision optics were introduced. Advancement in the technology then brought us Gen II, III, and Gen III Omni IV-VII. These advances increased the performance of the devices. The science behind it can be mind-boggling and is now developing to the point where nanocrystals can be fitted onto an ultra-thin film and placed on glasses reducing the bulk and size. The tiny crystals—500 times narrower than a human hair—are made of aluminum-gallium-arsenide, a stable semiconducting alloy used in mobile phones.

Further advances will reduce the size of these units to be fitted on contact lenses and allow one to see a larger spectrum of color than just blues and greens. With that said, the two going to the surplus store had their work cut out for them.

Zeni and Ari had a much easier time and were in and out of Home Depot in less than an hour. They rented a DeWalt 7,000-watt unit and would have no problem providing the warehouse with the power it needed through the 30-amp 240-volt twist-lock plug on the front should the power be knocked out. After getting two five-gallon containers for gasoline they got it back to the warehouse, hooked up, and started. It worked like a charm and they were ready if a blackout should occur, a blackout perpetrated by my team of bad boys.

Shpati and Valmir's man, Heinz, made their way to Kenmore Army-Navy store at 477 Washington Street in Boston. The store wasn't too busy, and they were greeted by a salesperson decked out in cammies. They laughed silently to themselves doubting that this clown had ever worn cammies except to go deer hunting, or more like pretending to hunt, and just drinking. From the looks of his bloated belly, it was probably the latter. He wore a nametag that read "Tom."

"How may I help you gentleman today? Are you preppers,

hunters, or looking for camping gear or just some good outdoor fun?"

Shpati thought to himself, *Is this guy serious? But hey, it is what it is.*

Heinz inquired, "Do you have any NVG in stock?"

Tom looked a little confused and asked, "NVG? Not quite sure what you mean."

"We're looking for night vision goggles. Does the store stock them?"

"Oh, I'm sorry, not many people come in here looking for them or refer to them just by NVG. You all must have military experience, but yes, we have several generations of goggles in stock and the prices vary. How many pair might you be needing?"

Boy, Heinz thought, *this guy sounded more like a college professor than someone who had any knowledge of military surplus equipment.*

"Why don't you just show us what you have, and we will decide how many we will take," responded Shpati.

"We have some nice Gen III models and they are a nice upgrade form the Gen II."

"Stop right there, we don't need an education on the goggles. We are familiar with them. You mentioned Gen III—do you have those in the Omni IV-VII models?"

Tom answered, "Well, I'm impressed you do know your stuff, but no, we don't. We do have some PVS-7 Gen III single tube goggles in stock. They run about $3300 apiece."

"How many do you have?" asked Heinz.

"I'll go check and see what we have in stock. Be right back."

Tom walked away and Heinz and Shpati looked at one another shaking their heads. Tom came back about five minutes later and the manager was with him.

"So, you gentlemen are asking about the night vision equipment? Gonna do some night hunting?" the manager asked.

Shpati dodged the question, his patience growing shorter by the second and responded, "How many pair do you have?"

"I have six pair in stock."

"Good, we'll take them all. Can we see them now?" said Heinz.

"That is quite the substantial purchase and how will you be paying?"

"We wouldn't be asking if we couldn't afford the price, besides, what difference does it make? But we are paying with cash, will that be a problem?" Shpati said.

"No, not at all," the manager replied.

"We would expect a nice discount for this kind of a purchase, wouldn't you agree?"

"Yes, I can arrange that," the manager said feeling a tad intimidated. "Come up to the counter and we will get everything in order."

Tom brought out all the units and the manager tested all of them to make sure they worked and totaled the bill up. It came to $19,950. The manager said, "I am able to give you a 15% discount bringing the price down to $16,957. Why don't we round it all off at $16,900?"

"Fifteen thousand works better for us, unless you want us to go elsewhere," replied Shpati.

The manager thought for a quick second, felt a bit intimidated again, and said, "Okay, I can do that. Hope you remember us for any future purchases this size."

"Have Tom bag them up, and here is your cash."

Shpati and Heinz carried the goggles out to the car and headed back to the warehouse. Tole should be pleased with this.

CHAPTER SIXTY-SIX

CHLOE'S STORY

CHLOE HAD BEEN BORN INTO A BROKEN FAMILY. HER mother became pregnant as an older teen and forced to quit school and go to work. Her mother did as much as she could for her daughter and tried to raise her with a proper upbringing. Because money was tight, Chloe's mother moved them into Chloe's grandmother's house and both women raised young Chloe. They were able to put enough food on the table and clothes on their backs, but they didn't have money for the extras that some of the other families had, which included games and vacations. Sometimes her mom had to go to the food banks to feed the three of them and at times shopped at the Salvation Army for clothes. She always found nice clothes for Chloe that were castoffs barely worn by those that just wanted a deduction on their tax returns, or who didn't believe in wearing something more than once.

Chloe's dad was a deadbeat, in and out of jail, and never contributed a cent to her support even though her mother took him to family court several times. He had been arrested numerous times for nonpayment but still never gave a cent to her upbringing.

Chloe was a good student and teachers always had a good word to say about the bright little girl. Her mother and grandmother were impressed with her scholastic achievement even at her young age and heaped praise on her for the grades she got. As she didn't have a lot of toys and the family couldn't afford vacations, she became an avid reader and books were her way of escape. Those books took her all over the world.

She explored mysterious, beautiful, and sometimes dangerous places through them and someday hoped to see the more beautiful and magnificent places she had read about. Of course, she loved *National Geographic* and made sure she was the first one at the library to read it each month. She skydived, and scuba-dived to the depths of the ocean through them and went to the moon and Mars. Chloe explored caves and pyramids and dug up old prehistoric bones. She read at several grade levels ahead of the other kids in her class and knew more about geography and world events than kids twice her age.

At one time the teachers and guidance counselors suggested that she skip a grade, but her mom and grandmother just wanted her to be like all the other kids and not set apart. They wanted a normal upbringing for her.

At age eleven, Chloe began to grow long-legged and started to develop the body of a lithe, athletic, beautiful young woman as a lot of girls did in this day and age. Her thick head of blonde hair cascaded over her toned shoulders together with a beautiful smile and thick pouty lips. Even at that young age she caught the attention of many boys, some a little too old. Both her mother and grandmother talked to her about boys and the changes she was experiencing and why she was turning into the pretty young woman she was transforming into.

Of course, it was difficult for her to comprehend it all, like any other girl of her age, but she noticed that boys looked at her differently and treated her differently. Sometimes it was a little teasing or pulling her ponytail, but it was what young boys did at that age to show affection, as they were further behind the girls in maturity. The attention made her feel special and Mom and Gram did their best to keep the young boys and some not so young at bay from their young girl.

Chloe aspired to go to college and with her grades she probably could have gotten a full scholarship. As she became more popular, she participated in school activities, student government, cheer and intramural sports, excelling in most if not all and could hold her own in a debate with the best of them. And that is when she met Kevin.

Kevin was a year older, a redheaded Irish boy, with both parents at home. He was tall for his age, which suited Chloe as she was taller than most of the girls her age, and he had a muscular trim physique. He was a bit wild but popular because he played sports, was captain of the football team, the typical All-American boy. He was very good, hoping one day to play in the NFL, maybe even the New England Patriots. He wanted to be another Tom Brady who was his idol.

He pursued Chloe with a passion, doted on her, walked her home from school, making her feel very special, and on her sixteenth birthday his dad allowed him to use the car to take her out for a dinner at a restaurant he could afford with the money he earned from a part-time job at Shaw's Supermarket.

She wanted pizza, and they went to Land of Pizza located at 445 West Broadway. They talked, ate, laughed, both enjoying the night and one another. When they finished eating, they went for a long drive along the waterfront and after a while found a secluded place to park and "talk" like most teens did.

Kevin produced a flask that one of his friends had provided for him from his dad's liquor cabinet complete with some good Irish whiskey. If Kevin's plan went the way he wanted, Chloe would not be a virgin after the night was over, just like the other girls he deflowered in this same spot. She would be another conquest and by far the prettiest one yet.

He and Chloe kissed and talked, and he got her to take a few sips and then a little more.

Just like the vodka did when Tole got her to drink, she began to feel the warm glow of the liquor and her guard dropped. He whispered sweet nothings into her ear, and she knew what her mom and gram had told her, but she was past the point of being responsible, and soon she was on top of him with her blouse open after Kevin sedated her fears. As they touched one another Chloe, with the help of Kevin, slid out of the panties she wore beneath her short skirt and he ran his hands up and down her legs and her firm butt. He touched and kissed her where no one ever had touched her before, pushed his pants down to his ankles, and all this led to a crescendo of heated lust.

He told her he loved her and would be there for her forever, and all the other lies that young boys tell a girl to get what they want. She said she loved him and for her it seemed real and they made love several times before she had to be home. They hadn't used any protection and the car was filled with the scent of their sex. Kevin would need to air the car out so his father wouldn't notice what he had been up to when he got in it to go to work in the morning. Chloe was dripping from the multiple discharges placed in her and now running down her leg. She tried to clean up as best as she could and by the time she got home she was starting to come to her senses and began to realize what they had done. She knew her mom and gram would know what had happened by the look on her face, and it's not something a young girl can hide well from other women especially in the same house.

When they pulled up in front of her house she asked, "Kevin, if I get pregnant you said you loved me and would be there for me, right?" It sounded almost if she was pleading with him.

"Of course I will be, Princess. Don't worry, it can't happen the first time," he said to her convincingly even though her mother had told her differently. She wanted desperately to believe him. He played with her emotions and her heart and that was a terrible thing to do to a young girl, any girl.

"Okay, I love you too and thank you for tonight, it was very special. You made me a woman tonight and I love you for that too."

She and Kevin were inseparable and united several more times until about a week later when Chloe missed her period and was in a mad panic. She had to go to her mother, and she knew it would crush both the older women as they had such high hopes for her. Her mother took Chloe to her OB-GYN doctor and she confirmed what Chloe already knew. She was now two weeks pregnant.

Chloe and her mother confronted Kevin and his parents, but he had already convinced them that she was the school slut and had been with a lot of boys in school and it could be any number of them. Where was Maury Povich when you needed him? Kevin refused to speak to her any further and spread rumors at school, telling lurid details about their night and the things that happened and didn't happen, but what did he care if he embellished a little. It made him look big to the rest of his boys. The lies along with the truth made it almost impossible for her to continue, and when she started to show at five months she dropped out. It killed her mother and gram, but she promised that after the baby was born, she would get a GED, work, and go to night school at the local community college. It was a far cry from what she could have accomplished.

When the baby was born, Kevin refused to show up and

would not sign the birth certificate, and his parents would not allow him to take a DNA test. They had gone as far as hiring an attorney to keep her from bothering him and his family. He stuck to his guns that he was not the baby daddy and his parents stood by his side. But Chloe got some justification as Kevin was hurt while playing football, blowing out his knee, and could never play again, ever. When that happened, Kevin started on a downward spiral and by his eighteenth birthday he had been arrested twice for petty crimes and drug possession. She knew she would never get any money from him despite her best efforts and he would never be a father to the baby, just like hers had never been to her.

Shortly after her beautiful baby girl was born, Chloe and her mom got a rare moment out and went to Victoria's one day for lunch and Chloe noted that they were looking for a waitress. She applied that day and was hired. So she started her career as a single working mom. All during her pregnancy she studied at home, worked toward her GED, and attained it when she was seventeen. All that reading she had done earlier in life was about to pay off now as Tole was dangling a golden carrot in front of her. Maybe now she would get to see all those places she dreamt and read about.

CHAPTER SIXTY-SEVEN

OUT OF DARKNESS, LIGHT

HEINZ AND SHPATI CALLED TOTI AS THEY CAME DOWN Topeka and had him open the overhead door. By the time they had gotten back all the doors had been reinforced and welded shut except for the one through which they entered. Tole came out of the office and asked the two men if they had any luck. Shpati held up the bags containing the goggles and Tole rubbed his hands together and said, "Things are looking up now. Tell me about them."

Heinz replied, "We got the best we could for what they had in stock. These are a PVS-7 Gen III monocle goggle. They ran $3300 apiece and Shpati convinced them to give us a lower price as we bought six units. They were all checked out at the store and everything seems to work."

"Let's kill the lights and see just how good they are," responded Tole.

Zeni went over to the main power panel and killed the lights, but even with the windows blacked-out there was the slightest bit of light still sneaking through. Heinz had powered up all six pair prior to Zeni killing the lights and gave a pair to Tole and five others.

"Damn," Tole said, "for not being the best they do a good job. Six of you will always have a unit with you in case they hit us, and we will still be able to see them." He continued to walk around the warehouse in the dark and was able to make out the men and other shapes as he approached them. "Zeni, turn the lights back on, Shpati and Heinz, good job."

Before Zeni could get to the switches Shpati said, "Wait, take off the goggles first, otherwise the light will be too intense."

After they had gotten them off and the lights came back on, Tole told them that tonight they would have a little extra fun after dinner. He was going to bring them a little surprise.

Tole had already made the reservation for eight that evening and requested a table in the back and checked to make sure the flowers had arrived at the restaurant. Tole made sure of that as he wanted the night to go perfectly, for him and his men, that is. He checked his supply of recreationals and decided the MDMA or ecstasy would be the best choice. He would put it in her drink before they left the restaurant and by the time they got to the warehouse she would be well under the effects of the drug as the drug worked within fifteen minutes. This drug would make her feel lovey-dovey with those around her and she would be less likely to reject their repeated advances or resist even if she wanted to. *Yes*, thought Tole, *this was going to be a good night.*

CHAPTER SIXTY-EIGHT

ONE LAST NIGHT OF PEACE

FORTUNATELY FOR LADY TATIANA AND ME, I HAD LOCKED the door of the armory from the inside and it couldn't be opened from the outside. There came a knock at the door and Lady and I hurried to arrange our clothes and get them buttoned up. We were both glad the knock hadn't come a few minutes earlier because there was no stopping us. "Just a minute, we're putting up some guns, be right out," I said. I had left the fans on, thank God, and the room and the range were well ventilated by the time I unlocked the door.

Much to my amazement, it was Max and Gina. "We wanted to shoot a few rounds together before dinner and check out some of the other guns," Max said not all that convincingly. I mean, they had a room to themselves but who were we to talk. Maybe they would have made too much noise and with everyone in the bunker, it didn't pay to advertise.

Lady spoke to Max's statement, "Knock yourselves out, we did, don't make a mess." Max looked a little embarrassed, but Gina took it all in stride. She knew the Lady was giving her a shot, but tigresses did that. There was no way these two women would ever be friends nor enemies, but they weren't here to be gal pals, no shopping trips or lunches.

Tatiana and I left the sanctity of the range and she told me she was going to change before she joined the rest of us. She kissed me and said, "I'll be right out. This is no show for everyone," meaning her state or lack of state of dress, as her shirt no longer had buttons.

I walked into the living area, poured myself a Booker's—four fingers worth—and I asked Brit to make a Long Island Tea for her sis.

Brit asked, "Where is she?"

"We were on the range and she wanted to freshen up and change before dinner, so she will be out in a few minutes."

"So, y'all were shooting?" she asked as if she were prying for another, much different answer.

"Oh, yeah, I let her shoot one of the MP7s."

"I bet you did," she said, and she walked away and made the drink.

I asked the others if there was anything newsworthy and they said it was the same old shit, just a different day. They had on *Family Feud* and were cracking up over the antics of Steve Harvey. I don't know how in hell he got away with saying half the stuff he did.

"So who's cooking tonight and what are we eating?" I asked.

Almost in unison they responded, "You are and we're eating whatever you make." I guess it was my turn to be batter-up and I checked out the walk-in and the three fridges.

"All right, you're all in luck but you'll get what I got when I give it to ya." I found a bunch of salmon fillets that wouldn't take long to thaw in some warm water. There was a bunch of zucchini and yellow squash in the vegetable bin and I found some sweet potatoes.

Lady came out finally looking refreshed and relaxed, got her drink from Brit, and came over, put her arm up over my shoulder, and asked if she could help. I had her wash the potatoes, pierce them, and put them in the oven while I cut up the veggies.

She asked, "You good with your drink or do you need a refresher?"

"Still good but that could change any minute."

"You let me know, babe, and I'll get it for you," she said. She planted a kiss on my still slightly swollen and sore cheek.

"Grab me that deep skillet," I asked her, "and put a good amount of coconut oil in it. Just warm it for now and I'll turn up the heat in a bit." I minced up some garlic and threw it in the skillet allowing it to slow-cook. I grabbed another skillet and put a small amount of the coconut oil into that too. The fish was just about thawed, and the potatoes were on their way to being done.

"Tat, bring me over that Jim Beam, I'll need it for the fish, and I'll need that big bottle of balsamic vinegar from the cabinet." She got me both items and asked what I was going to do. "First, I'm going to sear the fish in the hot coconut oil with a little salt and pepper then add a little bourbon, and finally when it is about finished cooking, I add the vinegar." When I did that the vinegar and bourbon made a nice, mildly sweet sauce. I had to repeat it with each panful of fish.

"Tat, take out the potatoes, cut them in half, add butter, ginger, cinnamon, and some brown sugar, no pun intended," which got a cute little laugh out of her. "Then place them in a broiler for a few minutes to brown up."

As a finishing touch I added some more bourbon, vinegar, and some real maple syrup, let it thicken, and poured it over the platter of fish. It was all good to go.

"Babe, I'll take that Booker's now."

The crew were all seated around the table as Tatiana and I brought out the food. Sly went over to the fridge and brought out six bottles of Vie di Romans Dessimis Pinot Grigio Friuli Isonzo, Friuli-Venezia Giulia, Italy, which paired very nicely with the salmon.

"Jake and J3, what's your take on all that's been happening, when do you think we should hit them?" I asked.

Just as he was about to answer, Channel 7 news at six came on and the lead story was, you guessed it, about the gunfire at the club.

Amaka was standing in front of police headquarters on Tremont Street and took her cue from Kim Khazei.

"Amaka, what have the Boston police told you about the ballistics that were conducted from the rounds recovered in the brick work at Chez Rendezvous?"

"I have been told that the rounds match a weapon that was used in New York City in a previous shooting there in 2017. What they don't know is how the gun got up here or if the same people that used it in New York are here. They suspect it was related to underworld activity involving the Albanian Rudaj crime family and the Italian Mafia. If that is the case, we don't know why a popular black club in Dorchester was shot up. Back to you, Kim."

Khazei continued:

"As of now no one has been able to get in contact with the owner of Chez Rendezvous, but we will keep our viewers posted with the latest breaking news regarding this incident."

It got quiet around the table really quick. Jake finally spoke up, "I don't think we have a lot of options. We are running out of time and they are playing stupid. I say we don't have a choice but to hit them tomorrow night, no later."

J3 responded, "I agree with Jake. If we wait any longer, this is going to be a pissing match that we can't win. Everyone will be on our ass."

"Can we all agree on that? And if we do, then I need you all to stay sharp tomorrow," Jake stated. There was no dissent on the part of anyone.

CHAPTER SIXTY-NINE

"Wanna Call You on the Telephone, Baby, I Give You a Ring"

— GEORGE THOROGOOD

As soon as the newscast was over, Sly's phone began to blow up. For Sly, this was turning into one major clusterfuck in a hurry. The mayor, commissioner, and of course Johnny Botts called within minutes of one another. He let the calls from the mayor and commish go to voice mail as he had time to call them back, but he had to take the call from Botts.

Sly excused himself from the table and walked back to his room to talk to Johnny.

"Sly, what the fuck is going on? The news is talking like a gang war is about to go down. I thought you had this all under wraps?"

"Johnny, I told you I got this, and the problem will be gone very shortly. I will double your gift for any heat your guys might take, but just tell them to lay low. Don't let them get a hair across their ass as it will only make matters worse."

"Sly, don't let me regret this, we go back too far for shit to go sideways now."

"I got the mayor and commish blowing up my phone, let me deal with them, but you and I are solid. I don't fuck my friends. We good?"

"We're good, come see me when it's over. Less calls the better."

The two men hung up and now Sly had to make two other calls he didn't want to make. *Screw it,* he thought, *I'm gonna enjoy dinner and I will call them later, let them both wait.*

Sly returned to the table and everyone looked at him and he said, "Don't even ask, I'm sure you can figure out who's blowing up my phone. I'll deal with it, but I am going to enjoy this dinner and I think we are going to need more wine. Carlo, you and Miss Tatiana did a hell of a job."

Sly was trying to deflect his uneasiness but not doing a good job of it. He may and probably did have the others fooled, but I knew the man all too well. The pressure was pushing down on him and I wanted this over so he could get back to whatever it was we considered normal. I knew a lot more about him now than I did a week ago and I believe he felt more than a little vulnerable. He had opened up his entire hidden life for us, for me more importantly, or so I thought, and I could see that it made him more than a tad worried.

But I knew my guys would never let a word slip about all that had happened in recent days and what was about to happen. Like I said before, we had become a family. I felt for Sly, he had grown to be a close and trusted friend, and I knew he was losing a chunk of change with having the club closed and still paying his men and the other unmentionable envelopes that were distributed or about to be. He was putting all that he had on the line for Brit and her sister, and you couldn't find a more stand-up guy than that. But a bill was gonna come due and I knew she, Lady, would be good for it. When the bottom line was made known, it would all go to Sly, because like I said from the start, I wouldn't have taken a cent.

Sly brought more wine over to the table but the mood was a bit somber than it was before the news. We all tried to end the dinner on a high note knowing that some of us may not make it back in one piece. But we had a morbid sense of humor when we were ready to go off to war.

When we had all finished and passed some time talking over coffee that Sly graciously made, he excused himself to make the other calls he knew he must make. The mayor could wait, and he called the commissioner first.

———

"It's about time you called me back! What the hell is going on? One of my beat cops let me know you had some trouble there the other day with getting your windows shot out. Do you have this or not? I need answers now because if the shit is about to hit the fan, I don't want the fan blowing on me!"

"Have I ever let you down? I already know the answer to that, No! I got this handled and you will only have to mop up like I told you after tomorrow night. Just keep your boys off my ass and everyone will disappear into the night like I promised. We need one clear route after we're done—straight down South Hampton to Dorchester Avenue. We need twenty minutes and we will be gone. Keep your guys at bay until then. After that you can start the game clock. Nothing will be traced back to me and I mean nothing. All you will have is a bunch of bodies to send to the morgue and then ship back to New York where those fuckers should have stayed. Maybe if the cops there didn't have their heads up their collective asses and the politicians had kept these assholes out of the country, we wouldn't be having this conversation right now. So, don't come blowing smoke up my ass, I got your back and you better have mine. Now do I need to address this issue with the mayor, or do you think you can handle it?"

Not too many people were able to talk to the commissioner the way Sly did. Sly had way too much leverage to hold his tongue. But that is a story for another time.

"I'll talk to His Honor when we get off the phone. I'll soothe his ruffled feathers and let him know to keep quiet and not shoot us all in the foot."

"Good enough for me," Sly said. He clicked off the call and let out an exhausted sigh.

———

Sly collapsed onto his bed spent from the stress rolling up on him. I passed his room and the door was ajar, so I knocked. "Okay if I come in, bro?"

"Yeah, come on in. At least I can carry on a conversation with you without having to coerce you to do something. Fucking mayor and the commish tried to play hardball and I gave it right back to them."

"You sure you wanted to do that?"

"I made it real clear that they wouldn't want anything to surface, they're typical politicians and running scared hoping they don't get a little shit on them. You know how the game is played, you were a cop. Politics sucks but everyone has to play to make things work."

"I do, unfortunately more than most, you know my past. You're looking a little tense, so just thought I might try to cheer you up a bit. Want a massage, big guy?"

Sly nearly jumped out of the bed, laughing and calling me a crazy ass motherfucker, but it got the job done and he wasn't so wound up.

"Sly, just remember, if we can't tell each other the hard truths then what are we doing here?"

"Then sit down, my man, I got something to tell you."

"Sure, Sly, what is it? You're not dying or anything like that, are you?"

CHAPTER SEVENTY

DAYS OF FUTURE PAST

"CARLO, NO, I'M NOT THE LEAST BIT SICK. BUT I'M LOADED, like I've got more money than I know what to do with. It boggles my mind when I sit and think about it and I ask God why did this happen to me? All this—the bar, the bunker, my other dalliances—are just diversions to keep me from going nuts. I have to admit I love the action, my connections, and the best part is no one knows just how much I have. They don't know I got it legally; they have no idea just how huge it all is. They all think I am some big badass, and to an extent I am, but they think I made it with drugs or some other illegal activity," Sly said chuckling, and I couldn't help but laugh too.

"Well, you are Sly, one big black badass! If I may ask, how did you come upon all the wealth? That is, if you care to share?" I was sitting there in awe of what he was relating to me.

"This is the part where you really need to be sitting. Years ago, I was driving up through New York and came upon a broke-down motorist, driving a nice Mercedes, and I stopped to help him. I was a young black man and this man was apparently wealthy and white, not that it matters, but it was how I was raised, to help folks. It was raining and blowin', and I almost didn't want to get out of the car cuz he probably thought I might jack him, but I did get out. The man was elderly, 60s and had a flat tire. He got out of the car and stood with me as I changed the tire and we talked a bit. It was way before cell phones where you could just call for help. When I was done, I asked if he wanted to get something to eat and get coffee, warm up, he said yes, he'd like that.

"We went to a little cafe just down the road, and we talked for several hours. He told me he didn't have any more family, his only son had died in Vietnam, a Green Beret, and I said he must be very proud. His wife passed just a few years earlier from pancreatic cancer and by the time it was diagnosed, she only had months to live. He told me it was a very fast-acting cancer for which there was no cure. Told me his whole life story and at times I saw his eyes mist up as he recalled memorable past moments in their lives. I could tell his family had meant everything to him. He had built up a big business, and he and his family were very close and wanted for nothing, they traveled, saw the world, helped those less fortunate, and did all kinds of other wonderful, philanthropic things. He told me that with all he had it meant nothing if he didn't have anyone to share it with and he thanked me for sitting with him and talking. I really felt sorry for him. I had my mom and dad still around and I don't know what I would have done if something happened to them. Then he asked me if I minded if he stayed in touch and we could talk from time to time as most of his friends had died, and I said I would be honored to.

"I gave him my phone number and through the years I would get a call from him. I mostly let him talk but he always asked about my life, what I was doing, school, work, family. It pleased him that I worked hard and tried to get a good education, and I loved sharing with that man, we both got a lot out of those talks and I hoped that I filled some void for him in his life. I believe I did, and he inspired me to be the best I could. About twelve years ago the calls stopped suddenly. I figured he became too old to call or he was incapacitated, and I wasn't far off. I tried to call but never got through as the line had been disconnected. I received a call from a lawyer, the managing partner in Arnel Law Group in Dedham, Massachusetts. He asked me to come to his office one day and of course I asked why. He told me that would all be disclosed when I got there but that I would find the talk very interesting. He didn't say anything else and I went down there on the day he said to come. I met with him and another gentleman, very distinguished-looking man with a British accent. The attorney from the Arnel firm left the room and allowed me and the other man, also an attorney, to talk. He asked if I remembered the man I had helped all those years ago, I said yes, I remembered very well and that I missed talking to him and wondered what had happened. He represented the man and removed a sheaf of documents from his briefcase.

"Carlo, there was no way I was prepared for what he told me. It was the gentleman's last will and testament, a trust actually, and this man left me everything he had. You know those cars in the garage, they were his. He had property, money, you name it. After he died one night in his sleep, his attorney, the man I was talking to, liquidated everything except for the cars because during one of our conversations we had talked about cars. We both loved classic performance cars. My old friend did that, as he didn't want me to have to go through all the trouble and legalities of selling everything. He put the money in accounts for me in the Cayman Islands and several other countries, which had very secret banking laws, planned everything very carefully. I had to sign a nondisclosure agreement that I would never divulge the source of the funds. I signed it."

"So what was the bottom line, you're keeping me in suspense?"

"He wouldn't say until I had signed the nondisclosure and then he dropped it on me like a bomb…the man left me thirty-six million dollars! I almost passed out. I couldn't believe it. The attorney said his client put the money in those secret banking havens, so the greedy government couldn't get their hands on any portion of it. The man thought a lot like me when it came to the government. The attorney gave me the contacts in the Caymans and other places and the name of a very trusted money-managing firm. You, my friend, are the first and last person I will ever tell, not even my son knew."

"Sly, I'm speechless, and you know that is definitely not like me. All the years I've known you, I had no idea. I mean, what do you do with it, besides invest, move it here and there, and obviously all this?" I asked meaning the bunker and such.

"I made up my mind to help those that didn't stand a chance, like my guys, and other gifted kids. But that doesn't make me a pushover or a softy; I wanted to pay it forward because of what he did for me. You know that or better know it. I've anonymously put more than a few kids through college that were very, very bright, attended their graduations at Ivy League colleges, set them up with a little something to help them get started on brilliant careers. All without them knowing, and I told Brit she could go to school, all she had to do was ask, but I guess she's happy just doin' what she's doin'. As you well know by now, I bought a lot of toys for myself. I make more on the invested money than I can spend so the principle keeps growing too."

"But the guns?"

"I have all the proper licenses for them if you can believe that. I collect very discretely, mostly private sales, but I also go through Mass Firearms and they are strictly by the book. The owner is a real stand-up guy. You know me, got to keep some mystery in my life. And I have gathered a lot of information on important people here, so yes, I do have them on a very big hook. Photos, recordings, transactions, trysts, you name it. I know a lot of good people and a few not so good ones. But you, Carlo, I've come to love and respect like a brother, and unlike most people you never asked me for anything other than to help you with one of your capers which I have enjoyed immensely. The reason I've looked stressed is because I didn't know how or if I should tell you. This all brought it to a head. You know how to put two and two together and had I showed you all this before, well, let's just say I'm glad you know now."

"I was a bit overwhelmed when I first saw it and with all that was going down, I didn't have time to think the backstory and just took your word on it. But you're good with all the stuff we are doing and about to do cuz that's a little more than crossing the line? Your guys are deep into this too."

"Look, man, it's the action keeping me alive. I could go live on some tropical island with a bunch of native girls catering to my every need for a minute, sipping on exotic drinks with tiny umbrellas in them, but that would drive me bonkers and I'd be very bored after a time. Besides, it would cost a fortune to get Booker's out there, unless you brought it! I like having my fingers on the pulse of the city and the people in it. If I want something I know where to get it and if I don't, I know people who I can go to. The Lady is a good woman and so is her sister, so we do what we gotta do."

"You don't feel bad about De'Londo?"

"Nope, I gave him more than anyone that works for me, and they have had tremendous opportunities. Some took advantage of them and others didn't. You know I said this before, but De'Londo stabbed us all in the back and someone who betrays family isn't worth my help any longer. He got what he deserved."

"My brother from another mother, you are a real enigma.

Come on, let's get us a big sip so the others don't think we got some man crush thing going on." We both laughed and walked out of his room. And yes, both men were like brothers to one another.

"Oh, what a tangled web we weave, when first we practice to deceive!"

Walter Scott

———

We exited the room shaking our heads and laughing and went back into the dining area. Some were still seated at the table talking and others were watching television or online. They saw a different Sly when he walked out, one that didn't look ten years older than the man that went into the bedroom to deal with you know who. Everyone was smart enough not to ask anything and figured all was good when they saw his mood had changed. I grabbed a couple of magnums of champagne, got glasses, and poured some for everyone.

Dave asked, "What's the occasion?"

"Well, let's just say we are toasting to good fortune." Glasses clinked and we all drank up.

CHAPTER SEVENTY-ONE

DATE NIGHT

TOTI HAD MADE SURE THAT TOLE'S BMW SHINED LIKE A mirror and there didn't appear to be a speck of dust on the expensive car. He knew Tole would want to be able to see his reflection in the metal well enough that he could use it to shave. Tole's was intact but Toti's did not fare as well from the other night when they were shot at; in fact, it was absolutely a useless piece of junk. But Tole's interior had been completely cleaned and the minibar was stocked.

The sidewalls of the tires shined a glistening black from the Armor All that had been applied, and the black rims were polished to perfection. Tole wanted tonight to reek of money and the finer things in life and did not want to leave one stone unturned. He donned a black Armani suit for which he had been fitted at the Armani Boutique across from Trump Tower in New York. He topped off the suit jacket with a red silk pocket square with green and white accents. Under the jacket he wore a white shirt that fit him like a glove, showing off his massive physique, and he left the top three buttons undone. He wasn't big on jewelry but put on a gold necklace with a double-headed eagle like the tattoo he bore on his right forearm. Lastly, he slipped on a white pair of $600 Gucci loafers bearing the red and green signature stripe. The big man looked like he had just stepped out of *GQ Magazine* and with a spray or two of Creed Pure White cologne he was ready to go. He texted Chloe that he was on his way and would pick her up at the same place down the street from the apartment.

Chloe texted him back saying she would be ready by the time he got there and was very excited, couldn't wait to see him again. With the money that Alban had left her, she was able to find a very hot-looking black dress that fit her like a second skin. She had gone to her favorite nail shop and got her nails done with silk-dip bright red powder—fingers and toes—and topped it off with her open-toed stilettos she rarely wore. But tonight was one of those nights.

She dispensed with panties as she didn't want a panty line showing but chose a black push-up bra that complimented the neckline of the dress. She may not have a lot of money, but she had fashion and style sense. She even splurged on a bottle of Coco Chanel Intense, which she luckily found on sale, and sprayed it sparingly in the most intimate parts of her body with a little extra between her cleavage. The night was warm, so she didn't need a coat but if it cooled, she was sure Alban would find a way to keep her warm.

She grabbed a black clutch from her closet and tossed in the leftover cash, her phone, her fake ID, and a small makeup bag. She wanted so badly to show Alban that she was worthy of the new life he had hinted at.

Her mom and grandmother saw her and asked where she was going, and she told them she was meeting a few friends out for some drinks and would be home late. "So, Mom, how do I look?"

"Beautiful as always, that dress compliments that perfect figure I am so jealous of!" her mom said with a smile. She loved her daughter dearly and couldn't help seeing herself as a young girl in Chloe.

"Thank you, Mom, and I got this figure from you, you know! You've showed me pictures of you from when you were my age, and Gram too. Now you and Gram behave yourselves, and no parties or men in the house!" she said and walked out the door.

Her mom and gram got a good laugh out of her last comment as it had been a while since either of them had been with a man. Chloe had no idea that that would come true, not for them but for her. As she walked to the corner to meet Tole, a few of the young bucks in the neighborhood made a few catcalls and told her the party was here. One of them called out, "Come on, girl, bring that sexy azz over here and give us a taste! I got somethin' for you right here," as he grabbed at his crotch. When the BMW Alpina B7 pulled up and they saw the big man get out and hold the door for her, you could have heard a pin drop. Tole just glared at the boys. The boys' jaws dropped, both seemed almost frozen where they stood.

She went up and gave Tole a hug and a kiss, told him how handsome he looked, and he pushed her back to arm's length and said, "Let my eyes drink you in, you look absolutely stunning." She gave the big man another kiss and got into the expensive car. She flipped off the boys as Toti pulled away.

So far so good, he thought. The boys just stared as the car pulled from the curb.

They got settled in the car and Tole asked her if she would like a drink, vodka of course. She replied, "Do you need to see my ID?" in a very sensual way.

"Only if you think I need too, *zuske.*"

"May I have it on the rocks with a little lime please, as it would be so refreshing with this warm weather," Chloe responded trying her best to sound so sophisticated.

"Certainly." Tole knew she was feeding right into his hand.

"When we go to New York will you teach me to speak Albanian? I've never been there but read so much about it, the restaurants, the shows, museums and galleries!" She had spoken like a woman who seemed much more culturally experienced.

"Most certainly, especially before I take you to meet my mother. You would have her heart in no time."

"Really, I would like that, and where would we live?" she said as the car pulled up to the front of Strega.

Tole answered before exiting the car, "I have the perfect place for you, my dove." Tole did not tell her it wasn't with him.

The parking valet opened the double glass doors and from the moment they walked in Strega, they were treated like royalty, just the impression that Tole had wanted to project. The host, Phil, asked if they had a seating preference and Alban asked if they could dine in private.

"Sir, that will not be a problem and I am able to afford you the luxury of a private room, it should prove to be quite romantic. It is usually reserved for private parties, but I have no problem giving it to you."

Tole replied, "You are most generous, my friend." He shook his hand and slid him two one-hundred dollar bills. It was a small outlay as he intended to pay for the meal with a stolen card.

Phil knew this man wasn't going to spend chump change and he took care of them like he did all his best customers. He assigned his best waiter to the room telling him to treat the man and the young lady like royalty. Phil knew that the elaborate bouquet of two dozen roses was for the young lady and brought them in to her along with two of his special drink shots he reserved for his best customers.

Phil handed Chloe the roses and said, "These are for you, young lady, a special gift."

No man had ever sent, let alone presented her with roses at a restaurant, and Chloe couldn't help but have tears appear in her eyes.

"Thank you so much, you have no idea what this means to me. You are the first man to ever send me flowers." She got out of her seat, sat on the big man's lap, hugged him, and kissed him passionately. Chloe was completely captivated by her supposed *nouvel amant*, new lover.

Phil waited a moment before he set the drinks down and toasted the young lady. Tole and Chloe raised the shot glasses, clinked them against Phil's, and drank them down. No one bothered to ask Chloe for her ID and Tole thanked him for the courtesy with a knowing nod.

The waiter appeared after Phil left and asked if they needed anything else at the moment and Tole asked for a bottle of Jewel of Russia Ultra vodka. The waiter, David, said, "I will check on that right away, sir, and by the way, such a great selection." It was one of the best Russia had to offer, and Tole loved a great vodka. Besides, it would mix well with the Ecstasy.

While they waited for David to return, Chloe and Alban browsed the appetizer menu and Chloe chose the Fragole E Pere salad and Tole the Scallops Grand Marnier. David returned with the bottle of vodka requested by Tole. He also set two rocks glasses on the table and asked if ice was needed. Tole declined the ice and David poured the rocks glasses half full of the top shelf vodka. Chloe was beginning to flush, but he did not want her too wasted before dinner and told her to sip slowly. Tole then placed an order for appetizers for both of them and told Chloe he would share the scallops as they were excellent.

She asked, "So not drink like the other night? You know what it does to me, makes me want you, but I really don't think I need vodka for that. I crave you already."

"I want you to enjoy your dinner, the food is excellent here, so please go slow, plenty of time for other things when we leave," he said smiling.

She sipped the vodka as Tole instructed her and she had a wanton look in her eyes. She wanted him all to herself, to be his one and only, and if she had any say in the matter that's the way it would be.

David arrived back about ten minutes later with the appetizers and placed the dishes on the table, poured a little more vodka, and asked if they needed a few more minutes before they ordered. Tole said they were ready and he ordered the Veal Chop Parmigiana for Chloe and the Bone-in Ribeye for himself.

"Very excellent choices, sir, and how would you like the ribeye done, sir?" and Tole responded, "Rare, please."

"Yes, sir, I'll get both those orders in right away."

Chloe was overly impressed not only with the restaurant but with Alban. She could see herself getting lost in his lifestyle and wanted desperately for something more than Victoria's restaurant and home. The two of them talked about their lives or lack thereof, of course Alban lied about his with a straight face. He painted a picture of himself as a businessman that had outlets in filmmaking, pharmaceuticals, and sporting goods—in other words human trafficking, drugs, and guns. Chloe took it all in, never once disbelieving him. Enthralled with all of it would have been a gross understatement.

David brought the meals to the table and had Alban cut into his steak to make sure it was cooked to perfection. As Tole cut into it, the blood began to run out and Tole said it was perfect. David said, "If there is anything you need please let me know and enjoy your meals." He topped off the glasses of vodka and backed away from the table. Phil, being the great host he was, had also checked on the table several times making sure Tole and the young girl were thoroughly catered to. Chloe was blown away seeing how the "other half" lived, and it was a life she craved for herself and eventually her daughter. She wanted to break out from her meager existence and be someone that people looked up to. She wanted to send her daughter to the best school, a chance that she had blown, and dress her little girl in the finest clothes.

After they had eaten Chloe excused herself to go to the ladies' room, and Tole knew this was the perfect opportunity to slip the Ecstasy into Chloe's unfinished drink. After she left the private room Tole pulled the drug from his pocket, placed it in the drink, and stirred until it had all dissolved. In another fifteen minutes she wouldn't care who did what to her.

Tole had David bring the check while she was still away and gave him the fraudulent card he was carrying. He would dispose of it tomorrow, as it would no longer be any good. Tole left a sizable tip for David in cash and had another several hundred for Phil that he would give him on the way out.

Chloe finally came back to the table and Tole had her down the last of her vodka. As Tole had bought the bottle, he had it placed in a bag to take with him. He had already texted Toti to have the car in front and Tole took Chloe's arm ready to walk out. He talked to Phil one last time and made a big deal of everything, more to impress Chloe than Phil. Phil was used to it and took it all in stride. Phil accompanied them to the front door, held the door and gave one last good night and thank you, giving Tole his personal business card should he need his services again. The valet was ready with the rear passenger door of the expensive BMW open, and Tole gave the young man a twenty, probably the largest tip he had received all week or month.

"I'm feeling so warm, is that the vodka or are you making me feel this way?" she asked.

"Probably a little of both but who knows. Would you like to see where I am working this week and meet some of my men?"

"Whatever you want, my babykins," she answered as the

drugs were most definitely kicking in. "Will we get to have some fun tonight?"

"Oh, we are definitely going to have some fun, you wait and see, my princess." Tole continued his act of making her feel special.

Toti had already contacted the warehouse and when they turned down Topeka, the one remaining functioning overhead, fourth door from the west side, rose up. Toti also instructed the men to conceal their weapons so the girl wouldn't lose her good vibes.

CHAPTER SEVENTY-TWO

RAPE NIGHT

"So this is where you work?" Chloe asked seeming a little disoriented and slurring her speech now that the drug had begun to work. Toti parked the top end BMW in the warehouse and held the door for both Tole and the girl. "What do you do here?" she asked and began to be very touchy-feely with Tole one of the side effects of the drug.

"We make movies here. Would you like to be in a movie?"

"I'd love that, will it make me famous, my love?" She was getting to the point where she could barely stand without Tole's assistance and it was just the way he wanted it.

"Most certainly it will, in certain circles that is. It will get you much work when we go to New York."

"Okay, what do I need to do and who else is in it with me? I want to make this movie with you." She was completely clueless and helpless at this point and would do as Tole asked.

"Remember what we did last night, my *zuske*?"

"Oh my God, yes how could I forget! That was the absolute best," the girl answered but slurred badly.

"Okay, let's go upstairs and you and I will start the acting and the others—remember I asked you the other night about them—well, they will join in. It will give them all pleasure and I am sure it will be wonderful for you too! Remember you said, 'if that's what I wanted,' and it is."

"Bring it on, big boy, anything you ask," she said again under the effects of the Ecstasy.

Tole had let his men know ahead of time that he wanted it recorded with a camera but not on one of their phones, as he didn't want evidence around that was not in his control. The "documenter" was already upstairs, and Tole and Chloe came up. A bed had been prepared and restraints were placed on the four corners. Tole also had one of his men, Zeni, load several syringes with high-grade heroin ahead of time so when the MDMA started to wear off in about three hours, they would start with the low doses to keep her helpless and high. It was obvious the girl no longer had a chance to back out and the men were bulging in their trousers.

Tole whispered in her ear, "Like last night, I want to restrain you and then rip your clothes off. It gets me so excited."

"Yes, please, I want you now, I'm ready."

Tole strapped her to the bed and ripped off the dress she had so carefully picked out and she gasped in delight at the violence of the act. As Tole stripped, she saw that the other men were doing the same, and with the last bit of clarity in her head she realized what she was in for.

She began a weak protest, "No, please, no, not all of them, just you, baby." Tole then plunged into her and the clarity ran from her, hiding far away, deep inside her.

One after another, the men took multiple turns with her using every opening her small body had to offer. None of them were gentle as they ravaged her, some took her two at a time, and all she could do was whimper. When she tried to resist, she was met with a hard slap. Her vaginal and anal tissue were traumatized from the repeated abuse, and she started to bleed along with the cuts from being hit. When they all had their fill about three hours later, Zeni injected her with the first shot of heroin and she nodded out. She no longer felt pain and drifted off into the haze of the drug. That first high was so incredible, but it made her slightly nauseous.

When Chloe started to come out of her nod, the brutality was repeated over and over, along with the injections, until a rising sun started to light the morning sky. His men were left physically spent and sleeping, more so from the vodka than the numerous times they had been "pleasured," and they couldn't care less about the damage they caused to the girl both mentally and physically.

She laid there uncovered in the chilly warehouse, shivering and coated with the seed of the men, dripping from her inside and out, adding to the chill of the air. One of the men, she couldn't remember who, not that she could have, saw her shaking as he staggered about the upper level of the warehouse, and with some slight bit of compassion threw a blanket over her. "There you go, *zuske*." She was beginning to understand that *zuske* did not mean dove.

By midmorning, Tole and Valmir's men began to stir and pull themselves together.

Chloe began to whimper in pain, both from the withdrawal and the injuries received the night before. She called out for help, not necessarily for rescue but just for the pain to stop, and Tole had Zeni inject her again with the heroin. It dulled the pain and stopped her whining as half the men left the warehouse and headed to a different place to eat. Tole was smart, he didn't want anyone to associate Chloe missing with their appearance at the restaurant. They had made enough of a spectacle of themselves with her when they were in there and they couldn't take that chance.

While she was still nodded out, three of the men picked her up, took her downstairs, and sprayed her with a hose to remove the accumulated blood and other coagulated substances. The cold jets of water caused her body to jerk and start to shiver. The cold spray somewhat awakened her from the drug-induced nod, but she went right back into it once the water was no longer spraying her. They dried her then took her back upstairs. One of the three put clean bedding on the bed while the other two helped her upright and then tossed her on the bed, covered her, and once again she was restrained.

Tole got back shortly after they had finished cleaning her up and asked if she was with it or needed another shot. They said she was all good and just coming out of a nod. "All right, you all go get something to eat but not at Victoria's," Tole mentioned as a reminder. "When you get back you can have some more fun with her."

When that time came, Chloe lay there helpless as the men's lust was taken out on her all through the rest of that day. The heroin did its job and by late afternoon she begged for the drug which Zeni dutifully and willingly gave her. Her weakened body began to crave the pure drug as it coursed through her veins, and she was on a downward spiral to addiction.

———

Chloe had never stayed out all night before and her mother began to get worried. Her mom had called her phone more times than she cared to think about, and eventually the phone just went to voice mail letting Chloe's mom know the battery had died out. She knew her daughter had a morning shift at the restaurant, and she called there looking to find out if Chloe had reported for work.

The manager told her he had not heard from her and had to call in another girl and that Chloe should call him when she got the message.

As the morning turned into afternoon and then into evening, she still had not heard from Chloe and called the police. Of course, the police asked all the right questions, what was she wearing, where did she go, who was she with, friends' names, etc.

Two patrol officers stopped by and took a written report to file back at the station along with a picture her mom had given them. It was all her mom could do to hold back the tears while giving the information to the two uniforms. All her mom could tell the officers was what she had been wearing and that she was going with friends and didn't know their names. In fact, her mom didn't really know any of Chloe's friends as Chloe was a homebody for the most part, or at work. The police asked if she thought her daughter had been abducted or having trouble with anyone like a boyfriend, and her mom had no idea. But as that statement registered, a chill ran through her, one that caused her to fear for her daughter's safety. "She's a good girl, never gives me any trouble, and she's a good mom too, please find her," Chloe's mom begged.

So Chloe's mom prayed for her daughter's safety and had she been abducted she feared the worst—that her daughter could be the victim of human trafficking. It was always in the news with victims found dead, or news of a lucky one that had managed to escape. Ads were prevalent on adult websites letting girls know where they could go for help, but for the most part, these young boys and girls were kept captive in primitive conditions and loaded up on drugs so they would do the bidding of their masters. These girls and boys were sold and traded like animals on the dark web on websites such as the now shutdown Silk Road using bitcoin for currency which couldn't be traced. And when these kids were used up, they were put out of their retched existence without so much as a blink of an eye to die alone.

Chloe's mom held out hope that she was sleeping off a bad hangover and her little girl would be home soon. It was all she had to hold onto and all she could pray for.

———

Chloe's eyes looked lifeless, staring out into a vast nothingness, lost to the present as the men repeatedly had their way with her. She felt the very urge to fight drained completely out of her, replaced by the overwhelming, compelling desire for the white powder they injected every few hours. She was broken, and even if she was rescued, doubted she could ever be fixed. She thought of her own daughter, the only conscious thought she had, growing up without her real mom and wondered if she would ever see the little girl again. It was almost like a voice you hear in the distance, through a fog and never quite being able to pinpoint where it was coming from. Chloe imagined the pain her mother and gram would feel if they never saw her again. She had been naïve to trust this man, this man that gave her hope for something better but lured her into a life she wouldn't wish on her worst enemy. She should have known he was nothing but a pig the first day at the restaurant when he had groped her and then paid her like a whore with big tips, and for their one-night tryst at the hotel. She would have been treated better by the boys on the block, they just wanted some, not to own her, not to do this to her.

She felt the sting of the needle once again as it punctured her vein, and the warming sensation of the drug engulfed her body again. Her eyes rolled back into her head and Chloe passed out, escaping the prison she was now in, and for a short time escaping the jeering and lewd comments and actions of her captors. The day began to fade like her consciousness, growing ever dimmer, and with the waning day so were her dreams of salvation.

CHAPTER SEVENTY-THREE

THE LADY SINGS THE BLUES

WE HAD ALL GATHERED AS WE DID EVERY OTHER MORNING since we had been in town. Breakfast had a bit different attitude among the men, as tonight was the night we would hit the Albanians. We knew this was our last chance to make sure all our weapons and tactics were nailed down with no room for error or Mr. Murphy. More rounds were fired, magazines loaded with rounds for the operation, guns cleaned, and all equipment checked and double-checked. It was the way these guys operated and brought me up a notch or two in tactics. I never professed to be a know-it-all and I learned all I could from these operators while I could. It may save my life tonight. We all were aware that any one of us could end up not coming out of this alive, but it was a chance we took with life every day. We knew for certain that some of us were going to get hurt; it was the nature of the game and the odds we accepted. Knowing what Sly had stockpiled, I knew we were better equipped, but who knows what surprises they may have. Hopefully we had an element of surprise and overwhelming force. As General George Patton would say, "A good plan violently executed now is better than a perfect plan executed next week." Today was our now.

Lady accepted under protest that she would not be part of the entry team and that was more than fine by me. She had no clue what it was like to be shot at, let alone take a round even with body armor, and "untutored courage is useless in the face of educated bullets" (General Patton). We all had at least some combat experience and there was no sense in letting rookies get caught in a situation they couldn't handle. Just the noise alone is enough to rattle even tested men. Even Sly's men and Ritchie would be delegated to getting those injured away from the scene and to the club, but they would all be armed, nevertheless. You never go to a gunfight without at least one gun; forget the knife.

Jake would have a last briefing later just before we rolled, so while we had time, we all did what we had to do to get ready. Some prayed, some wrote last notes to loved ones to be opened if they didn't make it, others sat in silence, and some joked around to dispel their pre-game jitters. We all had our superstitions and beliefs, like a baseball player wearing the same socks without washing them if he were on a streak. But I felt we were better armed, better trained, and more capable to complete the task at hand, and tonight would tell if I was right or wrong. Hopefully it would prove to be the former.

Lady came up to me, grabbed my hand, and just said, "Come with me." She led me to what I now considered our room, locked the door behind us, and we crawled up on the bed. I knew this wasn't for playtime by reading her nonverbal cues, nor was I expecting that.

"We need to talk and there are things I need to say to you before you go out there for me tonight. I don't know what all has happened this week...you, me, falling in love, my God and making love, these feelings. I don't know what will happen when this is all over. I know you have your life here in Boston, mine is in New York, and I wouldn't ask you to change that for the world. I have a lot to do with my business, I travel and quite frankly, I don't need an anchor, someone attached to my hip. I do my thing and if you want to be part of that thing, you have to accept that. Carlo, I do believe I love you, and I believe you love me too. You can travel with me, we can share time together here and in New York, but I'm not the typical woman who stays home and cooks and cleans and watches TV for hours on end. What I'm trying to say is I would love to have you in my life but on my terms."

I pressed my first two fingers to her lips and, she stopped talking. "I get it, I know the kind of life you have. We walk life down two very different paths. If you wanted, I could move down there, head up your security, or just be semiretired and play in the marvelous kitchen you must have while you do your thing. I don't have to do this anymore. These guys, I love them all. They came here for me and I would do the same for them, but I fell for you, hard. So, if you have room for me, I would like that. I need my time too and when I'm here, your sis will keep an eye on me for you and so will Sly, they're my family. I just always want to know where I stand with you, nothing more, nothing less, that's the only rule I have. Besides, it's only a five-hour drive to New York."

"If something happens to you tonight when you raid that place, my heart would be crushed. If you die, this would all be for nothing. There would be a void in my life that only you could fill, and I don't want to lose you," she continued.

"Look, baby girl, these people I'll be with are top-notch, you know that from sitting in on our meetings. Besides, I'll stand behind Tsuji, and I'll never get hit," I said with a smile. "I just want to kill the fucker Tole. I would love to send his head back to New York."

"Wow, no one's called me baby girl in a long, long time." She laughed at my Tsuji comment. "And you better make sure he comes back safe too or I'll whoop that white ass of yours!"

"Maybe cuz you wouldn't have stood for someone calling you that, baby girl?"

She shook her head with all those beautiful curls and a tear ran down her face.

"What's wrong?"

"You just get to me, I don't know how you do it. Just please don't die out there tonight." She didn't say another word. Her body shook as she cried, and we held one another and laid there in whatever peace we could find.

CHAPTER SEVENTY-FOUR

THE LAST SUPPER

SLY AND BRIT WERE THE COOKING TEAM FOR THE NIGHT, and they didn't let us down. Prime cut fillet mignon wrapped in bacon, lobster tails fresh caught that day with drawn butter, baked potatoes with anything you could ever want on them, sautéed mushrooms, grilled asparagus and broccoli, and for dessert, what else but homemade Boston cream pie! Sly and Brit had been just as busy as we were while on the range. Tonight's meal would have to forgo drinks and wine as we all needed to be as sharp as possible. It was a small sacrifice and if we all made it back in one piece, we could get drunk on our ass if we chose.

We all made the best of the situation and made small talk around the dinner table. Dave asked Sly, "You cook this because it's our last supper? You thinking we all ain't coming back? Just sayin'."

"Well, I'm not Jesus Christ and I don't see any of you with an extra thirty pieces of silver, and if that were the case there are no Judas's here. We took care of the last one, so the element of surprise should be on our side. Eat up and enjoy while you can and pray that there may be more," Sly responded, even though he knew Dave meant it as a joke.

When dinner finally finished, Sly and Brit cleared the table as they knew Jake and J3 would need it to plan strategy. Sly had his own work to do tonight and that was to get the staff in to get a makeshift hospital set up, plus he had one very important call to make before the crew headed out. He and his men had cleared enough space up above to make sure there was sufficient room. He had all his men certified in first aid and basic life support because you never knew what might jump off in the club. They would be a big help to Doc if the occasion arose. He and Brit would be on the phone and Doc Glen would get a few more experienced people he knew he might need to patch us up.

———

Sly hit number three on his phone as it was the speed dial setting for the commissioner. The mayor was number two and I was graced with number one. Numbers four through six were reserved for his lawyers should and when the time came that he needed them. They always took Sly's calls. Money was a tremendous motivating factor.

The commissioner answered on the first ring, excused himself from the family dinner table, and walked into his study.

"Good evening, Sly, am I being overly optimistic?"

"No, you are not. I want to give you a sitrep for tonight. I will call you when they get to the location and I will call you when they are gone. Are we clear on the route I want? That it will not be blocked off if it comes to that?"

"Sly, you know those are on main routes. Those would normally be the roads we would block, especially South Hampton."

"Sir, by the time your guys get there and find the mess we leave them, your commanders can make their decision, but by then we will be home free. It's not like this is going down in broad daylight at a shopping mall. And I'm guessing there won't be anyone around to call the cops in the first place. There won't be any witnesses to give descriptions, the bad guys aren't gonna tell, you can count on that because dead men tell no tales. You keep monitoring communication and if things start to get hot you let me know and we boogie. Just make sure we have a way out."

Sly hit the end button on his cell, placed it back in his pocket, and scratched one item off his list of things to do.

———

Jake and J3 pulled maps up on the sixty-five-inch monitor on the wall. "Okay, here's what we now know. There's a good chance that all the doors except this one, fourth from the west side of the building, are welded shut. Max and Mike were able to observe some big heat signatures inside and I don't think they're roasting weenies."

OMG, if they only knew!

"There's also the chance that they have the other two man-doors secured too. Here is what we do. Max, you will be on the roof and on my cue, you will take out the power. My team will be positioned on the west side of the building. J3, your team, as we discussed, will take the back of the building after we take out the lights. Your team will use the detcord to take down the door and then use the flash bangs before entry. Once inside, deploy more flash bangs into the main area of the warehouse as we hit the one usable overhead with more detcord. My team will hit them with more flash bangs as we enter.

"J3, your guys will stay in the office area until we are all in, take out anyone that pops their head up. Once we are in and have cover you follow with your team. Max will stay on the roof to provide cover until we are clear. Remember, Tole is Carlo's, don't kill him. Max, when we're ready to extract, you will have a car of your own to get back to the bunker. Don't wait, just go. We have one clear route and that is down South Hampton to Dorchester Ave. We will have twenty minutes at most to wrap this up. Drivers, once you drop us off you will stage at the Greater Boston Food Bank on South Bay. Once we're in the warehouse you will advance to the east side of the building and wait. It's your job to get any injured back to the club and to get us out. If this is quick, we all come out together and get the fuck out of Dodge. Doc, his team, and the rest of Sly's guys will be standing by to render medical treatment. Any questions?"

One of Sly's other guys asked, "Who are the drivers?"

"The drivers are Reshaun, Khaseem, Marcus, Cedric, and Ritchie. Cedric, you will be driving Max and you stay with him. Are we all clear on that?"

Khaseem asked, "Will there be medical kits in the cars?"

"Good question, we have that all covered. You drivers all had training so if need be use it."

"Who's riding with who? Looks like we got a Dirty Dozen," Mike said.

"Okay, listen up, here are the car assignments. Reshaun will drive J3, Sal, Bobby, and Dave. You all have the back door and remember, too much detcord is not a bad thing. Khaseem, you have yours truly, Brando, Mike, and Miss Gina. Ritchie, if you would, take Carlo, Lady Tatiana, and Tsuji, and do not let Lady Tatiana out of the car."

"I got it, I don't like it, but I will stay in the car, but I want to see Tole die."

"We will see if we can make that wish come true for you," responded Jake.

"What time do we go?" someone asked.

"We leave here at 0140 and be on set at 0200. The fireworks start then. Men, we all good to go, gear ready?"

Affirmatives were given all around.

CHAPTER SEVENTY-FIVE

Boom, Boom Out Go the Lights

"We few, we happy few, we band of brothers; or he today that sheds his blood with me shall be my brother."

— SHAKESPEARE HENRY V, ACT 4, SCENE 3

TOLE NO LONGER HAD ANY DESIRE FOR THE NOW-ADDICTED girl, and he continued to allow his men to use her well into the night. With the distractions of the vodka and the girl, most of the men had forgotten about security as had Tole. They were prancing about like young boys seeing a naked woman for the first time, and most with barely any clothing on if any, awaiting their next turn at the badly abused girl. Zeni had remained somewhat coherent as he was in charge of keeping the girl sedated and Tole's wrath was not worth him screwing up and giving her an OD. It would have been a loss of income for them all and likely the loss of his life.

———

Chloe had no idea how many times she had been taken, she was beyond feeling or caring. She just felt pressure of the men inside her and on top of her, nothing more. Death would have been preferable to this. This torture she endured was a slow, degrading death, the skag was there to keep her from thinking about it and she almost hoped that Zeni would give her a little too much and it would all end.

———

"This just in on News 7. Tonight, police are searching for a nineteen-year-old girl by the name of Chloe O'Malley from South Boston. She was last seen leaving her home that she shares with her mother, grandmother, and baby daughter. Her mother states that she left last night to meet friends and did not show for her shift this morning at Victoria's Diner. She was last seen wearing a black dress and heels. The Boston Police request anyone with information of her whereabouts to call."

A picture of the girl had appeared during the news alert along with the number for the Boston Police call center.

———

We were all geared up, body armor and night vision on, and waiting for the clock to tick 0140 hours. When the second hand swept to the twelve for the last time, Jake said, "Let's roll it up and go to war."

The drivers were waiting in the vehicles as we loaded in and Jake gave the command, "Let's go!" One by one the vehicles pulled out of the bunker, turned right onto Dorchester, and headed to South Hampton. For some reason it gets eerily silent on the way to a mission. I guess it's the way everyone was able to focus, but I knew at least it was that way for me.

The Lady held my hand, her eyes all misty with the occasional tear that ran down her face. But when I tried to wipe them away, she pushed my hand aside and said, "Let me feel it, Carlo, let me feel those tears burn into me." I remained silent and continued to hold her hand. It was as reassuring for me as it was for her.

The convoy rolled down Dorchester and took the left on South Hampton. When we got to Cummings Street, Reshaun took a right and stopped about one hundred yards from the back of the warehouse as he didn't want to risk setting off the motion sensors and tipping our hand. J3 and his crew bailed out and Bobby pulled out the bolt cutters opening a hole into the chain-link fence. The four of them piled through the cut fence and crept to within twenty-five yards of the southwest corner of the building. Reshaun shot down to the end of Cummings Street and parked in front of the Boston Food Bank as directed.

Cedric kept going straight before banging a right turn on Atkinson, parked in tight to the Trico building, grabbed the rope ladder out of the back, and helped Max set it up. Max threw the hook up and over and pulled the slack out of the line. The grappling hook held tight and Max headed up to the roof. He set up his silenced .300 Winchester Mag and started scoping the area. "Jake, you're not gonna believe this but it looks like they are having some kinda party. Half these guys are barely dressed, man, this is off the hook."

"You say they're partying?"

"Affirmative, that's the way it looks to me."

J3 chimed in, "We can hear music from our position."

"Roger that. Looks like this might be easier than we thought."

Ritchie and Khaseem had followed Reshaun down Atkinson Street and doubled back to Cummings. "All right, everyone out. Ritchie and Khaseem, go back down Atkinson and park up next to Reshaun. Once we breach, pull up near the northeast corner of the building and be ready to take casualties back to the club. Everyone good?" We were all good to go. "My team, through the hole in the fence and then over to the machinery parked near the northwest. Mike, you got our six."

One by one, me, Gina, Jake, Brando, Tsuji, and then Mike came through the opening in the fence and we trotted over to the front loader. "When Max takes out the power, we hit the corner of the building and then up to that fourth door, set the detcord and throw in flash bangs. We all ready?"

I said, "Let's get it done."

"Max, we are all in position, take out the power."

"Roger that." We heard a muted cough as the 300 magnum round hit the transformer and resulted in a shower of sparks. "Lights out, Boss."

We made our way to the corner of the building and Jake ordered J3's team, "Take out the rear door now!" Sal pushed the button on the ignition for the charge and a blast ripped the night air. The door flew inward and smacked full force into one of Valmir's men. Two flash bangs were tossed in the "hole" and the Albanian had no clue where he was and couldn't hear a thing. He finally made it up, stumbled, falling, to the opposite door and as he opened it Max opened up his head with another supersonic round. He never heard the round coming. Flash bangs went off in the main area of the warehouse and the rest of the men were now running around like chickens with their heads cut off. They were disoriented from the series of flash bangs and couldn't see or hear let alone find their guns or weapons.

"J3, what's the status?"

"They have no idea what is going on. They are running all over the place and we have not taken any fire."

"Lay down suppressive fire and take out who you can. We're going for the overhead."

"10-4. Jake, someone just got in the BMW and it looks like they may try to get out."

"Max, you see any movement?"

"Negative, wait, garage door going up. J3, stay down, I'm gonna hit the gas tank with an explosive round."

"Everybody down," J3 yelled at his team. They all hit the ground as ordered.

The BMW started to back up but was hit directly in the gas tank and two explosions ensued, the round and then the tank. A large fireball erupted frying whoever was in the car, his cries for help lost in the noise and confusion as the flames licked his burning body. The force of the explosion lifted the back end of the luxury car off the ground, and those that could see it watched it teeter on its nose before falling back down right-side up. When the tank went it sent a large, rolling, licking tongue of flame through the now open overhead causing Jake and crew to hit the ground.

"Let's go, showtime!" Jake ordered and we all piled through the door, weapons hot, and J3's team was laying down lead.

Zeni, the more coherent of Tole's men, grabbed an AK, drew down on us, getting a few rounds off, one of which hit Tsuji in the shoulder. Lucky shot as there wasn't much light and he wasn't wearing NVGs. The big man shook off the hit and stitched Zeni up the center line of his body with 4.6mm rounds from the MP7 that the mountain man carried, tearing Zeni's spine out the back of his body. Zeni fell forward over the railing and landed with a sickening splat when his head hit, cracking like an egg on the concrete floor.

The entire team in the building spread out the width of it and shooting as they went managed to take out anyone that offered resistance or poked their head up at a very unfortunate time. All received one last bullet to the head to make sure they never got up again.

Gina started to ascend the stairs on the south side of the building that led to the second level. She was followed by Mike and Brando. Jake and I took the stairs on the other side. J3, Tsuji, and the rest of his men cleared the lower level and it was like shooting fish in a barrel taking out a handful of the Eastern Europeans. As the Albanians were able to find weapons, we came under sporadic fire, but they couldn't hit what they couldn't see. They never had time to get their night vision on, but nonetheless, Mike and Brando took rounds, the shock absorbed by their vests. Even with the vests, the 7.62mm rounds packed enough punch to knock the wind out of them.

"We're good, we're good, keep going," they both managed, struggling to catch their breath, both down on their knees.

"Let's wrap this up, ten minutes left," Jake called out over the comms. We all knew that wrapping it up was to make sure no one was left to tell tales.

That was when Gina called out, "Hostage, hostage, hostage." She saw the girl laying there naked and blindfolded, filthy from the men's fluids, shaking and scared to death. Gina saw a used syringe on the floor next to the bed. This was the one thing that really set her off. She dropped her empty weapon, brought out her toys, and proceeded to eviscerate three Albanians that were closing in on her. She moved like a whirlwind as they tried to find weapons, watching them drop still alive in bloody piles of their entrails. They tried to scoop them back in, but it was an exercise in futility due to their vital fluids gushing out. They soon fell in lifeless heaps on the floor. We thought we had taken out the rest, as no one was moving.

It was then that the big bad man, Alban Tole, grabbed Gina by the throat. In her rage she didn't see him get up from the floor as she was locked in on the girl. But for that matter neither did any of us. He sprang at her with the speed of a cat. As bad as he thought he was, he had cowered like a little baby when all the shooting started, hiding, lying down next to one of his dead bloodied men. Tole thought she was easy prey and thought wrongly about using her as a bargaining chip for his life.

Brando and Mike leveled their weapons at him, and I yelled out, "Don't shoot, don't shoot, he's all mine."

When Tole grabbed her, she had dropped the knives she had in her clenched fists, she gasped for breath, her hands struggling to break his vice grip as it seeped the strength from her. Gina managed with her last bit of strength to reach her right hand behind her back pulling another knife that was concealed on her and she jammed the knife all the way to the hilt into Tole's left wrist watching it exit on the other side, and then she twisted the blade. Tole let out a shriek, more like a bull elephant's bellow, and dropped her as tendons, ligaments, muscle, and blood vessels were severed. We watched as he pulled the knife from his now useless left hand and started toward her where she had dropped to the ground. She turned and looked toward Chloe and hurried to cut the girl loose. Mike and Brando put rounds at Tole's feet stopping him in his tracks.

"Hey, pig fucker, over here. Remember me?" I yelled at him. He didn't have to look around to see who I was talking to as he was the only one of his now-decimated crew standing and for that matter still alive. All of them either shot, blown up, or gutted. It really didn't matter how, as long as they were all dead. "Come on, big man, you're real tough when you got someone tied up or it's a helpless young girl. Come on, let's finish this because there's no way in hell you're getting the Lady or her business."

Tole turned and glared at me with eyes that spelled death, his breath seething, anger and hatred running from his pores. I could smell the hate that emanated from his body.

Gina stood ready to pounce again but held back as a promise

to me. The look in her eye told me she wanted to gut him from balls to brain, but she had something much more important to tend to. Gina slung the limp girl over her shoulder, grabbed a sheet to cover her, and ran to one of the SUVs. Mike and Brando went with her and Gina called over the comms to Sly, "Get an OB-GYN doctor in there now. We have a badly hurt female hostage."

By now, all the guys were on the upper deck. They were not going to miss this showdown. Tole slowly reached down to the floor and picked up a Remington Tactical pump shotgun. My guys were all eyes on him, weapons at the ready. "Come on, Tole, make sure you got one chambered, cuz it's just you and me, motherfucker, you only get one shot, one chance. Old-fashioned shoot-out. You got your gun, I got mine," signifying the Glock 21 at my hip in a combat rig. "Just like the OK Corral, and you're the last of the Clanton Gang and I'm Wyatt Earp. Boy, how ironic, I just happen to be related to dear ole Wyatt, how do you like that? Whatta ya say, on the count of three?" All of this going out over the comms.

"So you want to play cowboys, huh? You think you're Wyatt Earp? What are you, a little boy?" he taunted barely able to speak through his anger.

"No, Tole, I'm not, real men like me don't need to rape little girls, but yes, I am defending her honor and Lady's. Come on now, times a wastin'," I said as I dropped into a Southern slang.

Lady, hearing all this, could no longer contain herself and she bolted from the Maybach before Ritchie could stop her. He had no choice but to chase after her. She sprinted into the warehouse, her breathing deep with panic and fear as her nostrils filled with the acrid air of gunpowder, detcord, burned gas, and a car with a roasting body inside. Her chest heaved as she tried to gasp for air in the putrid smoky building, trying to scale the stairs to where I was. Ritchie grabbed her before she could get all the way up the stairs telling her she couldn't go up there. She screamed back at him, "Don't tell me I can't go!" and broke free of him, heading to the top of the stairs.

"Come on, Tole, on the count of three, I'll put one hand behind my back to make it fair," I said goading the big man as blood ran out of his arm where Gina had savagely cut him. "J3, give me a count." My weapon was holstered with my hand on the grip, Tole's at his side. J3 counted, "One, two..." Before he could get to three my hand closed down tight on the grip of the handgun, cleared my holster with lightning speed, and I fired. Everything got really slow. I could almost envision the bullet travelling toward Tole, the air being compressed by the tip of the bullet, fanning out like a wake from the bow of a boat, smoke swirling as the bullet cut through it. No sooner had I cleared leather than Tole's shotgun raised up, fired, and a second muzzle flash lit up the room. I was faster, and I saw my round hit him in the center of his forehead as it traveled at 972 feet per second.

He smiled, how odd, and then dropped like a ton of bricks, facedown. Before he hit the ground, the slug fired from his weapon, moving at 1,252 feet per second and caught me square in the chest, hitting the trauma plate to be exact. I heard a crack before I dropped lifelessly to the ground. I don't remember hitting the ground, I felt no pain. The hydrostatic shock of the round had stopped my heart.

Lady reached the top step as I crumpled to the ground, and Jake called out over the comms screaming, "Carlo's hit, Carlo's hit. Evac now!"

She pushed everyone to the side, fell to her knees, screaming at me, "Damn you, Carlo, don't you die on me, don't you dare die. I love you, please don't die." The others tried to pull her away in efforts to resuscitate me, but she cast them off like flies.

"Let's go, get him out, we're out of time," yelled Jake and J3.

Lady began beating on my chest in grief with both hands, unwittingly giving my lifeless body a series of pre-cardial thumps. I watched as if I was out of my body. I could see the mayhem all around. I felt her tears running like rivers down her face onto mine, or the face that was mine. And then I gasped, and as I gasped, I could no longer see myself as I could a split second before. It was as if the gasp had sucked my ethereal being back into me and I couldn't resist the line from *The Gauntlet* when Clint Eastwood responded to Sondra Locke's character, Gus Mally, after she said, "How dare you die on me, Ben Shockley." I muttered just like Clint, "Nag, nag, nag." Man, what a beautiful line!

No sooner had it come out of my mouth and she said, "Oh, sometimes I just hate you! You scared the hell out of me." Then to the others she yelled, "Get him out of here, *now!*" She had one more thing to do before exiting the warehouse. She drew the Glock 19 that she wore on her hip and emptied the full magazine, 16 Hornady critical defense hollow point rounds, into the lifeless body of Alban Tole. I suppose it gave her some completion, satisfaction. But who was I to judge? She turned her back and as she walked away, she muttered, "Take that, motherfucker. Who the bitch now?" I couldn't have said it better.

Tsuji picked me up with one hand like a two-hundred-thirty-pound rag doll, cradled me in his massive arms, and made a hasty retreat to the Maybach. My rib cage screamed with pain, I labored for just a small breath of air. I heard him say, "Sorry, Boss."

Ritchie had already pulled up to the one open overhead. Tsuji set me down while Jake pulled from the back on the other side of the car and J3 in the front managed to get my full length into the car and the Lady jumped in, cradling my head. Tsuji jumped in the front and Lady, me, and Dave were in the back. It was more than painful to breathe and with the injuries I had received at the hands of Tole earlier in the week, my ribs were in no shape to let me inhale comfortably. All I could do was gasp for breath, but I was alive, which was much better than the alternative and what was left in the warehouse.

CHAPTER SEVENTY-SIX

"Goodnight, Goodnight! Parting is Such Sweet Sorrow, That I
Shall Say Goodnight Till it Be Tomorrow"

— ROMEO AND JULIET ACT 2, SCENE 2

WE COULD HEAR SIRENS IN THE DISTANCE DRAWING EVER
closer as our caravan pulled out onto South Hampton. Our time
had been up two minutes ago, and our luck could run out any
minute. If we were stopped, we were most likely headed to jail.
Ritchie lit the tires up on the Maybach and gave the rest of the
vehicles a bit of a smoke screen as we sped away from the scene
making identification next to impossible. Anyone outside at the
McDonald's on the other side of South Hampton only got a
cloud of premium tire if they even bothered to look. As promised
by the commissioner, we had a clear run back to the club,
making it into the garage without incident. Sly had also done his

job well. Gina and the girl had already made it back well ahead of us along with Mike and Brando.

Doc had called in a favor and had a "lady" doctor on the way to treat the injuries Chloe had sustained during two days of being continuously raped. Gina got her cleaned up after Doc gave her a little something for the pain. Except for the tears and broken capillaries inside of her, on the outside she wasn't in too bad of shape. Easing her off the "smack" would be a job for another day and another place. Gina fumed as she cleaned the track marks and if we hadn't killed them all she would have gone back and done the job herself.

We had gotten lucky, most of us made it back without a scratch, and those of us that got hit, well, Doc got us taken care of. Brando and Mike were going to have a little bruising and tenderness but other than that, they were good to go. Tsuji refused treatment until the Doc had taken care of me and the giant man stood there like it was another normal day at work. In this short span of time Tsuji not only gained my respect but became a trusted friend. I couldn't help being a bit envious that he would always be with Lady, but I knew she was in excellent hands. She loved us both in much different ways.

Sly was able to get his hands on an Amodeo P high frequency X-Ray machine designed for disaster areas and home use. Don't ask where he got it as it too had probably fallen off the back of a truck. Lady paced the floor while Doc took the pics and confirmed what I already knew. Several of the ribs that were previously cracked were now broke and there was a slight fracture in my sternum.

Doc laid it out to me. "I can tape them but that is old-school, and it will restrict your breathing. That could put you at risk of pneumonia. I will give you oral painkillers, you ice the area, and if that doesn't help, I can give you long-lasting injections of anesthesia around the ribs. It will help you breathe. You think you can just take it easy for a month and not get into any more trouble?" Oh, he knew me too well! I promised I would but between me, the wall, and the Doc, we knew that may be a bit of a stretch.

Tsuji had the bullet removed after Doc gave him a couple of locals, stitched him up, and told him to follow up with an MRI. For some reason I don't think he will bother.

The OB-GYN had arrived and began her examination of Chloe. Lady and Gina each had one of the girl's hands and held them letting her know she wasn't alone. That small act of kindness seemed to give her a bit of peace. The lady doctor conducted a colposcopy examination and determined that there was injury to her posterior fourchette with tearing. Along with broken capillaries in the vagina and anal area, a few stitches and tending to the wounds and rest, she would make a full recovery, physically.

She gave Gina detailed instruction for the girl's care. The lady doc finished patching her up and when she was ready to go Sly gave her a thick envelope and told her she was never here. As the Doc knew, so did she. She nodded and walked out of the club.

All of us had seen Chloe's picture on the news and how her mother feared she had been abducted. Gina was especially upset, as we all knew this was a very touchy issue with her and she took it upon herself to oversee Chloe's recovery. "Let's get her down to my room; I'll take care of her." Tsuji gently picked the girl up in his arms and took her to Gina's room in the bunker. Both the docs had left some morphine for those of us that needed it, but we gave it to Gina for Chloe, as withdrawal would start sooner rather than later. It was not the best alternative but here and now was not the time nor place to help the abused girl kick the joneses.

The rest of us knew this could be the last time we might all be together. We shared a few more drinks, toasting that we had made it out, and said our farewells. The crew thanked Sly for all he had done, especially for the first-class fares on the way home in the morning which was a few short hours away. They would enjoy the space and catch a combat nap on their flights. Lady had her own special farewell to the crew. She embraced each one of them, thanking them for their unquestioned loyalty and bravery. She knew they didn't have to come and put their lives on the line like they did. She told them if they ever needed anything, she would always take their calls.

Brit and Ritchie had this last night, whatever remained of it, together, and maybe it wasn't good-bye for the two of them. Fate and circumstances had brought them together and just might keep them together. She knew the boy traveled and when he was in town, he told her he would like to see her. He asked her if she had ever been to Paris or Rome, knowing that she hadn't, and told her not to be surprised if he told her to pack her bags, that is, if Sly would give her time off. Oh, hell yeah, he would!

It was tough saying good-bye to Jake and J3. It hadn't been that long since I had seen Jake, but J3, man, that took me back. I couldn't help the tears that flowed down my face. It had been years since the two of us were in the same room, let alone doing what we did. He was my mentor the reason I was the cop I was. The man even stood up for me at my first wedding, that's how close the two of us had become in such a short span of time. We always managed to stay in touch and on one of those occasions, he had told me one of our cases had been written about in a book, my fleeting fifteen minutes of fame. He was a big part of my life and I would never forget the adventures we had and some of doors he opened for me. But J3, grow a pair and take a sip of that Ghost Pepper vodka!

Dave got on his Harley the next morning. I couldn't resist giving him a hug and he headed back to Buffalo, his wife, and family. Dave knew a little about heartache and loss but was hard as nails when the going got tough. Peace be with you, my friend, and keep the rubber side down. I'm there for you anytime.

CHAPTER SEVENTY-SEVEN

AFTERMATH

"Once again, the fields we mow and gather in the aftermath."

— HENRY WADSWORTH LONGFELLOW

EVERYONE HAD EITHER LEFT TOWN OR HAD BEDDED DOWN for the night before leaving later in the day. Lady and I had a few moments of peace and quiet to ourselves as we sat in the living area watching some meaningless movie whose name I had already forgotten. We both sipped a Booker's and mine was enhanced with a Vicodin, which she diligently kept an eye on. As long as it allowed me to breathe, I was all good. She had her arm across my shoulders and gently scratched the back of my bald head. It felt good and was about the only part of my body that didn't hurt when touched.

The screen blanked for a moment and a news bulletin flashed across the screen. The announcer said, *"We interrupt this broadcast to bring you the following breaking news from Channel 7."*

Kim Khazei appeared looking a little haggard from her naturally perky self, due to the early morning hour.

"We ask if small children are in the room that you have them leave. Some of the scenes are quite graphic and may be disturbing to viewers. Amaka, what can you tell us?"

"The Boston Police have told me that it appears a military-style assault was conducted at this warehouse behind me on Topeka Street. Oddly enough, it is where the body of De'Londo Williams was found several nights ago. We also know now that Mr. Williams died from suffocation, wrapped in heavy plastic, and as evidenced by petechial hemorrhage of the capillaries in the white of the eye as determined by the medical examiner's office. The Boston Police found seventeen dead bodies in the warehouse, most shot, one burned, and several died of knife wounds that essentially gutted those men. It appears they were taken by surprise as many of them were in various stages of dress. There is no trace left behind of who may have done this except for spent casings. There is some speculation that it may be gang and drug oriented as small amounts of drugs and syringes were found. The Boston Police have rounded up several members of the Italian Mafia for questioning, but all were released for lack of evidence and having alibis."

Yep, Johnny worked his magic.

The camera crew were allowed inside and Khazei flushed at the sight of the mayhem.

"Amaka, if it wasn't a competing gang, who do the police think conducted the raid?"

"Kim, at this point in time they are not speculating but I was told the police commissioner will hold a press conference later today.

No other groups at this time are taking credit, as is no federal or state agency. If this was a gang war, at least one of them has been taken out of play for good. To be assured, the crime scene techs are taking DNA samples of blood, and fingerprints from the dead bodies will be sent to the Automated Fingerprint Identification System or AFIS. They will have their hands full as will the coroner's office."

"Amaka, do the police think this may have any connection to the shooting at Chez Rendezvous?"

"Kim, I asked the commander in charge at the scene about this and he didn't feel there was any connection. He believes this assault was highly organized and funded. He further stated that a small club owner could not have been involved in anything of this epic proportion."

If only she knew!

"Thank you Amaka, we now return you to the previously scheduled program, but we will keep you updated with the latest developments."

———

The commissioner poured himself several fingers of Johnny Walker Blue and looked down at his cell as it began to buzz. He picked it up. "Good morning, Mayor, I take it you have seen the news?"

"I have, it looks like our friend lived up to his word."

"That he did, but it is still one hell of a mess. I will tell the press we have collected DNA and prints from the deceased and see if it matches anything in our records, FBI or Interpol. We both know they will, but we'll do our usual song and dance and when there isn't any collateral damage the interest by the public dies out pretty quick."

"Good enough for me. We'll talk later." Both men clicked off the call.

Gina sat on the bed with her laptop next to Chloe and soon found a phone number for the address that the news had shown on TV. Gina dialed the number and a woman answered. Gina assumed it was Chloe's mother. "Mrs. O'Malley?"

"This is she. Who's calling?"

"That is not important, but I want you to know your daughter is safe. She has been through a lot, but she will stay with me until she recovers."

"What happened to my baby? Who are you and where is she?" she said almost frantically.

"Ma'am, I can assure you she is safe and will be well looked after. I will have her call when she is able. Nothing else bad will happen to her, she is in good hands. I will get back to you in a few days but in the meantime, please do not worry." Gina hung up the burner phone, removed the SIM card, broke the phone, and continued to make plans to take Chloe with her, away from Boston.

Sly too had his own plan for the girl and her family. Later that day Khaseem's white Town Car pulled up in front of 52 Costello. Reshaun exited the passenger side and knocked on the door. A tired-looking woman in her late thirties, bloodshot eyes from crying, answered the door and Reshaun asked, "Miss O'Malley?" The woman said yes and Reshaun handed her an envelope thick with cash.

"What is this?" she asked.

"From friends of your daughter." Reshaun smiled, turned, and walked back in the car. He didn't see the woman open the envelope but if he had he would have seen tears streaming down her face as she said a thank you through trembling lips to a stranger she didn't know, that no one would hear.

EPILOGUE

WHAT CAN I SAY, IT HAD BEEN A WILD ROLLER-COASTER ride during the past week and a half. Not only did we win the battle for Lady Tatiana, but we rescued a desperate young girl. My guys had all gone and disappeared into their former lives, but they were appreciative for getting to be a last action hero one more time. Not everyone got a chance at seconds.

Gina, I know, would get the girl mobile and vanish into the night as mysteriously as she had appeared at the club or anywhere else for that matter. I don't believe it would be the last I would hear from her as we always had dragged one another into one type of adventure or another. Keep your head down, killer. For her, the girl would be her challenge for some time and then return her to her mother, better, stronger, smarter than she had ever been. But I talk too much and that will be another story for another day.

The mayor and the commish both rode out the next couple of weeks answering questions from a host of agencies and the media as to how a gang of Albanian Mafia had been slaughtered with no trace of the perps. They spun it, lied, and it died out.

They even held good on getting Johnny Botts out of the can and Sly and I drove out to meet him when he got out. What a strange crew we were.

Remember Duncan? He was a little slicker than we all thought. He made a call to Reshaun and said he wanted to talk to the boss. Reshaun questioned it and Duncan told him he heard what the boss, mayor, and commissioner had talked about at Fan Pier. That got our attention. He made a deal with Sly to get him in the Academy and he would never speak of the incident again. Sly would get him in but he had to stand on his own merits. "Don't make me come find you now," were Sly's words to him. Before he hung up Duncan said, "I know."

Sly would get the club back up running with a good clean-up with the help of his guys and my limited help cuz I wasn't going anywhere soon. My apartment would keep. Besides, it was nicer in the bunker.

His guys had all learned a new lesson in loyalty and would be there for their boss until it was time for them to move on if they chose. Brit would be back at the bar serving drinks and putting down the boy's advances. She too had a new appreciation for the bald white guy with the tats and Sly. I guess we became like a small, somewhat functional family. Her and Ritchie, I think they are going to be a thing, but who can tell. He's a great guy.

Now I hear all y'all asking, "What about Lady Tatiana, dude?" She stayed a few more days but I knew her, and Tsuji had to get back to New York. She helped me those few days as best she could, but I could sense the edginess in her demeanor. It wasn't my fault nor hers, but she had her own "empire" to run and she was its "Cookie." As much as I wanted her to stay, I knew it wasn't her place nor my place to ask. Like the good businesswoman she was, she got what she needed to do to get the job done. I don't blame her, as I would have done the same. The day she and Tsuji left was bittersweet. Tsuji gave me a hug and didn't break my mending ribs, thank you, big man. Lady gave me one last long passionate kiss, told me to visit, and got in the Rolls.

Sly and I stood and watched it roll out of the garage and he let the door close. She didn't look back. Sly asked me, "You good, bro?"

"Yeah, man, I am. I still got your big black ass to take care of, don't I?"

"That you do, my man, that you do. Let's go have a Booker's."

"Best thing I heard all day."

THE END

———

Keep reading for a preview of the next *Cavazutti Crime*
The Rise of Chloe

———

Don't miss out on your next favorite book!

Join the Melange Books mailing list at
www.melange-books.com/mail.html

THE RISE OF CHLOE

a Cavazutti Crime Novel

Prologue

Kedainiai, Lithuania Eastern Europe / Present Time

Taking everything in that the quaint village had to offer, Mikhail Brozovitch sat in the tiny coffee shop run by an older couple. There were lines etched unkindly into their faces, plowed deep by the sun like the earthy folk they were. Here in Kėdainiai, Lithuania, was a well-preserved old town that dates back to the 17th century. Prior to WWII, Kėdainiai had a large Jewish population of approximately 3,000 people, several synagogues, and a Jewish cemetery. It was the kind of small village that Mikhail favored. Passing cars on the road spoke with a clackity-clack as their tires traveled over the cobblestone, along with the clopping of horses shod hooves pulling carts home from the market. The old alongside the new coexisted harmoniously.

Homes still had the same ancient stone foundations and

thatched roofs as they had for centuries. Visiting Kedainiai was like a journey into the past and Mikhail could imagine the horse- or oxen-drawn carts taking goods to the market in the square, folks milling about dressed in their ethnic clothing examining what the open air market had to offer.

Dogs lopped about the streets with their sideways gait that all dogs walk with, looking for a handout or a bit of discarded food. They growled at those that tried to pet them without something first to offer.

The coffee shop and bakery where he was seated was no Starbucks but far better in his opinion. There was no WiFi or music or the latest generation of computer nerds taking up all the seats sipping the latest overpriced fad drink. Residents sat reading papers or talking local politics while drinking the rich coffee, but Mikhail kept to himself.

A pastry case containing fresh baked goods indigenous to the region sat at the back of the shop where the register was perched on top of the glass counter. Nothing fancy. They did things the old way and roasted their own beans.

There were several brew choices available and he sipped from the tiny cup that contained the thick, black, aromatic coffee. The scent alone from the double-roasted espresso beans was enough to keep him on point and alert. Each time he lifted the cup earthy notes and hints of vanilla rose up to fill his nose.

His thick neck twisted from side to side deftly taking in his surroundings, every person, every action. Each person that moved or paced back and forth he eyed with suspicion. Or if they stayed too stationary for a second more than he thought necessary, he would perceive them as a threat.

He had not left the KGB and later the FSB, Foreign Security Service, renamed under Boris Yeltsin, without the skills necessary to detect a tail or surveillance. If they wanted him bad enough, they would throw numbers at him and he wouldn't be able catch them all. He might neutralize a few, but in the end, it would conclude with him lying in a pool of his own blood, hence him forfeiting his life. If they captured him alive, it would be a slow death, tortured for the trespass he had committed.

They would first have to find him as no one remained invisible forever, just a matter of time and logistics. More than likely they would send an assassin that would have no trail back to them, to the President. It was the way they worked when they didn't want to soil their own filthy corrupt hands.

They not only cared about the tens of millions he had stolen from them in his latest shady arms transaction, but that he had dealt with the Chechens—that was a no-no. Their greatest revenge would be that he didn't get to spend his illicit gains before they terminated him. Russia had been fighting with the Chechens for years and because they were Muslim terrorists, the entire deal caused issues for their allies, namely the United States, regardless of how loose the association was or how friendly Past-President Putin had seemed to be with one US President.

Most of the cash had been stashed in offshore accounts under assumed names and shell corporations, but he held onto an amount that permitted him to keep moving for the time being. For him it was the only way he might survive. He could make no friends. That would sign their death warrants. But all be told, he hated leaving the charm of this quaint village of Kedainiai and its better-than-average coffee shop. Besides, Europe was full of them, some more hospitable than others. Even with the progress after the fall of the old Soviet Union, many of these towns and villages had not stepped out of the 19th century let alone into the 20th. Yes, it was a much saner time.

Tomorrow he would have to leave. Too many of the townsfolk had seen him numerous times and therefore may remember him even with his unremarkable face. His plastic surgeon had made sure of that. When the FSB came looking, those same townsfolk would talk if they knew what was good for them. Who knows, it may make them a few dollars if they pointed in the right direction and he couldn't blame them one bit.

Money was hard to come by, especially greenbacks. The United States dollar could buy anything even cheaper than the local currency allowed.

If the plastic surgeon had done as good a job as he felt he did, then the pictures of him that his persecutors would show to the townspeople would be unrecognizable. His brow, nose, and jawline had all been enhanced or taken away, depending on the desired effect. His scars had healed fast and no one outside of a trained professional could tell he had the procedure. They would have to say they did not know him.

Unless of course the FSB or their delegates had gotten to the surgeon. He thought for a time that he should have killed the surgeon leaving no loose ends, but the doctor had treated him like family during his recovery. People like the doctor, well, let's just say it doesn't take a great deal to get them to talk and then he would be dead anyway. Mikhail's way was much more merciful. A muffled cough took care of the problem. But he couldn't bring himself to do it. He was not a murderer even though he sold arms to anyone for the price.

Tomorrow he would sort through his passports, cash, and other personal items and decide where his next move would play out.

THANK YOU FOR READING

Did you enjoy this book?

We invite you to leave a review at the website of your choice, such as Goodreads, Amazon, Barnes & Noble, etc.

DID YOU KNOW THAT LEAVING A REVIEW...

- Helps other readers find books they may enjoy.
- Gives you a chance to let your voice be heard.
- Gives authors recognition for their hard work.
- Doesn't have to be long. A sentence or two about why you liked the book will do.

ACKNOWLEDGMENTS

First, I would like to acknowledge Ms. Nancy Schumacher and her entire staff at Mélange Publishing for taking a chance on me, believing in me and holding my hand through this process. I have learned much.

To my editor, Lisa Petrocelli, who put in a lot of time getting my manuscript in shape for publication.

Without Miss Rae Monet I would not have the awesome website which she designed. Thank you for your ease of accessibility and listening to my ideas.

Jake, J3 and Gina, you all know who you are. I thank you for allowing me the use of your persona's and your never-ending encouragement. J3, without you, this book may never have been possible. You were a huge influencer in my life.

Phil, at Strega, I'll see you soon.

Thank you for my dear Albanian friends in Boston for helping with my research. Miss playing Vball with you all.

Ritchie, I miss our good times and to the other Italian friends of a friend of mine.

To the authors that I love and have read, Baldacci, Flynn and Box. You lit the spark.

To my dear wife Cynthia, her cousin Sandra and my family for enduring multiple rewrites and rereads.

Booker Noe, hat's off to you as you kept me company in the wee hours of the morning!

Thanks for the multiple sips!

ABOUT THE AUTHOR

Carlo has been in involved in the law enforcement community in NY. His career included successful undercover missions with the DEA and State Police. Carlo also coordinated inter-agency task forces and investigated all types of crimes before retiring as a detective. He furthered his career when he moved to Massachusetts where he worked as a private investigator, specializing in undercover operations and interrogation. Carlo also worked as an Executive Protection Agent with an impressive list of clients such as a presidential nominee; working closely with the Secret Service when they took over, federal judges, senators and congressmen. He also drove CEO's from several fortune 500 Companies. Carlo received his Bachelor of Arts, majoring in Criminology, from the State University of NY system. Today he writes from an undisclosed location in Texas and continues his education seeking a Masters in Criminal Organizations.

cavazutticrime45@gmail.com

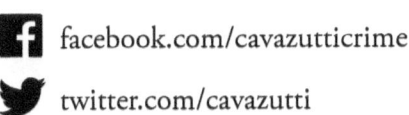

facebook.com/cavazutticrime

twitter.com/cavazutti